INK AND ICE

ERIN MCRAE AND RACHELINE MALTESE

AVIAN30
NEW YORK, NEW YORK
2020

Avian30
New York, New York
Ink and Ice by Erin McRae and Racheline Maltese
Copyright 2020
ISBN: 978-1-946192-16-5

www.Avian30.com

First Avian30 Printing: December 2020
Printed in the USA

A Note on the Setting

A significant portion of this book is set on a group of islands in Lake Erie.

While one of those islands – Whisker Island – is purely a product of our imagination, the others, including South Bass and Middle Bass, are perfectly real. South Bass, in particular, is worth a visit as it is the home of Put-In Bay, a lakeside village which has a small year-round local population and serves as a summer resort for the Ohio region. It is easily accessible by ferry in the warm season.

Several smaller islands, not all of which are accessible to the public, also dot the area. These include Mouse Island, Turtle Island, and Starve Island. Due to their small size, rocky soil, and the extreme nature of the environment in the winter months, none of these islands have a known history of permanent human settlement either by indigenous people or by colonizers and their descendants.

While seals are mostly saltwater creatures, freshwater seals do exist. The only true freshwater seal is the Baikal, which is native to Russia. Generally, what are termed freshwater seals are isolated colonies of saltwater species that became trapped inland and now persist in freshwater environments throughout Canada, Alaska, and Russia. To our knowledge there are no such colonies – or myths about such colonies – in Lake Erie.

PART I

PART II

1

Eight Months Before the Winter Olympics in Almaty, Kazakhstan

Lake Erie Islands

Aaron Sheftall was glad to be home for the summer, even if summer on the string of tiny islands in the middle of Lake Erie meant hard work, drunk people, and fish. So much fish.

Growing up, Aaron hadn't always appreciated how strange his life was. In the summers, his parents boated to and from the biggest island to work fourteen-hour days for the tourist crowd that wanted some fried perch and bottomless margaritas before the world turned cold. But once summer ended the tourists left and the one hundred or so full-time residents of the islands eventually became frozen in.

Now though, at twenty-three, Aaron knew exactly how odd his life had been. His high school graduating class had contained four people, including him and his twin sister Arianne (Ari, for short). The two of them had boated or snowmobiled, as the weather dictated, to Middle Bass

Island each day for classes. Whisker Island, where they and four other families lived, was much too small to have its own school.

But all of it – the isolation, the brutal winters, the intense sense of community born of both – had served Aaron well; he wouldn't have learned to ice skate if it hadn't been necessary to get around in those winters. And he wouldn't have picked up figure skating as a sport or moved into elite competition if he hadn't been so desperate sometimes not just to see, but live in, the world beyond the speck of rocks and trees from which he'd come. Sometimes Aaron wasn't sure the place existed at all.

But in summers it did. Tourist publications called it the Key West of the Midwest, and their brief seasonal attention was enough to keep the islands going year-round. Aaron's parents' restaurant kept their freezers full and funded Aaron's skating career. So in the off-season, while his fellow competitors were either on the road doing ice shows or showing off their beach bodies on social media, he was stuck here, in a place he loved and could never explain to anyone else, elbow-deep in raw fish.

Aaron's phone rang. More accurately, it barked; his ringtone was the sound of seals.

The device rested on the shelf above the counter where he and Ari worked. In unison they both went up on their toes to look at the screen and see who it was.

Ari frowned. "Your ex-boyfriend is calling."

While it was definitely Huy calling, Aaron did need to object to that description. Their thing had been brief, and they had been friends before, during, and most importantly, after it.

"He's my friend, not just…whatever. And we train at the same rink."

"Still, he's calling. He doesn't call much, does he?"

"No. And I'm not answering right now, I'm covered in perch." Not that Huy would know that, and not that Aaron

2

was embarrassed. But mentally shifting from summer restaurant help to chatty figure skater felt hard. Especially with an ex, no matter how amicable.

After a few more rounds of barking seals – Ari shot Aaron a dire look; she had never thought the seals were a thing to make light of – the phone fell silent for a moment. Then it started barking again.

The two of them both went up on their toes to check the screen once more.

"Your ex-boyfriend is calling…again," Ari proclaimed.

"Would you stop calling him that?" Aaron mentally paged through the summer schedules of the Twin City Ice skaters and tried to remember where Huy was this week. "I think he's on vacation, it's probably a drunk dial?"

Still, the repeated calls were odd enough that he peeled off his gloves and moved to the sink to wash fish bits off his hands.

The phone barked again.

"It's still him," Ari announced as Aaron was drying his hands.

He grabbed the phone off the shelf and accepted the call. "What's up?"

"Where are you right now?" Huy asked urgently and without preamble.

Huy Le, Canada's top men's figure skater who currently ranked third in the world, had a knack for both friendship and quad flips. He was usually energetic and outgoing, and Aaron had rarely heard him upset. He was definitely upset now. Aaron found it jarring. Whatever this was, it wasn't a drunk dial.

"The restaurant." Aaron took a deep breath and tried to calm the sudden pounding of his heart. Something was wrong.

"You're working?"

"Yes, I work all summer." Aaron hoped he didn't sound sharp but was quite sure he did. There were two types of people who skated: Those who could afford it comfortably and those who would always be struggling to afford it. Huy fell into the first category. Aaron did not.

"Take a break." The tone sounded suspiciously like *you had better sit down for this*, which did not lessen Aaron's sense of unease. He pulled the phone away from his ear.

"I'm stepping out for a minute; let Mom know?" he said to Ari, already on his way out the door.

Aaron stepped out the kitchen's back door and took a deep breath, letting his lungs fill with the fresh air. The sun was out, and the lake breeze blowing in off the water kept everything cool and somewhat damp. There was a bench by the door in the shade of the massive maple tree still in the process of putting out leaves. Summer came late to the islands and left early. Aaron propped his foot up on the seat to stretch while they talked.

"All right, I'm taking a break. What's happening?" He tried to keep the worry out of his voice as he continued to run through possible disaster scenarios in his head.

"Go on the internet," Huy said briskly. "Actually, no. Don't do that. There's video."

That was not remotely clarifying. Or reassuring. *Had something happened to the rink?* "Huy, what are you talking about? Is everything all right?"

"Luke Koval had an accident. At the ice show in Regina."

"What happened? Is he okay?" Luke and Aaron weren't close, but the world of elite competitive skating was like a family. Everyone knew and cared about everyone else.

"Well, he's not dead. But no, he's not okay."

"How not okay?" Aaron asked.

Huy paused. "It happened on a spin. A spiral fracture."

Aaron made an agonized noise and tried very hard not to imagine what that would look like, much less feel like. The physical pain would be agonizing, and an injury like that was career-ending. The fact was obvious to both of them, but neither said it out loud. Skaters – and, Aaron suspected, most competitive athletes – were superstitious.

"Yeah," Huy said. "Yeah, it wasn't good. And obviously he won't be skating for the rest of the season. Which means –"

"The whole field just opened up," Aaron breathed.

It didn't seem like the sort of thing that should be said too loudly. No one wanted anything bad to happen to a fellow skater, in part because you always knew on another day it could be you. But the reality was that the top U.S. men's skater was suddenly and unexpectedly out of the running for the foreseeable future. In an Olympic year.

Which meant opportunity.

Huy made a noise of agreement.

"I need to get back to Minnesota."

"My favorite ambitious murder kitten of the sea." Huy sounded proud. "Yeah, you do."

"But –" Almost as soon as the idea had occurred to him, Aaron saw the obstacles. Of which there were several. But one was the most pertinent. "Is anyone even there right now?"

"If they're not, they will be soon. Everyone's going to want Luke's – well, everything. Funding. Sponsorships. Grand Prix assignments...." his voice trailed off for a moment. Aaron knew what Huy was going to say next, because he'd done the math, too. "His Olympic team spot."

"That's such a long shot," Aaron said to try to contain the wild excitement that was building in his chest. Rushing back to training months early didn't necessarily make sense. And wasn't necessarily feasible. The restaurant needed every hand it could get this time of year, and training was expensive. His federation covered some of his costs, but not all of them; he wasn't ranked highly enough.

"I know," Huy said. "And I know the situation with your family and your island and your funding is

5

complicated. But you need to think about getting back to TCI."

"Lucky you're going to the Olympics anyway."

"Hush, don't jinx anything," Huy warned.

Huy was too good a skater and too good a friend for Aaron to resent his medals or his consistency. Still, Aaron was glad they were only in competition with each other for international medals, not national team spots. This upset was a sliver of a chance for him, not a guarantee. Aaron would have to fight tooth and nail for a chance to go to the winter Olympics in Almaty, while a spot on the Canadian team was Huy's to lose. But as Luke's accident proved, those losses did happen.

Aaron wanted to run inside and book his flights. Instead he sank down onto the bench.

"I'll work on it," he said into the phone. He couldn't promise more than that. Not to Huy, and sadly, not to himself. Not yet.

"You should," Huy said. "You've always been better than your results."

After they hung up, Aaron sat there feeling like he'd had the air punched out of him by Huy's last comment on his skating. There was validation in it, but it also stung. Aaron had a potential – he knew it, the people around him knew it – and he wasn't meeting it. And no one could figure out why.

He needed to get back inside; Ari couldn't deal with all that perch by herself. But first he needed to text his coaches.

Katie Nowacki and Brendan Reid had won Olympic gold as a pairs team. After they had retired – and resolved one of the longest-running and highest-drama on-again-off-again relationships in figure skating by getting married – they'd devoted themselves to coaching and, in Katie's case, to the bafflement of most of the skating community, dairy farming.

Aaron texted Brendan. He would have preferred Katie, who understood his brain and life best, but Brendan dealt with all things logistic. If he'd contacted Katie, she'd have made him talk to Brendan anyway.

> Aaron: Hi! I just heard about Luke's accident. What happens if I come back to training early?

Aaron didn't even know if they were in the Twin Cities right now. Probably, because of Katie's farm, but in the summers she and Brendan always seemed to be travelling all over the world for something for a week here and there. In either case, there wasn't anything he could but wait to hear back.

✦

For the rest of the day Aaron kept his phone muted and in his pocket so he wouldn't be tempted to check for notifications every five minutes. He finally let himself dig it out and look that evening while he was at the dock waiting for his mom to finish refueling the boat so they could head back home after a too-long day. His dad was sitting next to him, checking his own phone for the weather forecast, and Ari was somewhere along the shore, probably making friends with more seagulls.

There was, in fact, a reply from Brendan, and Aaron tapped on it hastily.

> Brendan: Hi! Good to hear from you. Hope your family's doing well. Short answer: Yes, if you decide you want to come back early, Katie and I will be here for you. Longer answer: Before you make a decision, think about what your goals are, think about resources you'll need outside of

federation funding, and think about whether the extra training is going to be useful to you vs overtraining.

Aaron breathed a sigh of relief at the first part of the message. As for the rest – well. His goal was obvious: He wanted to make the Olympic team.

More training versus overtraining was easy. Aaron could moderate himself once he got there. In part, because Katie and Brendan would make sure of it, but Aaron liked to think he was self-aware enough that he didn't have to put the burden of saying *stop* on his coaches.

Resources, however, were the question mark. Brendan meant Aaron's own internal resources of determination and physical endurance, yes. But *resources* was also code for money and time. And time was more complicated for Aaron than most.

He texted Brendan back.

Aaron: Thanks! I'll talk to my parents and figure some things out.

Brendan's reply came almost immediately.

Brendan: We look forward to hearing from you!

Aaron knew Brendan meant it, but there were times – like right now – he wanted a hell of a lot more handholding than that.

✦

The ride back to Whisker Island was one of Aaron's favorite parts of the day, and not just because work was over. In the middle of the lake, surrounded by water and sky, the world felt young and simpler. Tonight the lake was calm under a velvety lavender sky, silver-dark ripples spreading out to the horizon. Now that the sun had set, the air was cold, and the speed of the boat only amplified that.

As much as Aaron wanted to savor this moment, he suspected it would be easier to start this conversation now than when they were back on dry land.

"Something happened in skating today," he said over the rush of the wind and the steady slice of the boat through the water.

"What's that?" Aaron's mom asked. His dad was piloting, but Aaron knew he was listening too.

Aaron explained Luke's accident. He didn't need to use any more words than Huy had; his parents knew the realities of skating as well as non-skaters could. Ari, in the stern of the boat, sat with her face turned out over the water, her curls whipping back behind her. Aaron was sure she was listening too and that she would have opinions.

"This changes things...the lineup for the U.S. team," Aaron said. "I have a chance now. And – I know this is a big ask, and that there's going to be a lot of details to work out, but...."

"Spit it out, Aaron," his father said.

"I want to find a way to go back to training early."

"How early?" his mom asked.

Tomorrow, Aaron wanted to say. But he couldn't. Many things might or might not be possible, but that certainly wasn't. "As soon as possible."

"It's almost Memorial Day weekend," she pointed out. She wasn't saying no, but she didn't sound happy.

"I know."

"We open in two days and then it's one of the busiest seventy-two hours of the year."

Aaron was about to reply in the frustrated affirmative, again, when Ari shushed them.

He whipped his head around towards her. "What?"

"Cut the motor," she said quietly.

When her father didn't, she shouted. "Dad, cut the fucking motor!"

As the boat spluttered to its swaying stop in the middle of the dark lake, Aaron held his breath. In the darkness, something barked.

"It's a dog," their mother said.

"Quiet!" Ari hissed. In the dark the barking seemed to multiply.

"Someone's got an awful lot of dogs," Aaron said. The sound, whatever it was, was definitely *not* a dog.

"There," Ari said, pointing to a spot in the middle distance, somewhat vaguely in the direction of Canada.

What seemed to be the sleek rounded head of a seal rose up out of the water, before diving again. Then a few more, glimpsed and gone. Then dozens.

"It's the wind, stirring up the water," their mother said softly.

Aaron had to admit that was probably true. The wind could get so strong that eight-foot waves on the lake happened often enough. What looked like seal heads was probably just the breeze, lacing between the islands in the twilight and tricking their tired eyes.

The barking stopped, as if dispelled by reason.

"I don't want us to hit one," Ari said.

"Pretty sure magic freshwater seals are smart enough not to get hit by boats, kiddo," their dad said. He restarted the motor, but far more gently than before.

"We'll talk about your season Monday night," Aaron's mother said, as if they hadn't just been interrupted by the myth of the place they were all from and Aaron always felt guilty to leave.

✦

Memorial Day weekend arrived, and with it the rush of tourists that would swarm over the island all summer. That first day especially Ari was quiet, almost sullen; she never liked when outsiders came to the islands, and the beginning of the season was always hardest on her. So she took the kitchen shift, and Aaron took the front of house duties. The day wore on in endless hours, throbbing feet, and his first sunburn of the season.

Yet as tiring as the work was, he couldn't stop thinking about the Twin Cities and training. All he wanted was to be back on the ice. At the same time, he dreaded having to leave. What was summer, if not spent on the islands? He wondered what Brendan had told Katie of their conversation, and what Katie's reaction had been.

Late that night, once they'd returned to Whisker Island, he took a walk down to the edge of the lake and called Katie. Maybe that was too much, but he needed to talk to someone about this. She had always understood him, when it came to skating, in a way that no one else did.

Only after the phone started ringing did he realize that it was a weeknight, late for civilians, and later still for Katie, who kept skaters' hours during the season and farmers' hours otherwise.

She did, however, pick up the phone after only a few rings.

"Hi Aaron, what's up?"

Her tone wasn't exactly brusque, but it did make Aaron ask, "Is this a good time?"

"Depends why you're calling. Please tell me you haven't also had a season-ending injury out there on your island."

Your island would have made Aaron bristle from anyone else, but Katie had been a farm girl before she became a skater, and still was with twenty head of dairy cows ten miles outside Saint Paul. Why anyone would want two professions so hard on the heart, body, and wallet, Aaron didn't know. But he didn't need to. They were cut from some of the same stuff.

"Ah, no," he stammered. "But it's kind of about that."

"Brendan told me you texted him. Have you been able to talk things through with your parents yet?"

"Not yet," Aaron admitted. "With the holiday weekend, everything's busy. They want to wait 'til Monday."

"That's certainly fair. So why are you calling me?"

Aaron forced himself not to shrink at the question; he wanted Katie's approval, but was getting a challenge instead.

"Because I don't know what's possible and I can't stop thinking about it. And I can't wait 'til Monday night to make any kind of decision. I need to know what my options are, as far as you're concerned, so I can make plans. For every eventuality."

Katie seemed to consider that. "You already know Brendan and I will be here for whatever you need from us. Same as we are for all our skaters."

"Yes, ma'am."

"We're not your limiting factor. And you don't know what your parents are going to say yet. In some ways, the only limiting factor is you. Now what do you want?"

Aaron took a breath. What he wanted – a shot at the Olympics – was no more and no less than what any athlete at his level dreamed of. Expressing that, especially to one of his coaches, shouldn't have been difficult. But Aaron had always kept part of himself carefully tucked away from the rest of his life: The part that reveled in the lake's winter storms and calm summer dawns, the part that was happiest here by the water and wondered if maybe, just maybe, there was truth to the old stories about the seals. It was that part now that was making it hard for him to articulate the things he so badly wanted.

"If I leave early, I might make the team. *Might*. If I manage to, I won't medal."

"The team isn't the only thing at stake in the season," Katie said kindly, but Aaron would not be deterred.

"Not in an Olympic year."

Katie hummed down the phone line. "You coming back early may not be the thing that makes or breaks your shot at that or anything else."

"I know that," Aaron said. "But don't I have to at least try?"

"But you're uncertain," Katie led.

"Of course I'm uncertain," Aaron said. He was also exasperated, with himself as much as anything. "If I leave now, I leave my parents without my help for the entire summer. It's about money, but not just that. I spend maybe four months here a year. I've only been here a month so far. It's not fair to them. And it's not enough time for me."

"I see." Katie's voice was calm, nearly cold. Apparently, she was going to force him to figure this out on his own.

"You grew up on your family's farm. You know what it's like." Aaron took another deep breath to steady himself for the plunge, the way he always did before a performance began. There was one thing he had to know. "If you hadn't won a medal, and you'd gone into the Olympics *knowing* you wouldn't win a medal, would it still be worth everything you had to do in order to get there?"

There was a corresponding breath on the other side of the line. Aaron smiled. Skaters were all the same in some ways.

"Everything has always felt like life and death for me," Katie said. "And there was a lot going on for me that year."

Brendan, Aaron interpreted.

"I might have given you a different answer in the middle of it," she said, "but I never would have been able to live with myself if I hadn't made it." She paused for a long moment. "Honestly, sometimes the fact that I got there is the only reason I can live with myself now."

"Okay." Aaron took a moment to digest that.

Once he had, the way forward seemed as clear as it had when he had first heard the news from Huy. The island would still be here after this season. His family would still be here. But he only had one chance at this season. No matter what the cost, he had to take it.

"Okay," he said again, committing to the only decision that now made sense. "I still need to get through the next few days. And work with my family to figure out how to fill the gap I'll be leaving. But I'm going to get out of here Tuesday morning and I will see you at the rink on Wednesday."

"Good." Katie sounded pleased. "Once you have your flights, text Brendan and we'll pick you up."

"Are you sure? I can get the bus, or a car service or whatever – "

Katie laughed. "If you're coming back to work early, that means we're all coming back to work early. You want to get in the game now? That means talking and making a plan. Otherwise there's no reason for you to be running away from your family up there. Right?"

Katie was always a hardass about people keeping their lives in order off the ice. It cut down on distractions and made for good habits, she said. Aaron agreed in principle, but thought it was a little funny coming from someone who, when she had been competing, was legendary for being kind of a mess.

"Right," he agreed.

"We'll pick you up and we'll have lunch and we'll talk. Or rather, we'll have the first of what is going to be a long series of conversations because there's what you want, what you can have, and the options in between," Katie said. In the background, someone chuckled.

Which reminded Aaron that she had a whole life he was upending with his own desperate need to do the impossible.

"Thank you. Sorry if I interrupted."

Katie shushed him. "Don't worry about it. Do what you need to do there and we'll see you in a few days."

"Okay. Thanks." Aaron was about to say goodbye and pull the phone away from his ear when Katie's voice pulled him back.

"And Aaron?"

"Yeah?"

He could hear the smile in her voice. "Good boy."

✦

After he finished talking to Katie Aaron sat at the end of his family's dock for a long time, lying back and looking up at the stars. He knew he should go to bed; he had to be up at five to ride back to South Bass Island with everyone else for the morning shift. But he couldn't bring himself to go back to the house. Now that he'd started planning to leave, all he could think about was the summer nights under the stars he wouldn't have here, lulled to peace and restfulness with the soft slap of the waves on the shore. He could leave, and he would survive, but missing this place would still hurt. No matter the choice he made, there would be a price to pay. That was the nature of skating – and, he suspected, most of life.

Eventually he became aware that the soft sound he was hearing wasn't some nighttime creature, but footsteps. Ari's.

"How was it out front at the restaurant tonight?" she asked as she sat down next to him. "I didn't ask before."

"Eh." Aaron tried to think that far back. It had only been a few hours ago, but already it seemed like a separate lifetime. "Not bad. Only had to toss out one drunk and rowdy dude."

There was the soft tap of foam on wood as she kicked off her flip flops and dangled her feet in the water.

"Sorry you had to deal with that crap," she said.

"You'll have to deal with it when I'm gone," he pointed out.

"I always do, when you leave. And you always leave before the end of the season here," Ari said, that strange blend of easy and resigned about her role as always.

Aaron never stopped feeling guilty about it. How could he, when every one of his own career choices had been made with an eye to his own advantage, never mind how that left the rest of his family? Especially now. Especially with what he'd told Katie.

They were silent for a few long moments. The evening was calm, and the lake rippled in the moonlight. The quiet hiss and rush of water tossed tiny pebbles about as little wavelets crested on the beach.

"You're going back," Ari finally said.

"Yeah." There was no use demurring. "Were you listening?"

"Always. I'll miss you."

"I'll miss you too," Aaron said. It wasn't like she could come with him.

"I bet you'll miss hooking up with all the cute tourists, too," she teased.

"I don't *hook up* with them! I merely flirt with them." He couldn't believe they were talking about this, but it was better, he supposed, than addressing any of the actual repercussions of the departure he was planning.

"Because you live with your family and have nowhere discreet to take them?"

Aaron chuckled. "Well, yeah."

Ari laughed. "You're strange. And should have better taste than to settle for a mainlander."

"If you happen to encounter an eligible islander that we haven't known since we were babies, be sure to let me know."

They grinned at each other and the old terrible joke that was forever true.

Ari's expression sobered, and she looked at her feet in the water. "When are you leaving?"

"Tuesday. Mom and Dad don't know yet; we still have to talk about it. But I can still come back for some of the busier weekends," he offered, though he knew it made no sense.

"You won't," she said, that same even tone. There was no blame in it, but Aaron flinched anyway.

"Well, I'll try."

"You really think you can make the team?"

"I don't know," Aaron confessed. "If I did, if I was sure, I wouldn't hesitate to go."

"You don't seem like you're hesitating now."

"Not on the outside," Aaron pointed out. Being a competitive athlete often meant he was very good at squishing his emotions into a box and letting them out as infrequently as possible.

"If you're going to go regardless, why waste time feeling bad about it?" Ari kicked at the water, as if for emphasis.

"We're Jewish. We're very good at feeling guilty about things."

Ari laughed. "If you don't want your outside to match your inside – that is, if you're not going to let your guilt stop you –"

"I got that, thank you." So much was easier said than done.

"Then make your insides match your outsides!"

"I'm not sure my insides and outsides have *ever* matched."

"Yeah." Ari looked thoughtful. "Me neither."

✦

Aaron was almost grateful for the length of the days at the restaurant as the tourist season finally officially kicked off.

Business and exhaustion served to quiet his brain, and when Monday night came the conversation with his parents was less painful than it might have been. Aaron felt guilty through the entirety of it nonetheless.

There was enough money for ice time and coaching fees for now, and whatever difference the extra weeks added up to, Aaron knew that Luke's accident would leave some sponsorships and federation funding up for grabs. And he could always teach a few more basic skating classes if he needed to.

As for the restaurant, Aaron volunteered to do what paperwork and administration he could via distance and the magic of the internet. He knew that organizing spreadsheets and making calls to suppliers after a day of training would be the last thing he'd want to do, but being able to contribute mattered.

But even with those problems solved, he still had to get to Saint Paul. Aaron had to confess to his parents that he'd already called the Put-in Bay airport and arranged a flight to Cleveland for the next morning. Getting off the island itself was a little like taking a taxi: You let the airport know you needed to fly. If someone who could pilot one of the six-seat prop planes that served as a connection between the islands and the mainland was around, you paid them a hundred dollars and off you went. It was summer, so he could have taken the ferry to the mainland and driven to Cleveland, but flying was easier and faster. And he wouldn't have to rent a car. Once he got to Cleveland, he would need to get on a big plane like anyone else.

2

The Week Before Memorial Day

Miami, FL

Zack Kelly stood on his balcony and looked out at the ocean. It was supposed to be soothing. Compared to his recently ended career – rattling around the world's conflict zones in search of stories people didn't want to read about horrors they didn't want to admit were happening – it probably was.

But Zack was not soothed. Whatever healing he'd been supposed to find on Miami's beaches had largely been eclipsed by the book deal he was currently living off of, a somewhat hasty marriage, and a now even-hastier divorce. At least he had a decent therapist who was helping him get a handle his journalism-induced PTSD.

His cellphone, shoved in the back pocket of his shorts like an accident waiting to happen, rang. He fumbled it out, barely caring who was calling enough to check the ID. Was it his in-process ex, his supportive but exhausting local friends, more spam? It didn't matter. None of it was appealing.

He frowned at the screen; it was his best friend from college. Which, while his world was falling apart in the most boring way possible, felt like a halfway decent consolation prize.

"Sammy," he said, answering the call. "What brings you to rubbernecking my disaster life?"

"Work, if you want it. Assuming you're in the country."

Zack dragged his hand through his hair. "I'm here. Packing for my ex, who still can't be bothered to do domestic tasks even if they are the ones required for him not to be living here anymore."

"I don't want to tell you I always knew it would end in tears…." Sammy began.

"But you always knew it would end in tears?" Zack finished for him.

"Ten thousand percent. I don't know what you thought you were looking for, but you weren't going to find it in a trauma rebound six months after you got back from a shooting war."

"You know I have a therapist for conversations like this, right?" Zack tucked his phone between his shoulder and ear and went back inside so he could toss things that weren't his in boxes. "Anyway, I'm terrible company, but I still have a mortgage, because I got the condo. What's the gig?"

"That depends," Sammy said, his voice coy, almost flirtatious, despite his heterosexuality.

Zack chuckled. They'd been roommates their freshman year in college and had somehow survived getting journalism degrees together. But while Sammy had excelled at a life that didn't involve an excess of adrenaline and unwise risk-taking, Zack had not. Which made Sammy's call right now a bit of a godsend. Whatever the job was – and he really could use the work – it probably wouldn't mess with Zack's head too much.

"How soon can you get on a plane?" Sammy asked.

The words themselves were familiar. But the circumstance was definitely not. Zack stopped sorting DVDs and straightened up. "Dude. What the fuck? You edit a sports publication."

"With a circulation of over three million," Sammy said proudly.

"Yes, yes, you have an awesome job and seem almost as cool at reunions as I do."

"Almost?!" Sammy protested.

"I have more tattoos and also literal battle scars."

"Fair."

Zack went on. "But unless something bizarre has happened involving Division I NCAA players toppling foreign governments, 'how soon can you get on a plane?' is never a question you should be asking me."

"It's about figure skating," Sammy said, his affect completely flat.

Zack stared at a framed picture above the TV. It was one he'd taken of his now-ex, showing rope coiled against skin. This had to be a prank.

"Are you joking?"

"No."

"*Figure skating*?!" Zack trusted Sammy, but really, how was this not a prank?

"Yep."

"The only things your readers care about are basketball, football, and the swimsuit issue!"

"Baseball sometimes," Sammy reminded him. "And hockey's a thing."

Zack ran his free hand over his face. He should probably shave at some point, but he thought the facial hair thing was starting to work for him.

"Okay. Tell me why you want me to get on a plane right now for figure skating." He couldn't be sure, but he had a sinking suspicion his life was about to get more absurd than it already was.

"The number one men's figure skater in the U.S. just shattered his leg," Sammy said. "Super gory. Which our readers will love."

"I'm not in a mental place to do medical stories right now," Zack said immediately. No matter what the source of the injury, he suspected he would never be in a mental place to do medical stories again.

"Whatever, it's a paragraph," Sammy said, breezing by Zack's concern. "I'll shove it in if you can't deal. The point is, the Winter Olympics are in February in Almaty. The U.S. has two men's figure skating spots. Which everyone in the sport knew were going to go to Luke Koval and Jack Palumbo. But Koval fucked his leg up and now everything about every competition this season is in turmoil and his spot is up for grabs. There're two main contenders – Cayden Sauer in Phoenix and some kid in Minnesota. Aaron Sheffield... Sheftall? I don't know, something like that; you'll figure it out."

"You're making me chase ambulances to try to make America care about figure skating and you don't even want me to chase the actual ambulance? And can't remember the names of the people I'm supposed to write about?" Zack was pretty sure he was offended; he just wasn't sure on whose part.

"Kind of, yeah."

"Which is why you want me to get there before anyone else does?" Zack said, as if multiple reporters were going to be banging down the doors of skating rinks across the country. Which, for all he knew, maybe they were.

"Basically. Also figure skating is an absolute trash fire of drama, and it has hot ladies' skaters to appeal to our core demographics."

"I hate you." Zack sighed heavily. The reasonable thing would be to ask for time to think about it before uprooting

22

his entire life for an unforeseen amount of time. But his life here in Miami wasn't at all appealing at the moment, and work would give him something to focus on. "I don't get what you're thinking, but hey, it's your career's funeral. You still pay a dollar a word?"

"You bet."

"And this is why I love you," Zack said. "So, uh... do any of these people know I'm coming?"

"Yeah, I set up a whole thing. It'll be like an embed. With the Minnesota people at least. The other major training center hasn't gotten back to me yet, so that's on you."

"Okay, I'll go. On one condition."

"What?"

"Never compare covering figure skating to war reporting again."

✦

Two days later, after an endless series of mechanical delays, Zack was on what had become a late-night flight to the Minneapolis-Saint Paul airport. Once upon a time, boarding a plane would have felt not merely exciting, but like a relief. Being in the field as a reporter, ready to talk himself in and out of chaos and danger, was where he had felt most himself. *Had*, of course, being the operative word. Now, whenever he got on a plane, his mind, body, and adrenaline levels were convinced he was flying into danger again, and reacted accordingly. The entire experience was extremely unpleasant, and as his heart pounded in his ears during the taxi for takeoff, he wondered if he should have driven.

As soon as he was allowed, he pulled out his laptop and started trying to learn everything he possibly could about skating. He watched a video about how to identify each of the main jumps at least six times before he had to accept that he still had no idea how to tell the difference between them despite slow motion and arrows.

Watching the previous year's U.S. Nationals proved just as unhelpful. Zack may have intellectually understood why some programs with falls got better scores than those that seemed, to his inexperienced eye, to go off without a hitch, but he was emotionally baffled by it. At best, he was able to classify skaters into essentially meaningless boxes: lyrical, cocky, confident, and chaotic.

By the time he got off the plane at Minneapolis-Saint Paul he was overtired and motion sick and hadn't yet gotten around to watching any post-competition interviews with the skaters he was being paid to write about.

For bonus points, Brendan Reid, one of Aaron Sheftall's coaches, had arrived to pick him up at the airport. Which struck Zack as excessively courteous, but then, he supposed, this was Minnesota.

"Hey, you must be Zack," Brendan said brightly once they'd found each other at arrivals. "Glad you made it," he added warmly as if they'd been friends for years. He was exceptionally attractive, too, with neatly-cropped sandy brown hair, keen green eyes, and the faintest dusting of freckles across his fair skin.

Too bad he's married to his skating partner, Zack thought glumly as he shook Brendan's offered hand. "Sammy sent you a picture?"

"No, we googled you. Congrats on the book, by the way. Though I haven't had a chance to read it yet."

"Ahhh, that's fine," Zack said awkwardly; Brendan was a wall of charisma. And his own charming war reporter schtick felt grim and boring in the face of all this middle-American sparkle. "It would probably only make you more confused about why I got this assignment."

"I'm not confused at all. You and your editor have your expertise, and I've got mine." Brendan shrugged.

"Anyway, you got everything? I don't want to keep Marie up later than we have to."

Zack shouldered his backpack and his camera bag and trotted to catch up with Brendan who was already headed towards the parking lot. "Who's Marie?"

✦

Marie turned out to be an ex-nun who lived in Diamond Lake in a house with an in-law apartment. Usually, Brendan informed him as they drove, she rented it out to various elite skaters who came through the Twin Cities for choreography or a tryout for Katie and Brendan's team.

"Figured this made more sense than dumping you in a hotel," Brendan said as he leaned against the doorbell at the little bungalow. The neighborhood was quiet, the windows of the other houses dark. They were evidently the only ones awake at this hour. "If you want to get a handle on the skating life, staying at Marie's is practically a rite of passage around here."

Marie, bless her heart, answered the door with a plate of kolaczki and the offer of coffee, which struck Zack as a little odd given the hour until Brendan explained.

"Sometimes we start training days at the rink at five. Sometimes I'm on an overnight shift at the farm. If someone's still awake at..." he paused and checked his watch, "One a.m. around here, there's a better than even chance they're starting their day, not ending it."

"Let's get you inside," Marie said. "I have to leave for the soup kitchen at four thirty, but there's plenty of time to get you fed and caught up on some of the gossip."

Zack followed her through the door, then held it for Brendan once he was inside.

"Oh no," Brendan said. "I'm headed home and am gonna crash. But I'll see you tomorrow at the rink, yeah?"

"Definitely." Truth be told, other than making a call to Sauer's coaches to try to set up an interview, Zack had nothing else to do than get up to speed quick.

"Take some for everyone, all right?" Marie pressed a tinfoil-wrapped plate into Brendan's hands. "Tell them I say hi."

"Thanks! You're the best." Brendan gave Marie a hug and then, to Zack's great surprise, hugged him as well. "You're in good hands here, but call us if you need anything, okay?"

"Uh. Sure." Zack hugged him back awkwardly. He felt both relieved and a little guilty when Brendan had closed the door behind himself and he was alone with his new landlady for the next several weeks.

"Is he always like that?" Zack asked before he could stop himself.

"Brendan? Oh no. Sometimes he's worse. Midwestern meets figure skater sensibilities is a potent combination. Especially if you're not used to it. Which something tells me you're not," she said keenly.

"Not so much, no."

"Regretting whatever it was in your life that brought you here?" Marie asked, the short, grey curls of her hair looking far more alert than Zack felt.

"At this very moment, yes, I am," Zack admitted. Something in Marie invited confidences. And the briskness of her manner indicated she was practical and unlikely to judge him for whatever those confidences might be.

"Congratulations. You're not the first to stay here feeling that way, and you won't be the last. Now come on, I'll show you your room and you can get settled."

Zack followed Marie down the hallway, past a small living room and dining room and into a kitchen. Clean dishes were piled up on a dish rack and spread across several dish towels on the counter.

"You're down here," Marie said, opening a door that led to a flight of basement steps. They were somewhat steep and narrow, which made them difficult to navigate with his luggage. At the bottom of the steps Marie flipped on the lights to reveal the place he'd be calling home.

There was an open plan kitchen at one end of the living room, both painted a shade of green that had gone out of fashion at least a decade ago. The couch and armchairs, table and stove, were all clean and well-kept but also showed signs of much wear. There were framed photos on the walls – some of them were signed portraits of people Zack vaguely remembered from watching the Olympics as a kid, and some were larger ones of various landmarks in the Twin Cities. Shelves along the walls held books, board games, and more ceramic figure skating figurines than Zack had known existed. Also not a few pairs of figure skates, covered in sharpied signatures. Through one door off the living room Zack could see the edge of a bed, and through another a bathroom, tiled in remarkably vintage pink.

"That's your entrance," Marie said, pointing at another door. "Leads you out into the back yard, there's a path that'll bring you around to the front. Will you have a car?"

"Yeah, I have to pick up a rental at some point."

"That's fine, there's room in the driveway for you. I don't care what hours you keep, just don't make a racket coming home. Whatever you're doing, you won't be the strangest one who's ever stayed here. Your keys and the Wi-Fi info are on the table."

"Okay." Zack strongly suspected he was going to like Marie. "Does the offer of gossip cover some of those people who are probably stranger than me?"

"Oh, possibly," Marie said. There was no protest in it at all.

"You mentioned coffee," Zack said, eyeing a coffee maker on the counter. "Are you interested in partaking with me?"

"Depends. Are you any good at making it?"

"Well," Zack said, starting to open cupboards in search of supplies. He'd have to go shopping soon, but there were beans and a grinder in the cupboard. "Of the many reasons my ex-husband and I got divorced, my skill at coffee making was not one of them."

Marie pulled herself out a chair. "That sounds promising."

"Because coffee?"

Marie gave him a slow smile, and Zack loved it. "No. Because you seem to appreciate the rules when it comes to an exchange of gossip."

3

Two Days After Memorial Day

Twin Cities Ice Arena

Twenty-four hours after he'd left Whisker Island in its gray morning gloom, Aaron walked toward the doors of Twin Cities Ice Arena. The scrape of his skate bag's wheels across the parking lot asphalt and the feel of its duct-taped handle were comfortingly familiar. As was the presence of Charlotte Beaulieu, his roommate and the on-again off-again ladies French national champion, at his side.

Once he pushed through the glass double doors Aaron inhaled deeply. The scent of the rink - rubber floor mats, disinfectant, the indefinable smell of ice – surrounded him. He felt a weight he hadn't known he carried lift off his shoulders. He might have left his family, but still, here, he was also home.

Charlotte ran off to find Brendan to ask him something, and Aaron made for the men's locker room. He unpacked most of the contents of his skate bag into his locker – snacks, spare laces, a change of clothes, extra soakers, yet more snacks, a backup phone charger – and sat down on one of the benches to put his skates on.

He was the only one in there this early, which would have been unusual during the season and felt like a blessing now. Skating involved a tremendous amount of being watched – by judges, by coaches, by competitors. A respite from that was welcome.

Aaron tugged the laces on each of his skates tight and tied them off into double knots before tucking the ends into his boots. *Keep your eyes on your own paper*. It was a favorite saying of Katie's: Work on what you can control. Let go of the rest. There was plenty about skating no one could predict, but the biggest thing was the performance of others. As much as he was competing against the entire men's field, he had to train as if he was only competing against himself.

Still, it was hard. Aaron's first step onto the ice – that familiar shift from walking to gliding, the smooth slick of the ice beneath his blades and the rush of building speed – was marred by thoughts of his competition in the upcoming season.

Jack Palumbo would claim any top spot there was to claim nationally, plus a lot of the international top spots, that was for sure. Aaron wasn't sure which he envied more – Jack's stable of seemingly effortless quad jumps, or his consistency. And he had artistry, at least when his coaches let him pick his own music. But Aaron wasn't particularly preoccupied with him.

Cayden Sauer, on the other hand, was definitely living rent-free in Aaron's head. Not only did Aaron find him consistently unpleasant whenever they ran into each other at competitions and training camps, he edged out Aaron's scores more often than not. With Luke out of the running, if Aaron didn't get to the Olympics, it would be because Cayden had.

Aaron warmed up – edges and crossovers to get the feel of the ice, single jumps to get the feeling of his body and then doubles to find the physics of it all again after so many weeks off. As he went, Aaron tried, but failed, to shake off his worries about the season ahead.

What makes you different from all the other skaters? Katie was going to ask him, the same way she did every year when they started building programs. And as always, he didn't know. Which was a problem. With the stakes this season, nothing half-assed would serve.

His worries distracted him, and he popped what he'd meant to be a triple toe loop. Frustrated, he set up the entrance to the jump again. He got the full number of rotations in, but fell on the landing. Next try, he caught an edge going into it and went sprawling before he could take off.

Thank God for crash shorts.

Aaron knew he should give it a rest; there was no need to nail anything before he'd been on the ice an hour and for the first time in weeks. But that jump wasn't hard for him. He'd been landing it since he was a kid, and if he couldn't land such a reliable jump….

He gave it another go. In midair, half a meter off the ground, he already knew the jump was bad, and he yelled in frustration before he hit the ice. Again.

"Sheftall!" Katie's voice cut through the brisk air.

Aaron picked himself up off and readied himself for another attempt.

"Don't you dare!" Katie yelled again, like she might march right onto the sheet and drag him off of it if he didn't comply.

Aaron sighed and skated over to the boards where Katie waited, her brow furrowed. She was dressed as she usually was for a day of coaching, with no sign that Aaron had interrupted her summer vacation by returning early, except that she was wearing sneakers, not skates.

Silently, she handed Aaron his skate guards, a clear commentary that he was done for now. He slipped them on reluctantly as he stepped off the ice.

Brendan stood by the door that led to the lobby, talking to a man Aaron didn't recognize but who was wearing a hilarious number of layers. Aaron was only in a t-shirt, but this guy was wearing a down coat with a fur-trimmed hood. Still, he was definitely cute. Dark hair, a short dark beard that didn't hide how sharp his jawline was, and a general broadness of build that *probably* wasn't all the coat. And he was definitely at least six feet. Aaron approved.

"Good morning," Aaron told Katie cheerily, while he continued to check out the guy.

She gave him an exasperated look. "When I said we were going to get an early start I did not expect this."

Aaron refocused on her. "You told me I could use the ice. Who's the dude?" He tried not to grin. It was good to be back. Even – especially – when he was getting chewed out by Katie. She only bothered to be a hardass to people she liked.

"Journalist," Katie said. "He's here to write a piece about the state of the field as it stands now for *Athletics Monthly*. He'll be off to cover Sauer in Phoenix eventually. If I had to guess, he'll probably talk to a bunch of the juniors too. So in the meantime, make yourself a good story, preferably without being a giant flirt. You know narrative matters. The right sort of media coverage could mean a bit more respect from the federation and the judges."

✦

Aaron followed Katie through the warren of hallways at the heart of the Twin Cities Ice complex to the room they sometimes used for meetings, but more often for meals or impromptu naps. There were a few tables, no windows, an old microwave, and a refrigerator that rumbled ominously in the corner. Someone had made coffee in the communal coffee maker they all took turns bringing in beans for. Aaron helped himself to a cup – the bitter, slightly burnt smell felt like home – and sat down next to Charlotte.

Aside from themselves, Brendan, Katie, and the journalist, only those skaters who lived year-round in the Twin Cities and also weren't otherwise on tour or vacation were present. Which meant Sam and Morgan, who skated pairs together, and two junior men's skaters, Angel and Nikolai, who Aaron knew were both hoping to qualify for competing in the senior division soon. No one looked fully awake.

At the front of the room, Brendan waved haphazardly to get their attention. "Hi everybody. Thanks for being here. Normally we'd have a more organized welcome back, but this isn't the official start to our training season for most of you… you're just…here."

"There's like six of them," Katie said from the side of the room, sounding somewhere between exasperated and amused. Which was true – Katie and Brendan coached maybe thirty skaters all together, though most of them were younger skaters still competing at the novice and intermediate level.

Brendan waved that detail away and went on talking. "Which, honestly, warms my heart. That we love what we do and stick together in tough times. And with that out of the way," Brendan said, clapping his hands together. "We do have an actual announcement."

Katie sighed audibly. Brendan shot her a smile.

"God, they are so married," Charlotte murmured at Aaron.

"Jealous?" he whispered.

"Of the domestic bliss or that he gets to live with her hotness?" she replied.

"I'll take your word for it," Aaron said.

"You should."

33

"The man back there," Brendan said pointing, "Who looks like he wishes he'd packed a sweater."

Everyone in the room turned to look at the guy, who was leaning against a table, both hands wrapped around a paper coffee cup. He'd taken off his parka and definitely looked cold, but Aaron was more distracted by his elaborately tattooed arms. No one in skating had that much ink, not where anyone could see it. Aaron already thought the guy was hot, but the tattoos were definitely nice icing.

"Anyway, that's Zack," Brendan said. "He's a journalist–"

Charlotte cursed in French under her breath.

" – and he's here to write about all of you."

"It's a long-form, reported piece," Zack said, like that meant anything to any of them. "So, while the impetus is Luke Koval's injury and what that means for the men's field, I'll be here for a few weeks to soak up the atmosphere and community. You should all honestly ignore me as much as possible, except hopefully when I want to talk to you."

"Do you know how to skate?" Aaron asked. He didn't want to get skipped over for Angel and Nikolai and some premature look at the future of the sport, not when he was right here and ready to – hopefully – do great things.

"Ah. No," Zack admitted.

"I can fix that," he said and regretted it almost immediately as the rest of the room burst out with laughter.

"Do I want to know what the punchline is?" Zack asked.

"You really don't," Katie said, before anyone could say anything worse.

Brendan, meanwhile, looked from Aaron to Zack and back again.

"Can I have you two sort this out when we're not in the middle of a meeting?" he asked plaintively.

Aaron watched as Zack, trying to hide his confused amusement, nodded at the same time as him. Then he caught his eye with a wicked smile.

Aaron had a suspicion this was going to be all sorts of fun.

4

Very Early in the Morning

Twin Cities Ice Arena

Zack sat on the bench a few feet from the door to the ice and stared at the giant, glowing red clock that hung over the far end of the sheet. 5:05am. He still didn't know anything about skating beyond YouTube videos, but the early hour, the profusion of fluorescent lights, and the rink's industrial warehouse vibe were all familiar enough. He certainly felt more at ease here than he had in his own living room for the last several months, which was either situation normal given the divorce or something he should probably talk over with his therapist.

The heavy door from the locker room banged open, making Zack jump. Aaron, one of the main subjects of his article and now his skating instructor, appeared with a reusable shopping bag in one hand and a pair of skates in the other. Zack was freezing in several layers of long sleeves and a hoodie, but Aaron wore only a T-shirt and a light jacket, unzipped. Zack had seen him up close yesterday, but only briefly, and was struck anew at how small Aaron was. None of the skaters were tall, but Aaron seemed particularly slight and the top of his head barely came past Zack's shoulder.

"You made it!" he said cheerily, setting the bag down on the floor in front of Zack and the pair of skates – his own, Zack assumed – gently on the bench.

"Did you think I wouldn't?" Zack was curious.

"Five in the morning is early for most people." Aaron sat down next to him and started pulling on the skates, but with a sideways glance at Zack that instantly made him suspicious.

"Wait," Zack said. "Did you tell me to drag my ass out of bed and to this rink at five in the morning as a *test*?"

"Maybe."

"*Why?*"

"If I confess will you be mad?"

"No," Zack said, staring at Aaron in disbelief. "But I will be exceptionally curious."

Aaron shrugged as he tightened his laces with deft fingers. "If you're going to write about me working my ass off when none of us know if I'm going to make it to the Olympics, I thought you should suffer a little bit, too."

Despite the hour and energy required, a laugh burst out of Zack. "You're evil."

"I prefer 'feral.'" Aaron said with a sharp smile.

Zack felt completely off balance. While he hadn't expected the subject of an article about elite competitive sports to be mellow, Aaron's bright sharpness, not to mention the fact that he was apparently a little shit, was a shock. Zack was drawn to him in a way that he told himself, firmly, was about the piece he was here to write and not about the way Aaron held his lower lip between his teeth as he tied off his laces and tucked them in.

"I raided the skate exchange for some skates for you." Aaron said, nodding at the bag at Zack's feet. "I wasn't sure what your size was so I took a guess. Fitting skates is more of an art than a science anyway."

Zack peered dubiously into the bag, glad for something to do other than stare at his subject, who would hopefully let Zack photograph him at some point as well. In the bag were several pairs of black figure skates, the leather variously scuffed, scarred, and patched with black tape. He looked back up at Aaron.

"Doesn't the rink have rentals? Wouldn't that be easier?"

Aaron frowned. "No," he said seriously. "I don't teach anyone on rentals. They fit badly, they don't offer any ankle support, and the blades are shit. You'd get hurt."

"I might get hurt anyway," Zack pointed out, pulling out a skate and looking for a size indicated anywhere on them."

"If you do, it won't be because of something we could have prevented."

The serious tone of his proclamation made Zack remember that both of them were here because of a freak accident no one could have foreseen, much less prevented. Sometimes, life wasn't fair. Or kind.

The pair of skates he finally decided on – or rather, that Aaron decided on for him – felt snug, far more so than any shoe he had ever worn. They didn't hurt, but the sensation was a lot. He wasn't sure he liked it, but there also wasn't anything he could do about it. He had agreed to take a skating lesson, and this was apparently what was required to skate.

"I'll show you how to do the laces." Without ceremony Aaron pulled Zack's foot into his lap.

Zack sputtered. Whatever unprofessional attraction he might or might not have been feeling, he was not used to being manhandled so very effectively by someone a fraction of his size.

"Do you always have bad boundaries or am I special?" Zack asked, before his brain could wander into more dangerous territory, like noting how very good Aaron was with his hands or wondering what other things he might be able to tie.

Aaron's eyes stayed focused on his work. "I don't have bad boundaries. You don't know how to tie skates yet, and I can't describe the sensation to you. Sorry if it's weird."

He didn't sound sorry at all. Which probably should have annoyed Zack, but all it did was make him more intrigued. Aaron's mix of mischief, professionalism, and approval-seeking was not one he had encountered before.

"Jeez, that's tight," he said as Aaron finished.

"Does it hurt? Can you still feel your toes?"

"No. And yes."

"Then it's not too tight. It might even be too loose." Aaron shoved Zack's feet to the floor. "Stand up, let's see how that works."

Zack levered himself up and took a few wobbling steps forward. "I hope this is less awkward on the ice."

Aaron gave him a crooked smile. "In the abstract? Yes. In reality, because you've never done this before? Not so much."

With that, he took off a skate guard, set it on the boards, and stepped onto the ice in one fluid motion. Zack stared as Aaron glided on one foot and bent over to remove the other guard.

"Um...." Zack's brain was frozen. He was obviously not supposed to do *that*. But he had no idea what he was supposed to do. Aaron on the ice was mesmerizing, even when he wasn't doing any of the tricks Zack knew mattered from his attempt at in-flight research. On land Aaron moved with quick, energetic motions. On the ice, he seemed to flow with a grace that reminded Zack of someone gliding through water.

Aaron did a lap around the whole rink and came to a neat stop across the boards from where Zack was still standing, transfixed.

"Are you okay?" Aaron asked, his face concerned.

"Yeah. Totally."

Aaron was clearly not convinced. "Okay. Next steps. Sit back down, take your guards off, stand up, walk over to that door, and step onto the ice. Keep your feet under you. Hold onto the wall, and try to remember that frozen water is slippery."

"Thanks," Zack said dryly, but set about doing as he was told.

"It's not you," Aaron said calmly as Zack slowly managed to get himself onto the ice, mostly by holding on to the boards for dear life. "A lot of the time people are shocked that ice is wet."

Once Zack had both feet on the ice and one hand firmly gripping the boards, Aaron skated backwards towards the center of the rink.

"Come join me out here!"

"Are you kidding me?" Zack said. Aaron was appealing – way more so than Zack had anticipated – but he still wasn't motivating Zack to take his life into his hands in quite that way.

"You've seen people skate. Or use rollerblades or whatever. You also know how to walk. You don't have to be fast or graceful, you just have to get over here. Also, don't lean forward too much. The little teeth things at the front of your blades are toe picks, and you don't know what to do with them yet, so they're going to make you trip."

"Uh... great." It wasn't that Zack would rather have been getting shot at, but if he had been, he would at least have had a better idea of how to proceed. Carefully, he let go of the wall. That was okay. He tried to pick up one foot and decided that wasn't. "How do I tell where my foot is?"

"What?" Aaron asked. "You said you could feel your toes."

"Yes, but now I'm two inches taller than usual and I can't feel the ground."

"Ugh." Aaron skated back over to Zack and stuck out his hands. "Still not bad boundaries, although hopefully I'm cute enough for you to want to hold my hands."

Aaron winked. Zack wondered if this were hell and if so, what he'd done to deserve it.

"We're going to teach you how to walk," Aaron explained, "which is a thing you already know how to do."

It wasn't. Zack felt more absurd than he had in at least a decade as Aaron skated backwards so he could hold Zack's hands as he marched around the ice.

Then Aaron let go.

Zack took three steps before his feet slipped out from under him. He had a moment's sensation of being airborne before his ass hit the ice. Hard.

He gritted his teeth. "Damn, that hurts."

"Did you break anything?" Aaron didn't look particularly worried.

"I don't think so," Zack said as he tried to figure out how to get up. He felt like a crab skidding across the ice on its back.

"Hands and knees," Aaron said.

Once more Zack had few options other than doing as he was told. And really, this whole nightmare exercise might have been a little less hard if he wasn't fighting his brain's reluctance to take orders. At least until Aaron corrected him again.

"Ugh, not like that," Aaron said as Zack pressed his palms to the ice.

"Why not?"

"'Cause someone can skate over your fingers and cut them off."

"Tell me you're joking." Zack peered up at him. Which wasn't a bad angle from which to view Aaron.

Focus, he scolded himself.

"Nope. Everyone has a fingers story," Aaron said mildly.

"Is that like how everyone has a kidney thieves story involving a friend of their second cousin?"

Aaron shook his head. "Finger. Zamboni ice. Baggie. Ambulance."

"Great. Why am I doing this again?" *Because journalism*, his brain unhelpfully supplied. And worse, *because you're now a fool who wants to impress a guy.*

Aaron had his own answer, though. "So when you write your article you understand how hard this is and don't write a crappy opening about glitter, homosexuality, or tween girls."

"There's nothing wrong with any of those things," Zack said as he finally stumbled up to his feet, mostly by clutching onto Aaron, who might have been small but was also completely, freakishly immoveable.

"No," Aaron agreed sternly, "there's not." If he had more to say about the subject – and Zack was sure he did – he kept it to himself with pursed lips and a sharp gaze.

"Are people assholes to you because you're a skater?" he ventured.

"For that to be true, I'd have to know people who aren't skaters." Aaron took Zack's hands and slowly pried his fingers loose from his jacket. Zack hadn't realized he'd been gripping him quite so hard. "Now that we're done with *your* bad boundaries… try to glide, like push with one foot and then go. And please don't look at your feet, it throws your balance off."

Zack did his best to follow what felt like too many directions at once. Rather than look at the ice he locked eyes with Aaron, who smiled encouragingly at him.

The look was so appealing, sweet and come-hither at the same time, a smile just for him, as if they were the only two people in the world and Zack was doing right, exactly right, as he was.

That was not a thing that usually turned Zack's crank – usually he was the one giving both orders and approval – but oh this was working for him right now. Surely – *surely* – that look was calculated. Aaron was, after all, a trained performer. But it still made Zack's knees go weak. Which was a problem, as his muscles were way too tense to be able to incorporate any shift in balance. He went down again, this time forward onto his hands. It didn't hurt as much as that first fall. But it was still unpleasant. At least he sort of knew how to get up this time.

Zack looked up at Aaron, annoyed both at the sudden attraction that could only cause problems and at this entire venture that was going to turn him into one giant bruise.

"I hate this," he said. "And also possibly you."

✦

An hour later Zack was cold, sore, and, he assumed, wildly bruised everywhere he had fallen. When their lesson was finally finished, Aaron coaxed him off the ice and, before Zack managed to hobble over to a bench and sink down on it, was back in the center of the rink spinning at a rate that felt like it shouldn't be humanly possible. His head was back, his eyes were closed, and one hand reached upwards, the other pressed to his heart.

Definitely a different kind of creature, Zack thought. What Aaron had been teaching him had been a galaxy apart from what he was doing on the ice alone. Zack had known this, but seeing it in person was a different, almost sublime, experience.

I have been here less than twenty-four hours and am already in so much trouble.

Zack managed to get his skate guards on by himself and felt rather proud of that. He grimaced as he drained the rest of his coffee, gone frigid in the cold rink, and was about to lever himself to his feet again to find a drinking fountain when he heard voices.

Katie and Brendan were standing next to each other on the mats a quarter of the way around the rink, watching Aaron practice. Ordinarily they would have been too far away to make out what they were saying but sound travelled oddly in this space and Zack could hear them far too clearly.

"He's hungry the way you are," Brendan was saying, his voice low and with a note of urgency to it. "And he has the potential to be miserable the way you were. This season, the stakes for him, they're not going to help."

"He'll be fine," Katie retorted.

"I'm just saying –"

"I watch out for all our skaters."

Her voice was sharp. If Zack hadn't known Katie and Brendan were married, he'd be wondering when they were finally going to hook up. They had the vibe some couples had where conversations that seemed like arguments were things that happened so they didn't fuck in public. He suspected they were absolutely crazy about each other on top of being endlessly exhausted... and not only by skating hours.

Zack would have felt bad about the whole eavesdropping thing, but he was sitting in plain view and was overhearing only by an accident of acoustics. It wasn't like he was going to quote random chatter in his article anyway.

"I don't worry about all of our skaters. I worry about him." Brendan said, folding his arms over the boards and frowning as Aaron set up for a jump, went up into the air, and missed the landing. He fell with a hollow boom that made Zack hold his breath. But unlike Zack's agonizing climb back to his feet, Aaron picked himself up instantly.

Zack exhaled.

"Why?" Katie asked. "He tells us what he needs, and he does what he says he will. He's fine."

"He's not..." Brendan's voice trailed off. Frustration.

"He's not what?" Katie prompted. Zack's gaze moved between Katie and Brendan and their magnetic energy, and Aaron, who was setting up the jump again.

"Like other people." Brendan threw his hands up in the air for a moment and paced a tight circle. Zack recognized the impulse. This conversation was likely an old argument in a new frame. "Do you remember when you made me cut your hair? With the knife?"

Zack blinked, Aaron forgotten for a moment. Sammy had said skating was all drama all the time, but *yikes*. That was a lot by any standard.

"Yes?" Katie said. Still calm, still amused. A little defensive, but probably not as much as she should have been.

"You scared the shit out of me," Brendan said.

"Why?" She chuckled. "Because I was handing you a knife?"

"No. Because you didn't seem human. You seemed like the storm. Or a witch. Or a beast."

Katie looked at him, silently, and while Zack had no idea what Brendan was referencing, somehow he could see in her implacable face exactly what Brendan meant.

"Aaron's like that," Brendan said.

Katie gave a little shrug.

Zack suddenly had a lot more questions. Along with a sense he might have accidentally wandered into an even stranger group of people than he had thought. That sense was one that had never led him astray before. Into danger, many times. But there had always been a good story on the other side. And story was what he was here for.

✦

By the time Zack got his skates off and his shoes back on, Brendan had disappeared somewhere and Katie was talking to Aaron across the boards.

"See?" Aaron said, pointing over Katie's shoulder at Zack as he approached them. "Told you he survived."

Katie glanced at Zack. "Make sure you drink plenty of water today. Heat and arnica gel are your friends for the bruises you're going to have."

"Thank you." Zack was, unaccountably, touched by the simple gesture of care.

"You won't thank me tomorrow morning. Or him," Katie said.

"Don't *scare* him," Aaron protested. But he shot Zack a conspiratorial smile, which Zack returned.

"I've had rough workouts before," Zack said.

"Mmm." Katie looked at him consideringly. She was, he realized, sizing him up. For what, he didn't know, and the uncertainty left an uncomfortable prickling sensation at the back of his neck. Did she know he'd been eavesdropping on her and Brendan?

"Hey," he said to Aaron. "As a preemptive thank you for the lesson. Before I regret it too much, can I buy you a coffee?"

Aaron's face brightened and he opened his mouth, but before he could say anything, Katie cut in.

"No, you cannot. Unless you want to grab him something from the vending machine. We have ice time right now and a lot of work to do."

It was clear *we* did not, in this case, include Zack. Aaron looked crestfallen, but didn't protest.

"You two have thirty seconds," Katie said as she strode away to fiddle with the rink's sound system.

"I do have to interview you at some point," Zack said.

"Is that what the coffee is?" Aaron asked.

"No."

Aaron reached for his phone, sitting next to a box of kleenex and a water bottle on the boards, and handed it to Zack. "Quick," he whispered.

Zack hastily texted himself from Aaron's phone and passed it back.

By the time Katie turned back around, Aaron was scrolling through a playlist with a reasonable air of innocence. Zack had to admit he was impressed.

Feral indeed.

5

Later that Morning

Twin Cities Ice Arena

Done with his own skating for the day, Aaron dug in his bag for a clean pair of socks. He'd have to be back at the rink later to teach, but for a few hours at least, his time was his own.

His phone barked with an incoming text.

Zack: Hello, Aaron.

Aaron wondered where Zack was right now. For people who didn't live and die by the ice, the work day was just beginning. Perhaps he was holed up somewhere writing. Or recovering from whatever bruises he'd earned in his lesson. Aaron wasn't sure what journalists did when they weren't doing interviews or typing things.

But he wanted to find out. Zack had shown up yesterday, and this morning had submitted himself with a surprising willingness to Aaron's instruction. Aaron approved of that nearly as much as he approved of his tattoos, sadly not seen since yesterday's introductory meeting. Also his general physique, which Aaron had gotten to spend a lot of time assessing while Zack grabbed on to him and tried not to fall over.

Aaron: You still wanna do coffee?

Zack: If you do.

Aaron frowned at his phone. Either Zack was pissed off at him, or he was one of those odd creatures who precisely punctuated their text messages. Given the whole journalist thing, Aaron decided to assume the latter.

Aaron: Def. What time? I need to go home and shower, and I have to be back here at four to teach some of the little kids. There's a cafe not too far from TCI, I'll send the address... can meet you there at like two?

Zack: I'll see you there.

Aaron hummed to himself and went back to looking for his socks.

✦

Fortunately for Aaron, Charlotte had a class at Concordia that afternoon which meant he could get home and shower without offering her an explanation of his coffee date with Zack. If Katie had been askance at the idea, Charlotte was going to be downright appalled.

He took entirely too long deciding what to wear, given that Zack had already seen him in practice clothes and the rest of his wardrobe only provided two options: t-shirts and formalwear. He finally picked the shirt with a fish skeleton emblazoned on it that Huy had brought back for him from Vancouver a couple of years ago, made sure his curls were the appealing side of messy, and headed back to his car.

Zack wasn't there yet when Aaron got to the café, but that allowed Aaron to take his time catching up with his favorite barista before he settled in at a table by the window. There were exposed brick walls on two sides of the café, plus tin ceilings and lots of warm dark wood paneling. None of it was original; the building itself was maybe thirty years old. But Aaron liked the decor and was fond of the calm, workaday atmosphere. There was always at least one group of college students huddled over notebooks and laptops, and on Friday nights the café hosted a board game club. It was a frequent escape for the TCI skaters, and once the season started Aaron would have been sure to encounter at least one of his compatriots there. But with so few people back in town, the odds of running into anyone he knew were low.

He stirred honey into his tea as he people-watched out the window. The early afternoon sun was bright and very welcome; Aaron already missed the fresh air and sunshine of the islands.

Still, Saint Paul had its perks. Aaron watched as a deep blue Mazda crossover parked at the curb and Zack got out. The sight of his arms in a possibly too tight black t-shirt made Aaron sigh wistfully and wish that the rink was less cold or that Zack could tolerate it better.

He waved as Zack pushed open the door and didn't think he was imagining it when Zack's face lit up at the sight of him. A few minutes later Zack was sitting across from him, a steaming cup of coffee in front of him and a grateful look on his face.

"I needed more caffeine," he admitted.

"I'm not surprised." Aaron took a sip of his tea.

"You mean after you made me go to the rink at fuck o'clock in the morning?"

"Basically." Aaron had expected Zack to be somewhat more pissed about that – surely a typical human would have been. But maybe following inexplicable directives from subjects was just part of what journalists did.

"Anyway. Thanks for meeting me," Zack said.

"Thanks for slipping me your number."

"You handed me your phone. While your coach's back was turned." Zack sounded somewhere between horrified and in awe, and Aaron was flattered.

"Katie can be overprotective. That's not exactly what I mean, but…" Aaron trailed off, suddenly not sure what the appropriate or smart thing to say was. Aaron might have wanted this to be a coffee date with a cute guy, but Zack was a journalist and here to write about *him*. Assuming Aaron could be interesting enough.

Zack took a sip of his coffee. "If your life is anything like how my ass feels right now, your coach can be as overprotective as she wants."

Aaron laughed, nervous, shrill, and genuinely amused. He clapped a hand over his mouth. *Game face*, he reminded himself sternly.

"Sorry," Zack said, holding Aaron's gaze. "I didn't mean to make that sound dirty."

Aaron shook his head and slowly lowered his hand. "It's fine. Skaters are…." He trailed off. There was nothing he could say that was both appropriate for a journalist's consumption and that could be explained in under fifteen minutes.

"I'm not going to try to fill in the blank on that one," Zack said.

Aaron laughed again, started to answer, and stopped himself. "Before I make my life harder than it already is – "

"Is your life hard?"

Yes, and you're not helping right now. Aaron waved the question off and kept going. "To be clear, what is the context of this coffee we're having?"

"I think I spent a solid hour cursing you out this morning. Coffee was the least I could do," Zack swirled the dark liquid in his cup.

"So is this conversation happening for your article, or...?" Aaron asked.

Zack had raised his cup to his lips but set it down again. "Oh. No. This isn't on the record. Sorry. No wonder you're not finishing your sentences."

"But you can't like... forget what I've said." Now Aaron was curious. "It's all going to show up somewhere, right?"

"I mean, I'm always trying to absorb the atmosphere for a thing." Zack rested his forearms on the table, leaning forward slightly as if to emphasize his earnestness. "But I do try not to do things like that to people."

Zack's left arm was awash in colors that formed a full sleeve, dominated by a swirl of ink that looked like a cresting wave. It was inches from Aaron's fingers. Lost in his own curiosity, he reached out to touch the crest of it. He could feel Zack's pulse under his fingertips.

"Oh shit." Aaron suddenly realized what he was doing and jerked his hand back. His cheeks burned. "I'm so sorry. *That* was bad boundaries."

"It's fine." Zack didn't look upset. He also didn't move his arm. He looked curious and amused, the way he had every time Aaron had said or done something figure skater-y that, apparently, civilians didn't do. As if touching someone uninvited was on the same plane as tying their skates for them.

Aaron shook his head. "No, I'm sorry, I shouldn't have–"

A smile tugged at the corner of Zack's mouth. "Aaron. Relax. You're fine. I've dealt with some creepers in my day but, believe me, you are nowhere near being one of them."

"I–" Aaron tried to stammer out a reasonable explanation that wasn't *we spent all morning together and I apparently got used to being around you and having to touch you a lot and also your tattoos are cool and I wish I got to see them more.* Because that would have been way beyond bad boundaries.

He decided to shift the topic back towards something like professional. "The only tattoos anyone has around here are Olympic rings. Once they get there, that is. The judges hate anything else. So it's not something I'm used to seeing."

"Or feeling?" Zack looked arch.

Aaron's face flamed again, but they were smiling at each other.

"Is it cool if I ask about them?" Aaron gestured with his index finger, but otherwise kept his hands tightly clasped in front of him.

"Of course." Zack moved his arms forward on the table so Aaron could get a better look. "I got the first one before I went out on my first assignment in a conflict zone, and then I kept adding to it. There was no reason to stop, once I had started. My ex-husband thought they were me coping with stress badly, which was probably one of the few things he got right about me."

He paused, like he thought Aaron might have a comment about that, but he didn't. That Zack had been married was one of the first things that popped up on the internet about him, after glowing reviews of his book.

When Aaron said nothing, Zack went on. "I thought it was funny to keep telling people it would make it easier to identify my body. First of all, pro tip, I wasn't funny, I was an asshole. And what it did was make it easier to identify my live body as the asshole journalist no one wanted around."

"Oh, so we're both space aliens!"

Zack gave Aaron a baffled look. Which was justified. That probably wasn't how most people would have responded to such a confession.

"I'm from somewhere really weird," Aaron tried to explain. "I get excited when I meet other people who also can't make polite conversation about who they are."

"So which planet are you from, space boy?" Zack smiled at Aaron, his arms still on the table between them.

Aaron took a deep breath. "A string of islands in the middle of a lake that only a hundred people live on when it's not tourist season."

"Ah. I'm from Florida. It's always tourist season there."

"Yeah, not where I'm from."

"What are they called, your islands?"

"In the tourist brochures, the Key West of the Midwest."

Zack's face was bright with amusement. "No, fuck you! You have to be making that up."

"I am not, because if I were making it up it would sound cooler and I wouldn't spend my summers gutting perch."

He had to resist the urge to clap his hands over his mouth again. He hadn't meant to mention that – the island or the fish. Unlike Ari, he didn't resent every outsider who came on to the islands, but still, they were a treasured home for him, one that was too easy for outsiders to misunderstand. He didn't particularly want a piece about his dreams of the Olympics prefaced with too-intimate details of his life there.

Zack peered at Aaron, seeming to consider something. Aaron braced himself to be asked to have a conversation on the record regarding everything he least wanted to talk about.

But instead, the other man stuck his hand out across the table. "Well, Aaron, space boy from the planet perch, nice to meet you. I'm Zack and I'm a damn fool who thought covering wars would make me special."

Aaron shook his proffered hand. Zack's grip was sure and strong, with a hint of calluses on the palm. He didn't want to let go.

In his pocket, Aaron's phone barked. He reluctantly withdrew his hand to check it – a calendar reminder.

"I've got to go in a few," he said. "I've got a class in an hour. But can we do this again?" He still didn't know what *this* was, but he sure hoped it would prove to be something other than professional.

Zack looked surprised. "I got the impression your minder wouldn't be too happy about that."

Aaron stirred the dregs of his tea. "Katie has very good instincts about things that are significant, but she doesn't always know if things are going to be a problem." He paused, trying to find words that would make it make sense. "Sometimes, if she's wary about something, it's as much a sign to run towards it as away from it."

"Is she wary about me?"

"Not professionally, I don't think," Aaron decided to leave out the part where she had encouraged him to show off for Zack.

"That's good."

"But I don't think this coffee had particularly professional vibes for her," Aaron tried, hoping to get a sense of what Zack's intent had been.

Slyly, Zack clicked his own empty cup against Aaron's. "Indeed."

✦

Aaron drove back to the rink with the windows down and the radio turned up, singing along happily to the songs of the summer. Coffee with the journalist definitely wasn't a date. But Zack was very nice to look at, and weird in a good way, and Aaron was here for it.

He got back to TCI a little earlier than he needed to, and was standing at the front desk chatting with Cal, one of the zamboni drivers who Aaron had dated very briefly two years ago, when Katie brushed past him.

"Don't think you got away with that," she murmured as she passed.

"What?" Aaron asked, breaking off mid-sentence.

Katie kept walking.

"Uh, catch you later!" he called to Cal who, long accustomed to the oddities of figure skaters, waved him off with a chuckle.

"What?" he asked again, hustling after Katie.

She glanced at him over her shoulder as she walked down the hall. "You and Zack and your coffee date."

"It wasn't a date," he protested.

"You wanted it to be."

"Well, sure."

"I told you no. Him, too."

"Sure, then, because we had ice time. I wasn't going to skip out on work." Aaron was somewhat offended. He hadn't come back from the islands to fuck off from work with a boy.

"Aaron," Katie said slowly, like he was one of the little kids learning how to skate who needed reminding to bend his knees. "I didn't tell you no because we had ice time."

"Then why? You're the one who told me to show off and be nice."

Katie stopped at the door to the little office she and Brendan shared with the other TCI coaches. "Yes, but there's being nice to the journalist and there's being boy crazy at the journalist."

Aaron couldn't exactly defend himself against that one.

"I'm not saying you can't be friends with him or get coffee with him," Katie went on. "Just...be aware, okay? Because every moment I have known you, you've had a crush on someone. Usually ill-advised."

"You didn't mind when Huy and I were dating."

"Because Huy is sensible. He has good boundaries and knows how to balance his personal life and his skating." She shot him a sideways look. "I'd hoped he'd be a good role model even if you two want different things out of the people in your lives."

"Are you saying I have a bad work-life balance?"

Katie sighed. "It's hardly your fault. Your home and your family are out there in the middle of the lake and your work is exhausting. That's a big gulf."

"Maybe I want to close that gulf."

"Do you?" Katie gave him a keen look. "Or do you want a fun distraction because the work is hard and you're lonely? Look," she said, slinging her arm around his shoulders and steering him farther down the hall in the direction of the locker rooms. "You're a competitive figure skater. The work is brutal and involves too little reward most days. I get it; I've been there. But be smart about what you're doing. And seriously, don't fuck the reporter. Okay?"

"Do you want me to say 'okay, I hear you' or 'okay, I won't fuck the reporter?'"

She levelled her gaze at him. "Honestly? I'll take what I can get."

Aaron laughed and ducked out from under her arm. "That makes two of us!"

6

June and July

Minneapolis and Saint Paul, MN

Zack spent the next several weeks falling head over heels in love with Twin Cities Ice.

Aaron never let him miss his twice-weekly skating lessons – not that Zack was inclined to skip them. The hour was early and the rink was freezing, yes, but he'd have gone through more discomfort and lost more sleep if it meant spending more time with Aaron.

Aaron was funny, charming, handsome, and absolutely, unbelievably, strong. Not merely because he could and did keep catching Zack and picking him back up when he fell. But because the more Zack skated, the more he appreciated the ocean that separated his own physical abilities from Aaron's talent that had been honed by years of hard work.

Zack had always spent time in a gym when he could; living in conflict zones had made a certain level of physical strength and endurance a distinct asset. But now he was spending most of his time at the rink watching the TCI skaters do hours of on-ice drills and even more hours in the gym and dance studio. They didn't have the sort of bodies Zack had historically associated with strength, but they were, to a one, all stronger than him.

No one kept him at a distance; everyone from the front desk staff to the maintenance people at the rink greeted him by name and stopped to chat. The skaters bantered and gossiped around him while he sat in the break room transcribing notes or trying to thaw out. Brendan persisted in asking Zack how he was and whether he needed anything with a warmth and sincerity that made Zack relieved his inappropriate crush wasn't on him. Back at his apartment, Marie took to inviting him upstairs frequently for coffee, pastries, surprisingly good bourbon, and gossip.

There was a camaraderie here that came from doing something hard and dangerous that other people didn't understand. It made Zack miss the good things about the work he used to do: The friends, the teamwork, what it felt like when you'd done something almost impossible – whether it was getting the story or surviving the night.

And Aaron stood out from all of them, like a star serving as a beacon across a twilight horizon.

Zack didn't think that was only because he found Aaron devastatingly attractive, but it didn't hurt. Zack began to feel a thrill of anticipation every time he saw Aaron setting up a jump, and a bigger thrill of satisfaction when he landed them. When he finally did sit down to formally interview Aaron, Aaron was funny and odd and charming in all the ways that, Zack was sure, would make readers fall for him.

He came to know which jumps Aaron was stronger at – theoretically, at least; he still couldn't distinguish the jumps as they were happening in front of him. He watched Aaron spend days drilling a quadruple loop that would not happen as much as he and Katie seemed to think it should. And he watched as Aaron began working with Brendan on the choreography for what would become his programs for the competition season.

He wanted to write about it *all*. Not just Aaron and his hustle and the race to make the U.S. Olympic figure skating team. He only had three thousand words, not thirty thousand, and he needed to contain himself for this article, but Zack would be lying if he said he wasn't tinkering in his head with extended metaphors and an essay on how he'd gotten from there to here.

There was one, rather glaring, downside, which had nothing to do with the Twin Cities at all: He couldn't get Cayden Sauer to talk to him. Phone calls to him and his coaches were ignored; emails got one-line responses about getting in touch soon and then nothing. As much as Zack wanted to go out to Sauer's rink in Phoenix to conduct interviews in person so the two halves of his story would be equally weighted, there was no point in doing it if no one wanted to talk to him, and he was close to giving up on it. Generally, people who were good at things wanted media coverage about how intensely good at things they were. Why this dude had to be an exception, he didn't know.

After his latest attempt to call Sauer, which went to voicemail, Zack tossed his phone on the couch in his apartment and dropped down to sit next to it.

So far he hadn't been giving Sammy blow-by-blow updates on the problem. But if he kept that up, Zack knew how easily his attempts to get it solved or make do could turn into avoidance and a nasty surprise for his editor. But if he told Sammy about it, he'd inevitably tell Sammy everything, and his editor – and friend – was going to roll his eyes so hard at the whole mess they'd knock back and forth along the length of his office. Sammy would then ask Zack if he was – inappropriately because journalistic ethics existed – into Aaron. Which Zack would be helpless to deny convincingly.

Erin McRae & Racheline Maltese

"So that's spectacular," Zack muttered to himself. Afternoon sunshine gleamed on the trees outside, and he considered going for a run, or at least a walk, to get moving. Maybe he'd go skating. But he should probably let Sammy know what was happening before he got distracted by the ice again. Maybe he could get some damn help on solving both the Sauer problem and the wishing he had more words problem.

With a sigh of aggrievement at the universe, Zack picked up his phone again.

Sammy, for his part, seemed completely unsurprised by any of it and laughed about the mess with Sauer.

"Why do you think I sent you up to Minnesota and told you to figure out the rest yourself? I also got exactly nowhere, but since you're a journalist and I'm just some sort of word manager, I thought you'd work some magic that would leave me feeling inadequate yet thrilled."

"I wish you had told me that upfront," Zack said, feeling both too fond of Sammy and like he didn't want to express those particular feelings right now.

"Sorry. How is it up there anyway? Have you fallen through the ice yet?

"Um… it's not ice fishing?" Zack said

"Great, whatever. Tell me you've at least got good stuff there."

"I think so. Honestly, if anything, I'm struggling because everything is weird." Zack heard Sammy slap his hands together in delight.

"I told you! Figure skating is wild! Whatever you find, I trust you, write whatever you want, we'll figure it out."

"I have the suspicion." Zack said delicately, "that whatever you're imagining is probably not the sort of stuff that's fascinating me right now."

"What? Glitter and drama is glitter and drama, yeah?"

"No, not glitter and drama," Zack corrected. "I'm staying in an ex nun's basement, sometimes we drink hard

61

liquor together and gossip. The coaches also have a dairy farm. Everyone is wildly superstitious, and the rink has these wacked out acoustics where I'm constantly hearing shit I shouldn't. Also the guy whose last name you keep messing up is super cute and totally trying to get into my pants."

Sammy sighed in a way that Zack knew meant long-suffering frustration and a desperate desire for nicotine. "Zack. Zack Zack Zack. Zack."

"Yeah. Still here. What?"

"The story is not the nun. The story is not the cows. The story is not whichever random guy you want to fuck."

"Except that he is," Zack said. "I mean, not for that reason of course. But here we are!"

"I'm going to assume all your various adventures haven't knocked all the journalistic sense out of your head and that you're just venting at me."

"Pretty much," Zack said, and while he believed it in the moment, he wasn't sure how long that would last.

"Great. I'm going to pretend we didn't have half this conversation. Keep me posted on Sauer and tell me *nothing* about whatever I sincerely hope you're not going to do with Sheftall."

✦

Sammy hadn't given Zack his blessing for either more words or his desire to follow his very worst impulses. But what he had given him, no matter how inadvertently, was time and space to explore, which for now was enough.

Zack gave himself a mental pat on the back for achieving that much, and, feeling on a roll, turned to his non-journalistic to-do list. It was filled with things like calls to his ex, his lawyer, and his realtor, to deal with lingering issues of the divorce. He should also probably call his parents, so he could also reassure them that he hadn't fallen through the ice, it remained, in fact, impossible to fall through.

Before he could do any of that, though, his phone lit up with a text.

Aaron: Wanna do a thing?

Oh, so many things, Zack thought.

Zack: What sort of thing?

Aaron: Farm dinner, Friday night? I'll get u details

Zack was immensely curious and very game. The one place he hadn't been yet, that seemed central to the life of so many skaters here, was Katie and Brendan's farm. He very much wanted to go, and he was grateful for the gift of the invitation, regardless of what the motives behind it might be.

Zack: Sure, that sounds great.

7

A Friday Night in July

Katie and Brendan's Farm

That Friday night Aaron and Charlotte drove out to Katie and Brendan's farm, Charlotte at the wheel and Aaron in the passenger seat with their contribution to dinner – a giant fruit salad – on his lap. Signs of the city faded away, and soon they were in the midst of cow country. Green fields stretched as far as the eye could see, broken occasionally by a farmhouse, barn, or line of trees. This warm world of green and heat seemed worlds away from the eternal winter of the rink. Aaron rolled his window down and inhaled deep lungfuls of summer air.

Eventually they turned onto a gravel road, which they followed for nearly half a mile before they reached Katie and Brendan's house. There were no other buildings around, except for the barns beyond it. The house itself was small and in need of a coat of paint, but tiger lilies bloomed thickly around the front porch and a hammock swung between two trees in the yard. It looked like a daydream of a bucolic childhood. Aaron loved it all; it was the most home-like place he'd ever been off the islands. Not only because of the place itself, but because of all the hard work that was always happening here.

"Huy's back," Charlotte said, pointing to a gray car with a 'keep calm and figure skate' bumper sticker in the rear window.

"Ooh, yay!" But while Aaron was genuinely excited to see Huy, his car wasn't the one he had an eye out for. Zack's rental wasn't there yet, which was disappointing but also probably for the best; it wouldn't have been fair to make him face the others on his own.

Nobody answered Aaron's first knock at the door, but at the second came a distant shout from Katie.

"It's open! Come in!"

Inside, the house was in a pleasant state of not-quite-perfectly clean. Shoes were jumbled on a mat by the door. A sweater was tossed over the back of the couch, and blankets and throw pillows were piled on an armchair like someone had started to put them to rights but been interrupted.

The afternoon sun outside was muted by drawn shades, which gave the whole place an air of sleepy warmth until they got to the kitchen, where the windows were open, music was playing, and Brendan and Katie were moving around each other with practiced ease as they made food.

"Put me to work?" Aaron offered as soon as he and Charlotte entered the kitchen. He set their fruit salad down on the counter.

"You don't get enough of that during the week?" Katie looked amused. Her hands moved quickly as she chopped vegetables, but there was an air of relaxation about her here at the farm that there never was at the rink.

"He does not know what a day off means," Charlotte said, opening the refrigerator and helping herself to a seltzer. At Katie and Brendan's, no one stood on ceremony.

"Neither do you," Katie observed.

"And neither do you," Brendan said fondly, bumping Katie's hip as he passed behind her with a bucket full of corn soaking for the grill.

"I didn't say it was a bad thing," Charlotte observed placidly.

Katie narrowed her eyes at both of them. "You're supposed to be good influences on each other. Not egging each other on in bad decisions. Do I have to give you the Perils of Overtraining speech again?"

Aaron raised both hands. "No, I swear!"

Personally, he didn't think he could fit in more work even if he wanted to. Since he'd gotten back to TCI he'd spent his waking hours either at the rink, at the gym with his trainer, or at the yoga studio. At home, he had hours of accounting work to do remotely for the restaurant, plus cooking and cleaning and doing laundry; Charlotte had a devoted social media fanbase and insisted that their apartment always be clean enough to photograph. Things were only going to get busier as the season truly got under way.

"Where's Huy?" Charlotte asked, perching herself on one of the stools in the little breakfast nook. "We saw his car."

"Out getting the grill started."

"And your houseguests?"

"Still here. But doing things so they don't have to deal with all of you."

"But we're charming!" Aaron protested. He'd seen the guests in question – Fitz and Gabe – around the rink a few times recently, and had hoped they'd be here tonight. He was always vaguely fascinated that Katie and Brendan had lives and friends outside of figure skating; he couldn't figure out how they had acquired them.

"Actually," Brendan said. "Gabe's out working on the cow cams."

Katie gave an exasperated sigh. "I thought he'd finished that yesterday."

"He likes to tinker," Brendan said.

A knock sounded from the front door.

Katie frowned at Brendan. "Who else is coming? The juniors have that thing for the federation and Morgan and Sam are away for the weekend..."

Brendan looked equally as baffled but headed for the door. "Maybe Fitz left his keys?"

Katie shook her head. "Unlikely."

Aaron shifted his weight from foot to foot. Which Katie immediately noticed. She narrowed her eyes at him.

"What's up?"

"Wellllll," he began. "How do you feel about extra dinner guests?"

From the front door there was the sound of footsteps and Brendan's voice – polite, yet surprised – inviting whoever was there to come in.

Another familiar voice answered him, and Aaron smiled.

"Aaron Sheftall." Katie chided him.

"Yes?" He tried to look innocent but was certain he merely looked giddy and guilty instead.

"Did you invite the journalist to dinner at my house?"

"It's a dinner at the farm; this is the kind of life stuff he's here to write about!" He wasn't worried that Katie was going to kick Zack out. But he did want her to stop giving him the murder eyes.

"*Now* you choose to be strategic." Katie still looked more dismayed than Aaron thought the situation warranted.

"We're right here, under your watchful eye. Unlike with the coffee. Plus, Brendan said it was okay.".

"He did?"

"I did?" Brendan echoed as he walked into the room, Zack right behind him. "What did I do?" he looked between Aaron and Katie.

"I told you I had invited Zack. When we were finishing up a class with the little kids. You said it was cool, although it's possible you weren't quite focused at the time," Aaron said.

Katie briefly turned her murder eyes on Brendan.

"Hi, Zack!" Aaron said brightly to deliberately change the topic. "How was your drive?"

"Very peaceful. I would have been here earlier, but I got stuck behind a tractor." He held out a foil-wrapped casserole dish. "I brought food."

Aaron's stomach gave a pleased flutter at the sight of Brendan accepting the dish from Zack. Folding Zack into the little domestic routines of TCI was definitely promising. Also, he appreciated guys who could cook.

Behind Aaron, quietly enough that he was pretty sure he was the only one who could hear, Katie muttered, "You could have just asked me."

"Yeah, but this is more fun," he whispered back.

"Nightmare child," she retorted.

Another door squeaked and slammed, this time from the back of the house. Huy bounded into the kitchen from the back deck, glowing with the joy that seemed to be his default state of being.

"Aaron!" Huy beamed and threw himself at him, hugging him so hard his feet lifted off the ground. Aaron laughed and squeezed him back. They didn't spend a lot of time together off the ice, but the daily routine of training at TCI hadn't felt complete without his energy. Or his playlists of all Canadian dance music all the time at seven a.m. warmups.

Charlotte got a hug too. Once Huy had set her back on her feet, he turned to face Zack. He looked ready to tackle-hug him too, but Zack backed up a step, Aaron suspected unconsciously. Belatedly, he realized that Zack probably didn't know anything about his and Huy's history. Certainly, he wondered what he thought of the exuberant display of physical affection between them all.

Huy looked Zack up and down. "Who are you? Are you a hockey guy? I don't bite!"

Aaron recognized Huy evaluating someone he'd put in the 'potential hookup' category and had to stifle a laugh.

"He is the journalist," Charlotte said tartly, returning to her perch on the stool. "Here to write about Aaron."

"Ohhhh." Something in Huy's face shuttered, and Aaron watched in awe as Huy switched his public face on. "It's nice to meet you."

"You too. Technically, my assignment is to cover all the top U.S. contenders for the Olympic team slots. Not just Aaron. And I'm not here on the record tonight. Aaron took pity on me and invited me along."

"Pity, hmmm?" Huy looked between Zack and Aaron in a way that was entirely too knowing. Aaron wished he were close enough to step on his foot.

✦

Zack fell into the conversation at dinner as if he'd been part of the group for ages. He and Aaron sat next to each other at the table, occasionally bumping elbows while Aaron bantered with Huy and Zack talked hockey with Charlotte.

Aaron still missed home: The quiet summer nights on the island, boat trips on the lake, time together with his family. But on nights like this, Aaron was happy. The people gathered around the table tonight weren't his blood, but they were as much his family through shared work and commitments.

"Do you want a tour?" he asked Zack once the table had been cleared. Aaron wanted some time alone with

Zack, but if he was eventually going to write about TCI life, seeing the farm – off the record or on – was a must.

"Of?" Zack asked, setting a last stack of plates by the sink. Brendan was busy washing dishes and had waved away their offers of help. Katie, Charlotte and Huy were starting a card game and would probably be occupied for a while.

"The farm, obviously," Aaron said.

Zack's forehead creased. "What is there to see?"

"What is there – " Aaron repeated, staring at Zack's confusion in suddenly dawning realization and consternation. Was it really possible for someone to not know what there might be to see on a farm? "Have you never been on a farm?"

"Farms, yes. A Midwestern American farm, no."

"Why not?" Aaron was curious.

"Because I'm from Florida and write about wars," Zack said.

"Wars affect farms, right?" Aaron asked.

"Yes, but again, American farms."

"Well, now you're writing about figure skating. And we're figure skaters who take breaks on an American farm." Aaron grabbed Zack's arm and pulled him toward the door. "We'll be back later!" he called over his shoulder.

"What the hell does a farm have to do with figure skating?" Zack asked as Aaron towed him into the yard.

The evening air was warm and humid. Clouds were building up to the west, and the sun shone dramatically across them to make the sort of sunset worthy of any Instagram post.

"Looks like there's going to be a storm tonight," Aaron said, looking up at the sky.

"That's not an answer."

"On a farm," Aaron said. "Weather matters."

"Okay?"

They strolled shoulder-to-shoulder down the track that led to the barns. "Whatever you do, there's always factors that are beyond your control – on a farm and in skating."

"Ahhhhhh."

"Rain, the other skaters, not enough rain, the quality of the ice, bugs, the vibe of a competition," Aaron listed.

"External factors." Zack sounded both amused and exasperated. "Everyone deals with them. How are yours different?"

"Ugh." Aaron kicked at a pebble in the path. He wanted to show Zack this part of his life – of all their lives – that was so important, but so hard to explain. He didn't have the right words.

Zack waited patiently. Aaron could feel the weight of his attention like a warm hand on his arm.

"Katie asks me that too," he said. "Whenever we start talking about my programs for a season. She wants to know what makes me different, as a skater."

"What does make you different as a skater?"

"I don't know," Aaron burst out. "Except that I come from an island that's strange the way this farm is strange. And I don't mean farms in general, I mean, this farm. It has an energy to it, and it's why Katie and I get along so well. But no one else understands what it's like to be us," he said. "And that's an asshole thing to say, so don't write it down. Or find a way to make it sound better. But it's true. Right now the only thing that feels different about me is that you're here talking to me instead of everyone else. Usually I don't get that much attention."

"My job here is to talk to you," Zack pointed out. "Because of the narrative potential your season has. Although, to be clear," he added. "I do like talking to you. And as I told the others, I'm off the clock tonight."

"I know," Aaron said. "But your interest in me has no impact on my skating. On my career, maybe; media buzz drives a lot of calculations when it comes to funding and

Federation support and even what the judges think. In a season like this one, every little bit could tip the balance in my favor. But none of that impacts what I do on the ice. I have a literal once-in-a-lifetime opportunity this year, and I have no idea how I want my skating to look this season."

It was the first time he'd admitted that to anyone; he knew Katie and Brendan would tell him it was still early and he had time to work out a vision for himself, but he was starting to get frustrated.

They rounded the corner of an outbuilding and were suddenly standing in front of the barn.

Zack stopped suddenly. "There are cows." He sounded alarmed.

"Yes, it's a dairy farm." Aaron was amused, and also relieved to take a break from his own angsting about his season.

"There are *so many cows*," Zack said.

Zack, war reporter and tattooed god of attractive biceps, was so unnerved by a bunch of dairy cows that Aaron nearly doubled over laughing. "You've never seen a cow, have you?"

"I've seen cows," Zack said, sounding somewhat affronted. "Just not big American dairy cows that weren't in imminent danger of – well, anything."

Aaron laughed harder. "If you think this is weird," he said, catching his breath. "Wait 'til you see my island."

"Was that an invitation?"

Aaron stopped laughing abruptly. Instead he felt himself flushing to the roots of his hair. Which was the worst possible reaction to have to someone – especially a journalist writing about him – teasing and possibly flirting with him.

"Do you want to know what I think?" Zack asked. "What makes you different?"

"Sure?" The setting sun made Zack's skin glow golden. Aaron couldn't help but stare.

"The thing where you manage to convince everyone around you you're normal ninety-nine percent of the time, and then that last one percent – something flashes out of you. Like the ice, like the island maybe, is in your blood."

"It is." Aaron was acutely aware that his heart was now beating in his ears, almost drowning out the sound of his own words, the way it did whenever he stepped on the ice for a performance. "All of that."

Zack reached out a hand and traced the shell of Aaron's ear. "I've never seen anything like it. And I don't know why you hide it."

Goosebumps broke out up and down Aaron's arms. "The island's too strange," he said. "Too much mine. I can't walk around giving all my secrets away."

"Can't you, now?" Zack's words were half amusement, half-dare. "I've seen videos of Katie and Brendan skating. And I've seen them look at each other when they don't think anyone else is watching. They don't keep anything for themselves."

"Everyone keeps something," Aaron protested. The mere idea of sharing the island made him feel exposed and vulnerable. But there was, somehow, something appealing about that. He wanted Zack to have his secrets.

He leaned his cheek into Zack's hand.

Zack shook his head. "No sense in keeping something to yourself if it'll help you win." He shifted to trace Aaron's jawline.

Aaron's brain took a moment to be able to form words. "What do you know about it?" Unless he was mistaken, Zack was closing the space between them. His eyes gleamed in the fading light.

"People are people." Zack shrugged. He was close enough now that Aaron could smell his aftershave, warm and herbal. "Whether they're in a war zone or on the ice. You're holding something back. And," he said, his voice low and quiet, a command just for Aaron, "you should stop that."

Aaron leaned up onto his toes and kissed him.

Zack returned the kiss, long enough for Aaron to know that he was into it, before he pulled back a fraction of an inch.

"That wasn't what I meant, you know."

Aaron's knees felt weak. He'd gripped Zack's arms without realizing it; they felt as lovely to touch as he'd always hoped they would.

"I know." He loosened his fingers a little so Zack could step away if he wanted to. "Do you mind?"

Zack only moved closer. "Not at all." And with that, Zack threaded his fingers through Aaron's hair and pulled him in for a much more thorough kiss.

Zack was much bigger than Aaron, which Aaron had known from their skating lessons. But catching Zack's weight when he needed to was one thing. Zack, taller and broader and backing them up against a nearby fence was another entirely.

Aaron was really, really into it. From Zack's tongue in his mouth to his muscled thigh pressed between Aaron's legs and against his dick. If it weren't for the cow cams that made up Katie's freakish farm surveillance system, he would have been down to fuck Zack right here.

Is Gabe still out here working on the cameras? He was trying to figure out how likely they were to get away with surreptitious handjobs when his phone barked. Loudly.

Zack jumped back with a look so wild Aaron had to laugh at him again.

"My phone," he said, fumbling it out of his pocket.

"That's a messed-up ringtone."

"Our dog." Aaron told the usual lie.

"Hmm." Zack sounded skeptical, but Aaron didn't have the brain bandwidth to deal with that right now. His hands were so unsteady – Zack was a *really* good kisser –

that he couldn't get the fingerprint sensor to work and had to type in his unlock code instead. There was a text from Huy.

> Huy: Idk what you guys are doing out there, but Katie's heading out to make the rounds on the cows or sthg. Look lively!

> Aaron: Thx!

Aaron replied with sincere gratitude and shoved the phone back into his pocket.

"Katie's coming. We should probably look less like we've been sucking on each other's faces."

"Which would be…how?"

Aaron grabbed Zack's hand and dragged him away from the barn and away from the house. "Do you want to see the chickens?"

✦

They arrived back at the house as the fireflies started to flicker along the tree line. The rest of the group was gathered out back on the screened-in porch that looked over the pastures. Katie wasn't there, which meant that all Aaron had to deal with was a suggestive look from Huy and a pointed eyebrow-of-disapproval from Charlotte. But Brendan didn't seem to think anything was amiss, and soon Zack and Aaron were settled next to each other on the wicker loveseat.

Aaron leaned into Zack occasionally and was rewarded by the warm press of Zack, shoulder to thigh, against him. The heady memory of Zack's mouth pressed against his made Aaron deeply regret his early morning ice time and the fact that he'd driven here with Charlotte. Going home with Zack – he was pretty sure that was on the table if he wanted it to be – was both logistically unwise and more socially awkward than even his generally high tolerance for awkwardness could take. But despite the disappointment of that, Aaron's mind felt quiet in a way he hardly ever felt anywhere that wasn't the island. For a few hours tonight he had stopped worrying – about the season, about expectations, about letting his family down – and let himself be.

8

After Dinner on the Farm

Somewhere on I-35

There was something to be said for thinking things through while driving. Zack was glad for the rental car and the empty road when he finally pulled out of Katie and Brendan's at eleven – late, he was told, for skaters.

He flipped on the radio... and that was the thing about radio in the dark. No matter where you were, the experience of it was more or less the same: a bunch of songs you didn't necessarily love whispered into your ear by a DJ that felt like he was speaking just for you. The only thing that changed from state to state and country to country was the language and how much God was part of the mix.

Zack wished the farm were further out and the drive longer, because Aaron – who was apparently boy crazy and made of trouble – had kissed him, and it was completely a delight. And also a giant problem.

One, he had to admit, that he'd been courting since he arrived.

Zack knew the most obvious answer was to not entertain the situation further, wrap up whatever background he could pretend to himself that he still needed here, and go home. Or go to Phoenix and try to get an interview in person when he still couldn't get anyone on Sauer's team to answer his calls. He only had a week left on the temporary lease for Marie's in-law apartment anyway. Perfect timing.

If Zack hadn't become wildly, inappropriately, emotionally entangled with Aaron – and hadn't just spent half an hour making out with him in a field, what the fuck was his life? – he could give up on Sauer and make the story entirely about Aaron. But journalistic bias worked every which way. Focusing on Aaron because Zack liked him was as fucked up as avoiding focusing on Aaron for the same reason. Both versions of the situation were now a complete ethical nightmare, no matter the extent to which Aaron was complicit – knowingly or not.

Zack resisted the urge to bang his head on the steering wheel. He didn't want to leave the Twin Cities. He didn't want to go back to Miami and find a new place to live. To go back to the life he had before, writing little pieces here and there from the comfort of his apartment until he got bored enough to overcome his own better sense and fly back into the type of trouble he no longer believed his body and brain could handle.

Aaron was here, of course, but so were Katie and Brendan, and Twin Cities Ice and the other skaters he'd already met. Marie, too. It was a warm and welcoming community, with people who loved their work and were devoted to it. All of which Zack enjoyed. But there was also the feeling of something else, lurking under the surface, that Zack couldn't stop rolling around in his head.

There was a fuzziness here in the space that separated people from animals. The more that people relied on their instincts, the more their ears seemed to prick up at things seen or heard. This adventure was full of that, and Zack was aggressively interested. He didn't have that experience of the world himself, no extra senses and no animal instincts, but he knew it when he saw it. In a war zone he'd learned to watch the animals to know if he was safe, to know what would happen next, to know who the monsters were.

Finding people with that magic here – Aaron and Katie mostly, but also Marie – had suddenly made life outside a warzone seem a lot more interesting than it had in ages.

Zack knew he needed to stop thinking with his dick, to consider whether he was having addictive tendencies, and call this whole non-thing out as a rebound, but he also knew that if he did so, he wouldn't be being entirely honest with himself. The situation was ill-advised, yes. But it felt real and mutual.

The light in Marie's front window was on when he pulled into the driveway. And Zack, having already made a series of bad choices in his life (from war zones to marriage to kissing Aaron by the cows), decided there was no time like the present to make a few more.

Instead of following the walkway that led around to the back of the house and his own entrance, Zack banged on the front door. He realized only belatedly that the sound was too urgent.

From behind the wood, he heard Marie's irritated grumble.

"If you think a nun's gonna be alarmed by the end of the world, you're knocking on the wrong door."

Zack chuckled guiltily to himself.

The door opened. Marie, in a bathrobe and holding a coffee mug, stared at him.

"Oh, it's you."

"Were you expecting someone better?" Zack asked.

"I don't know. Depends what you've got to say."

Zack felt impossibly grateful for her kindness, masked as it was with brusqueness. It was a language he understood.

"Do you have anyone else due to take the apartment?"

She narrowed her eyes at him and took a sip from her mug.

"Why? Are you procrastinating writing your article?"

"No! I mean, yes, a little, but… can I come in?"

"You know nuns don't do Confession, right? And also that I'm not one anymore?"

"Yes, but you do keep bringing it up. Also, you're a gossip with good taste in bourbon and that will do?"

Marie tipped her head to the side in acknowledgement and offered Zack the mug.

He took a grateful sip and stepped into her house.

"What's going on?" Marie asked, leading the way to her kitchen. "I can't imagine it's a sudden uncontrollable love for the Twin Cities."

"It's a little bit that," Zack admitted.

"But not all?" she asked.

Zack shook his head.

Marie flipped on her coffee maker and dumped the old grounds in the trash.

"I'm too old for small talk, and it's too late for the same. 'Fess."

"I don't want to leave."

"Because?" She drew out the words, leading him, but Zack had to say all these things aloud sometime.

"Because I don't. I went out to Katie and Brendan's farm for dinner tonight, and I could breathe there, and I sure the hell can't in Miami. Sorry," he added, belatedly.

"What part of ex-nun are you not getting?" Marie asked as she refilled the coffeemaker with both water and fresh grounds.

"All the parts. Which is kind of why I want to stay."

"That requires an explanation," Marie said firmly.

Zack slumped down in a chair at the kitchen table. "I've got enough material for ten articles about this place. The people, the atmosphere, the work, the stakes, Katie's ridiculous cows. I could write it in my sleep at this point. The article's not the problem. It's this *place*. I don't want to let it go. Or the people. Every single person I've met up here is completely bizarre and I kind of love all of them. Brendan and his goofy all-American cliché. Katie, who's like a wild cat who mostly remembers how to be a normal human but only by trying incredibly hard."

"A not inaccurate assessment." The coffeemaker started percolating, and Marie slid into the chair across from his.

"There's whatever your deal is. And Charlotte, and the juniors, and Huy who I met for the first time tonight." He paused. "And Aaron."

"Oh yes," Marie said, her gaze far too knowing. "Aaron."

"And then there's me." Zack felt unaccountably emotional. "You have all welcomed me, in your ways, and made this the best place I've been for a long time."

"You haven't even been here two months," Marie pointed out.

"Isn't that enough?"

"Mmmmmmmmm."

"You don't believe me. And you haven't told me if the apartment is available," Zack said.

"It's available. But nothing you've told me is gossip. I was hoping you'd have gossip. Which is why I let you have some of my bourbon."

Zack sucked in a breath. What he had to tell surely qualified as gossip. And was probably necessary for Marie to understand the rest of his choices, questionable and otherwise.

"I kissed Aaron."

"Of course you did. I bet he kissed you too." There was something almost pitying in Marie's eyes.

"I know. I know."

"Oh, darling," Marie said. "I don't think you do."

✦

Zack returned to his own apartment full of both relief and urgency. While he had solved several of his problems – including wanting to kiss Aaron and staying on in the Twin Cities – he had also created several new ones for himself.

There was no way around it: He was wildly compromised when it came to the article he was writing for Sammy, and there was no way to become less so. He couldn't undo either his actions or his feelings when it came to Aaron. The only truly ethical thing to do would be to withdraw from the assignment. That, however, would leave Sammy in the lurch and make his own life more of a disaster than it already was. If he couldn't bring himself to extricate himself from the situation, his only other option was to uncomplicate the situation as much as possible, as quickly as possible.

Zack was going to write this article tonight, send it to Sammy, and never confess to when, exactly, he and Aaron had first kissed. Was that sketchy? Sure. But life was full of sketchiness. If anyone was keeping an account of his sins, he rather imagined this one wouldn't even rank.

There were, of course, issues with this brilliant idea. It was already after midnight, and Zack was supposed to be up early to be at the rink, and Sauer, who was supposed to make up half his article, was still perpetually unavailable. *Oh well*. He'd write what he could and let Sammy sort out the rest.

An hour later, Zack had written and deleted a half-dozen openings. None of them had been bad; they just hadn't been about what he'd been sent here to write about.

They hadn't been about Aaron, who he was infatuated with, or Sauer, who he had decided was a dick and who he kind of hated. They'd been about himself: His own strange path that had brought him to Twin Cities Ice, and the experience he'd been having there since.

Fine, he thought to himself, opening a fresh document. As a procrastination tool, he'd done far worse before. *I will get this out of my system, and then I will get the rest of my work done.*

'This' turned out to be four thousand words of what could only be called personal essay. For that length of time, Zack could pretend he hadn't landed himself in a quagmire of ethical concerns and overall bad choices, and wallow in the atmosphere of this place that he had fallen in love with so quickly. If Zack had been more rational or less caffeinated, he would have stuck it in a drawer and pretended it never existed. Instead, he fired it off along with an email to his agent.

After that, he was exhausted enough that he banged out a draft of his article that was at least passable and sent it to Sammy as the sky outside was starting to get light.

He collapsed backwards into his chair and stared up at the ceiling. He fell asleep there, his laptop whirring quietly in his lap.

✦

Zack woke up an indeterminate amount of time later to his alarm blaring at him, an overcast sky, and an email from Sammy which merely thanked him for the draft and said he'd get to it soon. Zack wasn't sure if that was a reprieve or a reminder of the sword hanging over his head.

Tired as he still was, he got to the rink early for his lesson with Aaron. That was a place where he at least knew what he thought and felt. And he needed to tell Aaron what was going on – with the article and with his presence at TCI.

When he got there an all-too familiar figure was out on the ice. Zack watched him, transfixed. He and Brendan were working together, doing footwork side-by-side. While Brendan was a more than capable skater, Zack only had eyes for Aaron. His grace. His power. The smooth flow of his movements. He was a singular creature on the ice, and Zack wanted him.

He wanted Aaron's body wrapped in his arms again while Aaron tipped his head back to be kissed. He wanted Aaron's clever sharpness in conversation and to always have a seat next to him at the dinner table at Katie and Brendan's. He wanted to watch him pursue his dreams, not only this season but next year and the year after that.

He didn't realize Aaron had finished and skated over to him at the boards until he spoke.

"What's wrong?"

"We need to talk." Zack cringed as blurted out the words. He didn't blame Aaron one bit for the frown that creased his forehead. That was not a sentence anyone ever wanted to hear.

Aaron looked at the clock, then back at Zack. "We have a lesson right now."

Which was true, but Zack didn't want to leave Aaron with the idea that the conversation was going to be something terrible. "I know, but –"

Aaron cut him off with a shake of his head. "The way life works here is that skating comes first. Always. Whatever you have to say can keep."

The idea of focusing on skating for an hour with a conversation looming wasn't appealing. He realized suddenly that he had no idea what Aaron would think about his staying on here. Maybe Zack had more problems than he knew. But they couldn't be dealt with now. Aaron's eyes watched him keenly; This was a challenge. It was not one Zack could fail to meet, especially right now.

"All right," he agreed. "But can we go get coffee or something afterwards?"

Aaron nodded. "Of course. Now go get your skates on."

✦

They were halfway through what Aaron called stroking drills – Zack tried hard to suppress his desire to make cheesy innuendo about that – when there was a yelp and a hollow boom from the other side of the rink.

Aaron whipped around gracefully; Zack managed to turn without tripping on a toe pick. On the other side of the rink a woman in hockey skates was woozily trying to sit up from where she'd clearly fallen, and judging by the blood trickling down from above her eyebrow, had hit her head.

"Shit, Tasha" Aaron hissed. "You, don't fall over," he snapped at Zack, and zipped off across the ice.

Zack knew he could probably manage that. But there was also an emergency at hand involving head injuries and blood. Other than the fact it had happened on the ice, he'd been in enough dicey circumstances that he definitely knew how to handle a situation like this. For one thing, someone who'd hit their head like that should not be trying to sit up.

He looked down at his feet and decided he could get to the other side of the rink on his own. The rush of adrenaline probably helped. There was hearing about injuries – like Luke's career-ending one – and there was seeing them happen. The sight of blood didn't particularly bother Zack, but the visceral reminder that skating was a high-risk endeavor jolted him.

As Zack made his gradual way across the ice, Aaron slid to his knees next to the woman and gently helped her lay back on the ice.

"Maddie," Aaron called, to one of the junior girls nearby. All the skaters had stopped to watch, but were mostly staying where they were when the fall happened, evidently not wanting to crowd.

"Yes?" Maddie stepped forward.

Aaron glanced sideways at her. "Go have Cal at the front desk call the EMTs and show them the way in once they get here, okay? Let's not have a repeat of that time Deb broke her arm and they got lost."

Maddie was skating off before he had finished speaking, her braids whipping in the wind of her speed. "I'll bring back ice!" she called.

"You're overreacting," the woman – Tasha – said, as Aaron knelt over her.

"And you're bleeding all over the ice," Aaron retorted. "Did you hit anything else on the way down?"

"I'm *fine*," she protested.

Aaron took one of Tasha's hands between his and rubbed it gently. "You might have a concussion."

"I've had a concussion before, that fall was not nearly hard enough for one."

"Are you hearing yourself right now?" Aaron was exasperated. "What day is it?"

"Saturday," she said promptly.

"Who's the president?" he asked.

Tasha grimaced. "Fuck you."

"Yeah, right there with you," Aaron agreed.

Zack snorted at that; he couldn't help himself.

Aaron jerked his head around, and Zack watched as he let himself be surprised by his proximity for only for a split second.

"You see the cones in the hockey box over there?" Aaron said, pointing. "Do you think you can go grab those and get them back here?"

Zack nodded. "I think so."

"Go do that, and set them up so no one skates through the blood," Aaron said, before turning his attention back to Tasha.

Zack went without question. Aaron – who was playful and sweet and liked approval and for his kisses to be led – knew how to delegate in a crisis, so Zack was trusting that doing as he said was going to result in the least harm possible. Honestly, aside from being terrified by his own lack of skating skill (swizzling with cones in his hands was difficult), Aaron was impressing the hell out of him.

It was not what he would have expected from him or from any skater. Which was, he realized, unfair. Especially after all the time he had already spent around the rink. Skating was kind of metal; there was no other way to put it.

By the time Zack arrived back with the cones, Aaron was holding a wad of clean paper towels to Tasha's head while Tasha wiped blood off the side of her face with tissues.

"A-minus on the skating," Aaron said, glancing over at Zack as he set them down. "D-minus on common sense. Next time, you put the cones down and slide them over."

"I didn't fall," Zack protested.

"No, you did not." Aaron's eyes had gone back to Tasha. But he did sound impressed.

Zack was still not used to how much he enjoyed Aaron's approval. "Is there anything else I can do?"

"You can tell him I'm fine," Tasha said, clearly eager to get up and go back to her day.

"You probably are," Zack said. Aaron didn't need any help, but he figured he should be supportive where he could. "You also probably need a few stitches, so I'm pretty sure you have to wait for the EMTs."

"Ugh."

"Can you go find Ashley?" Aaron said.

"Who?" Zack asked.

"The zamboni driver. We're gonna need her to scrape up the blood and maybe cut the ice when this is all over. You're going to have to get off the ice, put your guards on, and walk around for this assignment," Aaron added, when Zack hesitated to move.

"Oh, right. Okay," Zack said, as if he'd only been confused by the directions. But the truth was he was disappointed. Despite the circumstances he was enjoying being on the ice as much as he was enjoying being by Aaron's side.

9

On the Way to their Usual Café

Near Twin Cities Ice

Once Tasha had been taken off to the hospital by the EMTs Aaron did his best to muddle through the rest of Zack's lesson. He was used to working with nerves, but competition anxiety was a different beast than whatever adrenaline rush had hit him. He felt jangly and untethered, and, despite his best efforts, he was prickly with Zack.

The memory of Zack's serious face when he had said *We need to talk* didn't help either. Aaron didn't have a great feeling about that and suspected Zack was going to give him a speech about why they couldn't do what they certainly seemed to be on the precipice of doing.

Aaron was used to compartmentalizing and grateful when anyone outside of skating could avoid bringing their problems to the ice. That Zack had kept his mouth shut was a significant point in his favor, even if it had weakened Aaron's own resolve and focus. Of course, then he'd gone and been helpful when Tasha got hurt. It had all added up to leave Aaron unfairly annoyed at him but also very much wanting to bury his head in Zack's shoulder so he could soothe away all the emotions of the last hour.

And now, he was probably about to get dumped.

"Coffee?" Zack asked as they sat down next to each other on the bench to undo their skates.

"I've got work to do for the restaurant," Aaron said shortly. He was irritated at Zack, at the universe, and at himself, but Zack was the easiest one to take it out on at the moment. "And I have more practice time tonight."

"Okay," Zack said. Aaron could see him out of the corner of his eye, looking back at Aaron out of the corner of *his* eye as he unlaced his skates. "What did I do wrong?"

Aaron sighed. "You didn't. Yet. You're probably going to though. And I'm already mad about it."

"If I say you're cute when you're pessimistic…." Zack nudged his knee against Aaron's, and it was all Aaron could do not to throw his arms around Zack and hide from the rest of the world.

"I will stab you with your skates," he said in lieu of doing anything of the sort. If Zack was teasing, maybe he wasn't about to tell Aaron all of this was a bad idea. A faint bubble of hope rose in his chest, adding itself to the already too-large pile of emotions he was dealing with.

Aaron forced himself to take a deep breath and reminded himself that adrenaline was a nasty drug. Of course he was reeling. Fresh air and a change of scene would probably do him good. Especially if he was about to get preemptively broken up with.

"Gotcha." Zack gave him a half-smile, and Aaron's stomach fluttered pleasantly. "Same place we went last time? I do need to bring you up to speed on some stuff, and I'd rather not do it here"

✦

The café was close enough to the rink that they walked. Zack never seemed to mind getting out in what, to Aaron, was sweltering late-summer heat, and Aaron needed to burn off his itchy energy.

"How are your programs coming?" Zack asked as they walked.

Aaron twitched one of his shoulders up in an approximation of a shrug. "Okay."

"Just okay?"

Aaron drummed his fingers against his thigh. "My short program is great but Brendan and I couldn't agree on a song for my free skate so I'm stuck with Katie's pick. Which… it's a good song, and I trust Katie's taste, but I haven't clicked with it yet. How's your article coming?" he asked. Talking shop with Zack felt so natural. Why couldn't they rewind to last night at the farm? Not just the making out – although also that. It was the warm ease between them that he needed.

"All right. I sent in a draft last night. This morning, technically."

"Really?" Aaron was surprised. "I didn't know you were so close to done."

"I wasn't, but this is what I wanted to talk to you about." Zack hesitated. "If you don't mind doing it before we arrive at coffee."

Aaron stopped walking and turned to face Zack. "Sooner would be better than later. 'We need to talk' once is forgivable. Twice is bordering on sadism."

Zack laughed quietly to himself. "I'm sorry. That's fair." He scrubbed a hand through his hair; Aaron caught himself staring at the tattoos on his arm.

"After last night," Zack went on. "I went back to Marie's and babbled to her for a while."

Aaron smiled, forcing himself to look at Zack's face instead of his arms. He had a good face. "That is a rite of passage."

"Yeah, I got that impression. And we talked about you and this place and my mess of a life, and I realized I had two choices."

"Which are?" None of this was making Aaron's nerves diminish in the least.

"Be a responsible journalist, confess my ethical lapses –"

"The kissing?"

"Definitely the kissing. Confess that to my editor, and go back to Florida or on to Phoenix and do my damn work and forget any of this happened."

"Or?" Aaron prodded, when Zack paused again.

Zack dropped his hand from his hair, his gaze intent on Aaron. "Accept that I am happy here and that I am not done with this place or you, but that that means I am compromised in every way with no way to undo that."

"Which did you choose? "Aaron's voice was barely a whisper.

"The one where I'm happy," Zack said softly. "But the only way I could entertain that was to get the article off my desk as quickly as possible. That doesn't mitigate my lapses, but it theoretically stops them from getting worse. The piece is full of holes about the Sauer kid and my editor will be pissed, but I will deal with that later."

"Did he ever call you back?" Aaron asked, because it was better than seizing on all his giddy hope. He didn't trust it yet; he couldn't.

"Nope. Which means that right now most of the meat of the article is about you."

Aaron considered that. "That feels a little overwhelming," he admitted.

"Blame the big stage," Zack said with a shrug.

"I'll try," Aaron said, but then another, much less pleasant, realization hit him. "Wait, if the article has been submitted, that means you're headed back home, doesn't?"

Zack shook his head. "Nope. I said I wasn't done with this place. Or you. So if you're not horrified by my impulsive life choices, poor journalistic ethics, or fooling around with a divorcé who is possibly mildly afraid of cows, Marie said she'd let me reup on her basement apartment for a bit."

Aaron grinned from ear to ear, flickering hope blooming to full-on elation in a moment. "Does this mean I have a disaster boyfriend?" he asked, before he could tell himself to reign it in.

Zack stared at him, but a smile tugged at the corner of his mouth. "Emphasis on disaster. Because look, this is the other thing, I don't want to cause you problems, and I can think of a lot of ways I might."

"How?" Aaron demanded.

"When that article comes out…. It's pretty glowing – because you earned it, not because I want to get in your pants – and if we're together people are going to have opinions about that, with consequences for both of us."

"Who's going to notice?" Aaron crossed his arms over his chest, impatient.

"Someone always notices," Zack said. "That's how the world works. But Katie, for one, who didn't want you to have coffee with me that wasn't on strictly professional terms."

Aaron shrugged. "It's a little late for that now. I'm an adult; she knows that. I do my work; she knows that too."

Zack scratched his hand across his cheek. "Okay. Maybe. But… like you said… skating is the most important thing."

"Sure. But it's not the *only* thing." Aaron tapped his foot to emphasize his point. "Ask me out, or I'm going to get in trouble for nothing and this conversation makes no sense."

Zack seemed ready to leap at the command. He grabbed Aaron's hands, gently uncrossing his arms. "Have dinner with me tonight?"

Aaron bit his lip, and considered if Zack would be annoyed if he pushed things now. If Aaron hadn't scared him off yet....

"No," he said, making up his mind and secretly enjoying the momentary crestfallen look on Zack's face. "A boy is never available at the last minute. How about...." he drew the words out, thinking about them. "We get coffee, you walk me back to the rink, we make out somewhere we won't get busted, and you invite me over for dinner sometime this weekend?"

"There are some bold and intriguing ideas there," Zack said. He rubbed his thumbs over the back of Aaron's hands.

Aaron squeezed their fingers together. "I should hope. No one calls me boy-crazy just to be mean, you know."

10

A Few Days Later

Zack's Apartment in Marie the Ex-Nun's Basement

Zack spent Friday grocery shopping and cleaning the little basement apartment. He'd barely picked up pantry staples in the time he'd been in the Twin Cities, relying far too much on takeout and convenience food. And, while he could tidy the apartment, it was not a space that could impress anyone. In a way, Zack was relieved. Whatever was happening with him and Aaron, it was progressing entirely on their own merits as people rather than any metric of American material success.

Aaron arrived punctually at six, ringing the bell as Zack finished chopping the vegetables for a stir fry.

"Hi!" he said brightly when Zack opened the door. He was holding a small bouquet of flowers and a bottle of sparkling water, both of which he pressed into Zack's hands. "These are for you! And also, us. Since I don't really drink, and I don't know if you do."

"Thank you." Zack said, touched. He stepped back to let Aaron in. When was the last time anyone had brought him flowers? It was such an unnecessary gesture, and yet one that was so very Aaron in its concern for detail. What an absurd and lovely creature he was.

"You know, I've never been in here before." Aaron toed off his shoes, looking around. "It's nice. In that skater kitsch way."

"I'd say thank you, but I'm not sure you're being nice," Zack said, amused. He moved into the kitchen to find something to use as a vase.

"I am being nice! I'm a skater; I'm kitschy." Aaron said.

From the back of one of the shelves Zack pulled out on a giant ceramic mug emblazoned with a cartoon dog wearing figure skates.

"Like this?" He held up the mug so Aaron could see.

Aaron's face lit up. "Oh my God, yes. That's great!"

"Marie deserves the credit." Zack filled the mug at the sink and put in the flowers.

"Tell her I said so, then."

"Are you hungry?" Zack asked, returning to the piles of vegetables and meat on his cutting boards.

"Starving."

There was something effortless about having Aaron in his space. As he cooked, Zack watched him walk around the living room taking in the art on the walls and the few of Zack's own possessions scattered around. He touched things and picked them up to see them closer without any kind of self-consciousness or embarrassment.

"You didn't tell me you were a photographer too," Aaron said, running his fingertips over Zack's Nikon where it was sitting on the TV stand.

"It's a hobby more than work. It lines up sometimes though. Sometimes, I can get pictures no one else can get."

"Show me?" Aaron asked.

"Maybe." That was going to be another potentially fraught conversation, and Zack thought he deserved at least a week of enjoying Aaron before that needed to happen. He wanted to pick him up, set him on the kitchen counter, and make out with him.

Aaron caught Zack staring as he ran his fingers across the spine of a spiral notebook next to the camera. He flushed, but didn't retract his hand.

"Is this weird?" he asked. "Am I being weird?"

"You don't normally date people who aren't skaters, do you?"

Aaron paused a moment, his gaze a little distant, like he was calculating. "Uh. No. Not dated, anyway. But mostly skaters either way, yeah." He drifted over to the kitchen. "What can I do to help?"

"Sit there and look pretty?"

Aaron gave him an exaggerated show smile and laughed. "No, really. You know I work at my parents' restaurant, I'm good at this kind of stuff."

"I thought you did accounts for them? Not the chopping and cooking."

Aaron shrugged. "I'm doing accounting now because it's one of the things I can do remotely, and I need to help out somehow. But no, it's usually messier. Lots of fish. Peeling, slicing, dicing, cleaning, bouncing...." he trailed off to steal a bite of pepper out of Zack's skillet. "Hey, that's good."

"Thank you. Wait. Bouncing?" Zack asked. He was sure he'd heard wrong.

"Yeah. Lots of drunk and rowdy patrons on a summer island."

"But, you're...." Zack didn't know if it was all right to say, but Aaron tiny, at least compared with the size and stature of the bouncers he typically associated with venues and bars.

"Not all bouncers are huge. And I've been keeping you on your feet for weeks." Aaron stole another piece of vegetable out of the skillet. "When I skate I have to fill the entire rink with my 'presence.'" He licked a bit of sauce off his thumb and made the air quotes. "Up close and personal, it tends to grab people's attention. After that I just have to talk them into chilling out and doing what I want."

"Which you're good at, I've noticed," Zack said. Aaron did, indeed, seem to have a distinct talent for getting what he wanted.

Without invitation, Aaron started opening cupboards and taking out dishes. "Mmm. Ari's better at it, though."

"Who's Ari?" Zack asked.

"My sister."

Zack rapidly searched his memory for any conversation they'd had about Aaron's home or family where he'd mentioned any siblings. He came up blank. "You have a sister?"

"Yeah?" Aaron sounded surprised the question had been in doubt.

"Older or younger?" Zack asked, in lieu of saying *why have you never mentioned her*? It wasn't that Aaron owed him any information, but Aaron always seemed so open about everything the omission seemed odd.

Aaron was now laying plates on the table. "Older. Technically. By a few minutes."

Zack stared at him.

Aaron stared back. "We're twins?" he said, as if Zack was missing something quite obvious. Which apparently he was.

"You have a twin and you never mentioned her to me? I wrote a whole article about you!"

"About my skating. Ari doesn't skate competitively. And she doesn't like it when I talk about her to outsiders."

"Outsiders?" Zack was confused again.

"People not from the islands," Aaron explained. He returned to the little kitchen corner and started opening drawers.

"Silverware's to the left of the sink. And why?" Zack asked.

"Because people who aren't from there don't know what life there is like."

"I thought it was a massive vacation destination."

Aaron found the drawer and started pulling out forks and knives. "It is. But only for a few months of the year. And that's the main island, they have about fifty families there. Our island only has four families."

Zack was frozen, mouth open, with a wooden spoon in his hand. It was probably not a good look. But all the hair on the back of his neck was standing on end. Six weeks he'd been here, talking to Aaron and learning about his life. Six weeks and he hadn't known Aaron's family was all but alone on their own island or that he had a twin. Zack's journalistic instincts were good, but Aaron had somehow managed to do a complete end run around them.

"Did you wait to tell me this until I'd finished your part of the article?" he asked.

Aaron shook his head. "It never came up."

But it was an evasion, Zack knew, and he was pretty sure that Aaron knew he knew it.

"Okay." Zack put the spoon down, wiped his hands on a towel, and turned around to lean back against the counter. "What do I have to do to see the island?" he asked.

Aaron shrugged. "Fly to Ohio and book a ferry ticket like everyone else."

"No. Not that one. Yours."

Aaron laughed and tipped his head to the side as if Zack was the biggest fool in the world. And, truth be told, he probably was. "Why, be very, very good, of course."

✦

While they ate, Aaron chatted happily about his day and updated Zack on little happenings at the rink. It was a disgusting portrait of domesticity, and Zack wasn't quite convinced that he wasn't dreaming. Life with his ex had never exactly been about domestic bliss. Zack hadn't known he wanted someone to do the pleasant little niceties of home life with and yet, here he was, listening to Aaron with rapt attention.

Aaron nudged his socked toes against Zack's ankle in the middle of a story about a lesson he'd taught the other day when his student had landed their first single jump. It was a little thing in itself, next door to innocent, but the touch sent a bolt of heat through him.

"You're used to getting what you want when you want it, aren't you?" Zack asked, in lieu of focusing on the story.

Aaron scoffed. "If I was used to getting what I wanted when I wanted it, I wouldn't be trying to get on my first Olympic team; I'd be expecting to get on my second."

"I wasn't talking about your career." Zack wasn't offended that that was where Aaron's mind had gone first. He adored Aaron's drive. Also, Aaron's foot was still pressed against his, and there was a knowing gleam in his eyes.

Aaron tilted his head from side to side as he thought about it. "Maybe. I don't feel like I'm particularly demanding or persuasive. It's all performance. So what that gets me is what other people want to give me. Or what I earn."

Zack had a lot of questions, but as much as he was fairly sure he'd have Aaron in his bed by the end of the evening, he knew it was too forward to ask any of them directly.

"You mean on the ice?" he asked instead.

Aaron shrugged. "Sure. Or with my family. Or Katie and Brendan. I had to earn my place here as surely as I've had to earn my life off the island."

"Does that feel fucked up?" Zack didn't want to lean in to Aaron's self-confessed desire for winning other people's approval if he had issues about it.

"Nope. I know where I stand with people and I know what is and isn't under my control. It makes things clear. And…" he added, with a look from under his eyelashes at Zack, "most importantly, I enjoy it."

✦

Somehow they managed to finish eating. As soon as they had, Aaron stood and started collecting plates. Zack took the plates out of his hands, set them on the counter, and looped his fingers loosely around Aaron's wrists.

"Dishes later," he said against Aaron's ear. "This, now."

"Oh, good." Aaron all but melted against him. "I thought you'd never ask."

Zack chuckled. "Does that mean you want to skip the awkward makeouts on Marie's couch and get right to the main show?"

"If I say yes, does that mean you'll throw me over your shoulder and drag me off to bed?"

"Yes." Zack tightened his grip on Aaron's wrists and watched as his eyes fluttered closed. Aaron took a deep breath, his features schooling into some sort of calm, then snapped his eyes open.

"Yes, please," he said.

Zack obliged. He'd never be strong in the ways Aaron was, but he had height and breadth on Aaron and enough athleticism that it was an easy enough thing to hoist him up in a fireman's carry.

Aaron yelped briefly.

"You all good?" Zack asked.

"Fantastic," Aaron said.

Zack grabbed Aaron's ass – which skating had made *perfect* – with one palm, and walked him into the bedroom to dump him across his bed. Zack looked at him, sprawled there, breathless and flushed.

"Take your shirt off," he said quietly.

As Aaron did as he was told, Zack swooped in to grab the shirt once it was over Aaron's head but before his arms could get free of it.

"I'm tangled," Aaron said, laughing awkwardly.

"Do you mind?" Zack asked. He didn't like to think there were tests in sex, but this trick served as one. It had always reliably told him where he could or could not go, although he was pretty sure he'd already clocked Aaron on this.

Aaron, as he expected, shook his head.

Zack let himself take Aaron in for a moment. His body was almost that of a dancer's, but not quite as lithe or corded. But even just sitting there on Zack's bed, he had definition and grace and a defiant sort of fearlessness. Zack leaned in to kiss him. Aaron's lips parted instantly and it was desperately clear how eager he was to go where he was led. Zack twisted the shirt in his hands and hooked it over one of the bedposts so that Aaron was pinned and slouched against it.

"Okay?" he asked Aaron.

"Okay."

"Say red if you want –"

"I know. And I won't."

Zack wasn't into the type of play that took that type of statement as a challenge, but it was still hot as hell. He ran his nails up and down Aaron's sides, to watch how he squirmed with the sensation and to see also how the blood rose to the surface of his pinking skin.

That wasn't the only thing rising. Aaron's dick was obviously hard and miserably trapped in his jeans. Zack grabbed his thighs through the thick material and kneaded, his hands slowly drifting towards, but never reaching, where Aaron clearly wanted them.

"I am suffering here," Aaron breathed out, still with all that lovely laughter.

"Is that a problem?" Zack asked.

"No."

"Good. Then keep suffering."

Aaron moaned and dropped his head back against the bedpost. And Zack used the moment – so perfect, so hot – to pull out of his own clothes.

Naked, he stood next to the bed, and waited for Aaron's eyes to open and focus on his body. He watched as they tracked up and down him, lingering and returning, lingering over and returning to his tattooed arms and his thickening dick.

"See something you like?" Zack asked.

"So much," Aaron said. "You're ridiculous, but so much. Are you going to give me any of it?"

"What's going to make it the most agonizing for you," Zack asked, "if I don't let your cock out?"

"Fuck my mouth?" Aaron asked in a small eager voice.

Zack wasn't going to make him beg today, but he would bet anything that he could make Aaron beg and love every second of it.

He fisted himself in his hand and gave himself several sharp tugs before holding his dick out to Aaron barely an inch from his face.

"If you want it," he said, "you have to stretch for it."

Aaron did, leaning forward and stretching his neck out the best he could with his arms still trapped in his shirt and bound to the bedpost.

"That's it," Zack cooed as Aaron flicked his tongue over the head of his dick. This was, he knew, going to be amazing.

"That's it, that's a good boy," he said as Aaron got his lips wrapped around the head. "Now let me feed it to you, nice and slow."

Aaron whined back in his throat and shifted and squirmed on the bed. Zack forced himself to keep his eyes open to see Aaron thrusting up into the air, desperately trying to get friction against his jeans.

"You don't come until I'm done," he said.

Aaron, his mouth full, nodded in agreement, and made a small noise of assent.

Zack gripped the back of his head and started to thrust gently.

"Close your eyes," he said. "Trust me. I don't want you to think or feel or *be* anything else right now."

Aaron moaned and Zack nearly did too as he felt the other man slip under the spell of a moment he was determined to drag out as long as possible.

After Zack came, panting and having to shove a hand over his own mouth to make sure he wasn't heard in Marie's house above, he let himself linger in Aaron's mouth. It was overwhelming, almost too much, but Aaron's soft whimpers as he tried to hold onto Zack's dick with his lips while he made shallow circles with his hips on the bed were hard to let go of.

Eventually, Zack let himself slide out of Aaron's slick mouth. He watched as the man took three sharp, shallow breaths, his lips glistening with what they had done.

"Please," Aaron said like a prayer, his eyes still closed.

Zack crashed to his knees to get Aaron's jeans open, his dick popping free.

"Please please please," Aaron started begging now, eyes pressed shut so tight.

"Can you be quiet?" Zack asked. He doubted this apartment was any type of sound proof.

Aaron shook his head frantically.

"Can I put my hand over your mouth?" Zack asked.

"Yes," Aaron said. Zack clamped his hand there. Aaron pressed up into it, as if he liked that confinement as well.

As Zack took Aaron's cock into his mouth down to the root, he felt the vibrations of Aaron's cries against his palm. He wanted to keep them forever.

11

The Next Morning

Zack's Bed

Aaron woke up as light was starting to show outside the small, curtained windows that hovered close to street level. He lay still, cocooned in blankets and pressed against Zack's side, resolved not to move until he had to. Any morning he didn't have to rush out the door to the rink was a good morning. A day he got to stay in bed, warm and blissfully comfortable, with the person he'd just had some pretty incredible sex with... that was sublime. He eventually fell asleep again, lulled by the sound of rain drumming on the windows and Zack's quiet breathing.

He was pulled back to consciousness an indeterminate amount of time later by Zack's voice.

"You're stealing the blankets," Zack complained, tugging at the duvet that Aaron had burritoed himself in.

Aaron mumbled his displeasure at the disturbance and rolled toward the nearest source of warmth, taking the blankets with him.

"Okay, now you're on top of me *and* still stole all the blankets. How did you do that?" Zack sounded equal parts dismayed and amused.

"I'm cold," Aaron mumbled into a bare patch of Zack's skin that might have been his shoulder.

The warm lump that was Zack shifted, and he wrapped his arms around Aaron's shoulders. Aaron snuggled further into the embrace. "You're never cold," Zack protested.

"Rink cold is different," Aaron said.

Zack laughed softly. "I don't think that's true, but okay."

Aaron blinked sleep out of his eyes and peered down at Zack. His eyes were very pretty from this close. "Hi."

"Hi." Zack brushed a stray bit of hair off Aaron's face. The touch sent goosebumps sparking down his arms. He was tempted – strongly – to lean down and kiss Zack and continue where they'd left off last night. But the more he woke up, the more nervy and uncertain he felt. Aaron had done enough mornings-after following hookups of varying degrees of wisdom that he had been sure he knew how to handle any variation. But right now, he was at a loss.

"I'm not sure what I'm supposed to do now," Aaron blurted.

"If you wanted to share the blankets, I wouldn't mind," Zack said, evidently amused.

"Ugh." Aaron protested for the form of it. He shuffled himself around until his head was on Zack's shoulder and the covers were reasonably distributed over both of them.

"Why ugh?" Zack asked once they were settled again, his arms wrapped comfortably around Aaron.

"This – you – are very pleasant, but...." Aaron squirmed with uncertainty.

"But what?"

"I've never done anything like what we did last night. And now I am kind of at a loss."

"Really?" Zack teased. "You seemed like a natural."

Aaron shoved at him with a laugh. "Thank you and that's not what I meant."

"Fair. Sorry. But that's not uncommon," Zack said. His matter-of-factness made some of Aaron's nerviness dissipate. At least one of them knew what they were doing. "What do you need?"

"I don't know," Aaron said. "Which I think is part of the problem? I always know what I need. At least in training. And sex is usually straightforward."

"But last night wasn't?" Zack asked.

"Not in the least." Aaron shook his head.

Zack's forehead creased. "Did you not like it?"

"No! No no no no. I liked it. I liked it a lot," Aaron said emphatically.

"Oh, okay. Good then." Zack sounded relieved. He tightened his arms around Aaron. "I liked it too, in case that wasn't clear at the time."

"I just...." Aaron searched for words. "I don't know what to think about it."

"If it helps, you don't have to think anything about it."

"I know, but. I'm a competitive athlete. I like structure. I'm wired to like meeting expectations, or maybe, I've wired myself to like meeting expectations. Which is probably why that worked for me the way it did. But you saying there's nothing I have to do – I get that you're being generous. But it's not helping right now."

Zack narrowed his eyes, evidently considering. When he spoke again, his voice was lower. Warmer, with a hush that promised good things to Aaron if he listened and listened closely.

"Is what you need reassurance?" he asked.

Aaron nodded.

"Easy enough. Especially for you." Zack drew his nose along the line of Aaron's jaw, from his mouth to his ear. "You are good. You are very good. Especially for me.

Whatever you want me to say – or do – to prove that to you, I am more than happy to oblige. And if you don't know what that might be…." he trailed off, and pulled back enough to give Aaron a wicked grin.

Aaron shook his head, his eyes wide. He wanted another chance to feel amazing as much as he wanted another chance to not think at all.

"Do you want me to get you off again?" Zack asked.

"Yes," Aaron said. "But –"

"But? I am many things," Zack replied, "But definitely a crappy mind-reader."

"I want to focus on you first," Aaron said. "Like last night."

"Ohhhhh." Zack looked beyond delighted. "Then why don't you come down here," he said, holding the blankets up for Aaron. "And warm my cock. Just hold it in your perfect mouth."

Aaron scrambled under the covers into the heat and warmth and musk of being so close to Zack's body like this.

"That's it," Zack crooned above him. "Don't do anything. Just breathe," he said as he stroked Aaron's hair. "Let me take my time getting hard. When I want to make use of you I will."

It was so filthy and hot Aaron thought he would combust on the spot, but he did as he was told, enjoying the heavy weight of Zack in his mouth and the idea that he could be this incredibly good – and be rewarded for it – by doing almost nothing at all.

✦

Aaron got ready to leave Zack's apartment reluctantly, and only because he had ice time that afternoon. He felt giddy, tired, and remarkably clear-headed, like he suddenly knew what silence was for the very first time in his life.

"When we do this again," Zack told him, pressing him back against the door and sucking a bite below the collar of Aaron's shirt. "Bring your skating stuff here and save yourself a trip."

So much for the quiet in his head.

Aaron was dizzy with desire on the drive home. Nothing but years of discipline kept him from turning around and diving right back into Zack's bed with him. He needed to snap out of it, but he didn't want to.

Focus, he told himself, twiddling the radio dial to find a suitably high-energy station to get into the right mode. *You have work now. Be boy crazy on your own time.*

Which was always easier said than done. And Zack seemed to make it particularly difficult.

He unlocked the door to his own apartment to find Charlotte perched on the couch, her computer on her lap and a half-empty smoothie bottle on the coffee table.

"Where have you been?" she demanded as soon as he came in.

"I told you I was going to Zack's."

"All night?" She narrowed her eyes at him.

"I mean, demonstrably, yes?"

Charlotte sniffed. "You might have come to your senses and gone to the gym this morning instead. You have ice time at two and an Olympic team to make. He can't be that good."

"I can keep my own schedule," Aaron pointed out. There were ways in which he was a mess, but blow off his obligations, he did not.

"When is he leaving? His article must be nearly done." Charlotte quite clearly wanted him gone. Which Aaron could accept to some extent as the care of a concerned roommate and a fellow skater who didn't want the distraction in the rink, but it struck him as a little extreme.

"It is," Aaron said. "But he's not. At least for now. He's staying on to do some work of his own. Or something. I'm not positive he's sure what."

Charlotte's mouth opened in dismay. "In Marie's basement?"

Aaron dropped down beside her on the couch. "It's a good basement."

"The basement is not the point!"

"Okay, what is the point?" he asked, squinting at her. Zack's presence at TCI had never thrilled Charlotte, but she'd never been this abrasive about him before. "What's wrong?"

"Has Marie googled him? Have *you* googled him?" she demanded.

"I read one of the war book reviews, but you know, I'm a little busy here." He squinted at her. "Why?"

"You have questionable taste in men, even more questionable judgment, and no research skills. All the good google stuff is always two or three pages down."

"What did you find?" Aaron asked, curious. "His high school Myspace page or something?"

"No. Not that. Here." Charlotte shoved her laptop at him.

Aaron didn't have that much time before he needed to get back out the door and to the rink, but he took it with trepidation. What was he about to find? Was Zack not really divorced?

"See?" she said.

Aaron didn't at first. He squinted, trying to make out the subject of a series of black-and-white photos on the screen. The reflection from the window behind them made it hard, and he reached behind himself with one hand to tug the shade closed.

Ah. Discussing erotica photography with Charlotte wasn't how he expected his afternoon was going to go.

"That is a very attractive mostly naked man, but –"

Charlotte huffed and yanked the computer back into her lap, gesturing at the screen. "Do ropes count as clothes? I think he's just naked."

Aaron didn't feel prepared to get into that particular philosophical conversation at this particular moment as his brain tried to catch up to why they were having this conversation at all.

"But that's not Zack. What do these have to do with anything?" He realized the likely answer only as the words flew out of his mouth. Zack had a very nice camera, a photography hobby he was super vague about, and he'd hooked Aaron's arm over the bedpost and put him on display within moments of their agreeing to have sex. *Oh.*

Somehow over the screeching of metaphorical brakes in his own head, he heard Charlotte make a noise of disgust that sounded like all the consonants in the English alphabet exhaled in one single breath of supreme annoyance.

"He's the photographer, Aaron."

"Of course he is," he said softly.

Aaron yanked the laptop back from her and did some more squinting at the sun-obscured screen. He was still fascinated, and not just by how hot the pictures were. Who was the guy in them? A random model? Zack's ex? They'd had sex last night – and again this morning less than two hours ago. These photos were as intimate as those moments, no matter how artful. He felt adrift again.

Zack's past didn't matter, and neither, really, did the photos. Certainly, Aaron had no moral objection to them. But he was a public person who hated that reality of the sport. Zack had helped him feel okay and contained in his own skin again, but Zack could, just as easily, ask to expose him like this. Aaron didn't know how to reconcile that.

"Oh," he said again because he didn't know what else to say. "You should have told me what I was looking for, otherwise I'm gonna look at –"

"*I know!*" Charlotte gave him a glare illustrative of her done-ness with the entire masculine portion of the species.

Aaron angled the laptop to get a better look. Patterns of ropes and knots danced over skin as surely as shadow and light. They were, truly, beautiful photographs, even if they were also complicating his life immeasurably. The ropes were something he wanted, but now Zack's camera, idle on a table, felt wildly dangerous.

"He's good," he said, because it was true and simpler than the rest of it.

Charlotte's murder eyes could have rivalled Katie's at their best. "That's your reaction!"

"What else am I supposed to say?" Other than *Zack is very good at getting people to do what he wants*.

Aside from the somersaults his brain was doing – talk about information overload – he couldn't track Charlotte's dismay. She was never bothered by displays of the sensual or explicit and was often very vocal about her impatience with puritanical American prudishness.

"You want to make Team USA, and yet you're sleeping with a journalist who also ties people up and takes pictures of them and puts those pictures on the internet! I don't know, Aaron, that seems like a bad plan!"

"They're not pictures of me," he protested. Though now that Charlotte put it that way, his own concerns had coalesced to a bright, vivid point.

"Are you being dense on purpose?"

"No! I get what you're saying. But I don't get why it matters." That was true. He didn't want this to be an issue, and he was angry that it already felt like one.

"In an Olympic year, everything matters."

Charlotte wasn't wrong. But life at Twin Cities Ice was never as regimented as it was at some of the other training centers. Yes, food and sleep and training regimens were tracked rigorously in ways that were intrusive, exhausting, and not always fun. Unlike a lot of athletes elsewhere,

Aaron got to eat dessert once a week, but that was seen as a wild, unorthodox risk. Olympic years were hard. Brutal, even. But Brendan and Katie were constantly telling him that he couldn't only be a skater, he had to be a person too. Otherwise no one would care about what he did on the ice, not even himself.

But what if everything *includes my body feeling something other than constant pain and my heart feeling something other than desperate fear that I won't pull this off?*

If Zack untethered Aaron, he also anchored him again and made him feel like a person in his own skin. Now that he'd had a taste of that, Aaron didn't want to give it up.

✦

The biggest problem with discovering the guy he had been crushing on for ages and who he'd finally slept with last night wasn't just kind of into bondage but was a world-renowned bondage photographer in his spare time was that it was, as far as the facts went, kind of distracting.

Aaron lost complete track of time scrolling through the photos – there were a lot of them, with a variety of subjects – and arguing with Charlotte about how bad an idea dating Zack was. He ended up grabbing his skating stuff in a rush, bolting to the car, and sticking to the speed limit only because he knew Katie would kill him more for getting a speeding ticket than for being late. He ran into the rink, sparing only a wave for Cal at the front desk, and dropped himself onto the benches closest to the ice as the giant clock ticked over to the top of the hour.

Katie approached as he dug through his bag for his skate guards, still out of breath.

"Are you okay?" she asked, pulling on her own gloves.

"What? Oh, yeah, I'm fine."

Katie looked unconvinced, but she didn't press. Aaron was thankful.

"Good," she said. "Let's start from the top of your short program, okay?" She brandished the remote for the rink's sound system. "It's time to make decisions about jump composition."

Aaron wondered if Katie somehow *knew* he'd spent last night with Zack and was testing him on purpose, or if the universe had the worst sense of humor. In the end, though, it didn't matter. His run-through was choppy at best. When they moved on to trying out different jumps in different places, he couldn't land anything, not even his old standby, the triple lutz. His attempt at a quad toe-triple toe combo ended with him sprawled halfway across the ice.

Katie stood there and watched him, the line of her mouth getting thinner every time he fell. Finally, he two-footed a triple sal, wobbled precariously, and crashed onto his ass.

"Okay," she said. "Break time. Before you break yourself."

At the boards Aaron gulped water, as if that would somehow help him find stability, and pulled off his hoodie so he was just wearing a t-shirt.

"Aaron," Katie said, looking up from her notebook.

Aaron ran his fingers through his disaster hair in the vain hope he might smooth it down somewhat. "Yes ma'am?"

"Charlotte has talked to you about training at other skating centers, right?"

"Um… some?" Aaron had no idea what this had to do with anything.

"I presume she's told you all about the rules a lot of coaches have. Not only about how to work out and what to eat but who you can date. When and how you can have sex. With other people or yourself."

"What makes you think I had sex?" Aaron blurted. His face, unhelpfully, was burning.

A quiver of amusement tugged at the corner of Katie's mouth. "Did you look in a mirror before you left – wherever you left, this morning?"

"Why?" Aaron glanced down at himself. "Ah. I see." Dotted across the upper part of his chest were numerous hickeys and other bruises. He could only imagine how many more were on his throat and jaw that he couldn't see.

Katie continued as if he hadn't interrupted. "Here, you will notice, we have *no* such rules. Because we are coaches, and we are here to help you, and we want you to have satisfying lives both on and off the ice. Right?"

"Right." Aaron resisted the urge to pull his hoodie back on.

"To be clear, you can do whatever you want. In your own time. As long as it does not leave you *splattered* across my ice."

"Er." Aaron said. His face was on fire. He was fairly sure his hair was blushing.

"Whatever you did last night, restrain yourself in the future, okay? At least until after the Olympics."

Aaron was sure his face did a thing at the word *restrain*. "The problem isn't what I did last night," he said before he could stop himself. Discretion was probably the better part of valor here, but he couldn't help himself.

"It's not?" Katie looked wary.

"I mean yes, I hooked up with Zack, and you're probably right that's not a distraction I need but Charlotte got mad when I didn't come home last night and googled him and showed me this morning and apparently he's like, this big bondage photographer and –" Aaron ran out of air and had to gulp some down. "Now I'm freaking out about a lot of things?

Katie took a deep breath. In for four seconds, hold for four seconds, out for eight seconds. Aaron recognized it because it was a breathing pattern she'd made all of them learn for regulating anxiety and stress. He bit his lip; she was trying not to kill someone.

"Skates off," Katie said, slinging an arm around his shoulders and guiding him toward the door to the ice. "Let's see if the yoga studio is free."

✦

The yoga studio was one of the little rooms in the warren that made up the rink complex. It had probably been a conference room in a former life. Aaron appreciated the choice, because it meant he could sit on the floor, fold his chest to his knees, and make no eye contact whatsoever.

"What do you need?" Katie asked him. The fact that she was echoing what Zack had asked him a few hours ago didn't help his equilibrium.

"Self-control and the ability to google?" he mumbled.

"Self-control isn't your biggest problem, and we all could have googled. Do the pictures bother you?"

"No," Aaron told his knees. "Not really. And I guess I don't mind that I didn't know. Everybody has hobbies. It's just… distracting."

"I can see why it might be, yes."

"Also, I think I really like him," Aaron confessed. "No matter what ridiculous thing I do or say, he just nods like it's as unsurprising and miraculous as the sun rising and setting."

Katie was silent for a moment.

Aaron hoped she wasn't going to do the must-not-commit-murder breathing thing again. "I know I sound ridiculous. I know I've known him for all of five minutes. I know I always do this. But this is different. I promise."

"You don't sound ridiculous," Katie said, her voice gentle now. "You sound like someone who wants to be seen. Now, do you want my opinion about this as your coach or as your friend?"

Aaron looked up at her. That was a choice he did not want to make. "I'll take whatever's useful."

"All right. Everyone will make you think they can get to an Olympics by being absolutely regimented about every single aspect of their life at every second of every day. And I am here to tell you that is not possible. No matter how regimented you are, the fact that you're human will come out somewhere. For Brendan and I it was the screaming matches and the panic. For you, maybe it's how you're always looking for love. Or maybe it's this one particular guy. It is, of course, also possible that you just need a hobby. I don't know, and I don't care. My only job is to help you find what you need and make sure you don't blow up your life in the process."

"But you don't like Zack. Or don't trust him, or something. You didn't want him at the farm."

Katie shook her head. "I don't have any feelings about him one way or the other. He was supposed to be useful and then... you were you."

"Sorry about that."

"We both know you're not sorry, but Aaron, listen to me. I don't care about the photos or whatever. I really don't. I think the world is wildly fucked up for the ways it judges people. But it does judge people. If you want to have a boyfriend who's a war reporter and bondage photographer...." Katie trailed off and pinched the bridge of her nose. "Why is this happening to me?" she muttered to herself. "Look... don't let him take any photos of you, and if you're only in it for the sex, find someone else. This will all be funny after the Olympics. But not right now."

Aaron stared at the faded pattern on the carpet, absorbing that. He felt strangely light, a burden he hadn't known was there lifted off his shoulders. He didn't need his coach's permission or approval to date whoever he wanted to date – or fuck whoever he wanted to fuck. Like Katie had said, TCI wasn't that kind of training center. But still. Knowing that being with Zack wasn't going to be an issue was a relief.

"Do you think I'm going to get there?" he asked. "To Almaty."

Katie looked at him for a long moment. "I don't know," she finally said. "You're still looking for something, probably in the wrong places. But if you find it? Yeah. You'll get there."

12

The Same Morning

Twin Cities Ice

Once Aaron left, Zack set about doing the cleaning they'd ignored last night in lieu of sex. The temptation to crawl back into bed and sleep for another few hours was strong, but getting the dishes done now instead of later was probably the more responsible thing to do.

Sleeping with Aaron had probably not been responsible, however. Zack had been divorced for less than six months. He was definitely still in rebound territory. Aaron was trying to get to the Olympics. And the campsite rule probably didn't approve of introducing aspiring Olympians to bondage weeks before the most important season of their careers began.

Oh well.

Zack whistled to himself as he put clean dishes away and wiped down the counter. He couldn't bring himself to feel remorse or regret. Aaron was adorable and hot and eager and had been more than happy with everything Zack had offered. And as unwise as it may have been, Zack was pleased with himself. He liked Aaron. A *lot*. And last night, and this morning, had been excellent.

With the kitchen once more clean, Zack considered his options for the rest of the day. Revisions on his article draft wouldn't come back from Sammy for a few weeks. Unless there was yelling. Then they might happen sooner, but they still weren't going to happen today.

He didn't need to burn time chasing down Sauer for a comment at the moment either. There were probably emails he could send to his lawyer about his place in Miami, but that could wait. And he could noodle around with the personal essay that he was suspecting might become a full-fledged memoir, but.... He had time and a city to settle into.

It was probably only natural that he gravitated to the rink – and for once, not because Aaron was also going to be there, although Zack did see his car in the parking lot as he walked in. The sight made him smile even as he had no intention of being a distraction or otherwise interfering with Aaron's work day.

Cal, the front desk guy, greeted Zack warmly and waved him back as usual, but Zack stopped at the counter. "Actually, I'm here to skate today."

"You mean unlike every other day you're here?" Cal grinned.

"I mean, on my own. If that's a thing I can do?" Zack realized belatedly that he didn't know anything about the public side of skating at TCI at all. He probably should have called. Or googled. Or just asked Aaron.

Cal, though, was enthusiastic. "Oh yeah, of course! The schedule's there," he said, pointing to a bulletin board across the lobby. "There's public skate, that's for anybody, any level, and you can rent skates if you need, though you've got your own, right?"

Zack nodded.

"Then there's practice sessions for the people taking the intro-level group lessons. The kids are great but you probably don't want to deal with those. A bunch of six-year-olds with hockey gear and no fear is chaos. We've also got stick and puck and pickup hockey sessions if you're interested in that. It's a good group and they're always looking for new people."

"That's more choices than I was anticipating." Zack said. He paid for the afternoon's public session, and held out his arm for Cal to put a wristband on.

He couldn't help smiling as he followed Cal's directions down a different route than he usually took. TCI had four sheets of ice, and while Zack had been coming here for weeks he had never spent time in any of the rinks other than the one Aaron and the other high-level skaters principally used. But the smell of the rubber mats and industrial disinfectant was the same throughout the complex, as was the bite of cold, the fluorescent lighting, and the constant hum of compressors. It felt pleasantly familiar and a little bit like home.

Public sessions in the middle of the day, as it turned out, were more or less empty. Getting his own skates on and getting onto the ice felt like a much less daunting task when the only other people there were a woman who might have been in her seventies practicing footwork and a father with his young daughter clinging to his hands.

The woman who had fallen and hit her head – Tasha, if Zack remembered correctly – came out on the ice as he was skating laps to warm up. She caught his eye and waved, looking none the worse for wear. Zack smiled and waved back.

Since her accident Zack had felt more confident on the ice. He could stay upright, go fast, and if Tasha had survived her fall, he'd probably be fine. Although he was starting to get the sense that skaters were as easily as tough as anyone he'd known when he'd been in the field. He wasn't sure he, himself, was that tough, but he'd probably survive.

The real problem – if he allowed himself to view anything about his skating as a problem – was grace. He did not have it. Not like this. He also wasn't sure if he wanted it. Sometimes, Zack knew, it was best to play to your strengths.

As he practiced stroking and worked on his stops, he thought about his options. Until Cal's little spiel he hadn't given hockey much thought. Much like public skating at TCI in general, he knew it existed, but the figure skating community was so self-contained, that it and hockey might have been in two separate universes.

But there was an instant appeal in the idea. He could keep skating – which he enjoyed – without undue overlap with Aaron's sphere. Which maybe was giving himself too much credit, but given the whole introducing-aspiring-Olympian-to-bondage thing, he wanted to score karma points where he could. Besides, if he was going to be in the Twin Cities for the next little while, he could stand to have something to do and to meet more people.

At the end of the session, he went back to the front desk to ask Cal for more information. As they were chatting – and Cal was happily inundating him with various schedules and flyers – Katie walked by. Zack nodded at her and was surprised when she stopped to say hello.

"You're thinking about starting hockey?" she asked, with a glance at the calendar Cal had laid on the counter for him.

"Yeah," he said, curious what her reaction would be. Katie had never been an obstacle to his work covering Aaron and the TCI skating program, but she had never seemed overly thrilled at his presence either. Zack could both understand and respect that. They each had their own professional priorities to attend to: him, his writing; her, her skaters. He wondered what it was like to be responsible for so many people's high-stake careers. Perhaps someday she'd let him write about her.

"You can't play hockey in those," she said with a glance at the skates he was holding, the ones Aaron had liberated from somewhere for his first day on the ice.

"Do you think I can play hockey at all?" he asked. He realized, with no small amount of surprise at himself, that he wanted Katie's approval for this endeavor.

Katie looked him up and down. Zack found himself standing up straighter under her gaze.

"You're big enough and you're stubborn," she finally said. "Any rec league could do worse, that's for sure," she added, with what might have been a smile.

It was the kindest thing she'd ever said to him, and Zack gave her a crooked smile. "Thanks."

"You're welcome. Now. Niceties over. We need to talk." Katie grabbed his arm and started walking.

She was easily as strong as Aaron. Zack could only follow.

✦

Katie pulled Zack into the break room where he'd first met the TCI skaters and shut the door behind them. Zack braced himself; he could think of only one reason Katie would want to talk to him like this: Aaron. It wouldn't be the first time he'd gotten the shovel talk, but he didn't think this time was going to be any more fun than any of the others.

"I told him this, and I'll tell you," Katie said briskly. "What Aaron does on his own time is his business, even if I have opinions."

"Does Brendan have opinions?" Zack asked. If this was going to happen, he might as well know where every potentially involved party stood.

"You mean, what does the more rational, easygoing man think?" Katie said sharply.

"Oh. Fuck. I didn't mean – I'm sorry," Zack said, chagrined at his own inadvertent sexism.

"Thank you." Katie gave him a stare he could feel himself wilting under. "Brendan is too nice to have opinions. And look, everyone needs a life off the ice. I understand and support that. But Aaron is a competitive figure skater and he needs to get through this season without getting injured."

"Did I hurt him?" Zack felt a lurch of horror. That wasn't the kind of kink he was into, and pain had never been any part of his intent with Aaron.

Katie shook her head sharply, but Zack's relief was short lived. "You did not, and there are any number of details I don't need. What you need to know is that he was so distracted during our session today that he kept falling over. On stuff he never falls on. Camp is coming up soon and he's going to have to show off his programs for the federation for their approval. I don't want him tempting fate, and I don't think you understand the problem your *photographs* present."

Zack could feel his brain catching up with her words and screeching to an abrupt halt before it slammed into the inside of his skull.

"Oh," he said foolishly.

"Yes. Oh." Katie's tone was mocking.

"I'm... sorry?" Zack knew this was a thing he needed to bring up with Aaron eventually. He hadn't thought he needed to, and admittedly hadn't wanted to, last night.

"You're not; he's not; and neither of you have a responsibility to me regarding this in any case," Katie said. "Believe me, I want to be having this conversation less than you do, so I'll keep it to the point. I'm not telling you to not date him, or...." She trailed off with a wave of a hand and a pained look. "But I am telling you not to distract him. Whatever that means to you two. Which probably includes him not getting any more surprises via google."

"Oh yeah. It's not a thing you casually mention, you know?"

"You're the one who put the pics with your name on the internet. It's definitely the sort of thing you casually mention."

Ashamed, Zack stared at his feet. All the time he'd been focusing on whether introducing Aaron to bondage was too much of a distraction, he never considered how his own projects – and his failure to talk about them – might be a bigger issue. "Yeah. That's fair."

"You owe him a conversation," Katie said. "About three weeks ago, but I guess late will be better than never. And now, if you're serious about hockey, go talk to Tasha, she's the coordinator for the adult league. She can get you sorted. And really, don't do hockey with those skates."

✦

That evening, back home – or rather, back at Marie's in-law apartment – Zack sat on his coach and stared at his phone. Katie was right; he did owe Aaron a conversation. But he didn't feel ready for it.

He did not, in fact, feel prepared for anything. Everything he'd done from the moment Sammy had called with the figure skating assignment up 'til now, he'd done at the spur of the moment. Moving to the Twin Cities. Getting folded into the TCI crew. Falling in – something, with Aaron. Deciding to stay, without a plan for who knew how long. Deciding to sleep with Aaron without considering what the long-term consequences might be for either of them.

And if he was honest with himself, that pattern went back much farther than his move to Minnesota. It had been there for the entire miserable process of the divorce when he could only cope by taking one day at a time. And when he got back from his last assignment in a conflict zone and hadn't been able to sleep for weeks. The short term had been all he'd been able to manage, and that barely. With, he knew, good reason. He hadn't been handed a PTSD diagnosis out of nowhere.

But now he was here. In a place where he felt, if not *okay*, then better. Where he'd been able to do work and interact with people and want to join a community again. People and a community, he realized, that specialized in long-term planning. Aaron knew what his life was going to look like from now until February – at least, what he wanted it to look like. Whether he got there or not, he had a day-by-day plan to try.

I want my life to be more like that, Zack realized with a jolt. He'd never been one for thinking too much about the future. He often hadn't had the luxury. But being here and seeing the stability that Aaron – and Katie and Brendan and the rest of their skaters – had, he wanted that stability too. Maybe, just maybe, he was finally in a place where that could be possible. At the very least, he could try.

So instead of texting Aaron with an awkward and belated apology, he made a list of the things he needed to deal with and that he wanted to achieve. *Any lingering divorce paperwork. Sell the condo. Figure out what my next book project is. Make friends who aren't skaters. Join hockey?*

He didn't write *figure out what to do with Aaron*. That went without saying.

It turned out Tasha's contact info was in one of the flyers Cal had given him, so he emailed her about joining the adult rec league. She replied within minutes, and quicker than Zack would have thought possiblehe was signed up for one of the teams and had, at Tasha's urging, scheduled an appointment at the TCI pro shop to get fitted for hockey skates of his own.

That business concluded for the present, Zack opened another email message to deal with another issue much less fun, but more important. His ex was the last person he wanted to contact right now, but the divorce being finalized hadn't meant they were done with each other logistically. The apartment still needed to be dealt with.

I'm still in Minnesota for work and am going to be here for the foreseeable future. Since I'm not going to be in the condo, please take advantage of my absence and get the rest of your stuff out of it. It's all in boxes already.

– Z

Zack was pretty sure he deserved a medal for getting through that email without any profanity.

13

Later That Day

Aaron's Apartment

By the end of the day Aaron's brain was so worn out from everything that had happened – and all the information he'd acquired – that after he and Charlotte made dinner it was all he could do to lay on the floor in front of the TV and eat while watching a cooking show. He'd done a lot of processing already today, and while he wanted to talk to Zack at some point, for now his brain needed a break.

The universe did not agree, apparently, because halfway through the show his phone barked. The caller ID said *Ari*.

"Oh no," Aaron muttered to himself as he swiped to answer. Ari rarely called him. When she did, it was usually because something had gone wrong on the island. At least it was still summer, which meant the ferry was still running and the islands weren't ice locked from the mainland.

"What happened?" he asked.

"I was going to ask you the same thing," Ari said.

"Why?" Aaron frowned at the ceiling. "You don't usually call to say hi."

"I don't know. But it felt like a good time to talk."

Both Ari and Aaron protested against the idea that there was any sort of magical emotional or psychological connection between them as twins. Even so, there were times when intuition seemed to tug between them more strongly than it did with other people. For the most part Aaron found it comforting: A connection, however small and possibly imagined, to home.

"All right. Just a sec." Aaron levered himself up from the floor. "I'm gonna go outside."

"You have company?" Ari asked.

"No, but Charlotte disapproves of the company I had." He winked at Charlotte as he toed his shoes on. She stuck her tongue out at him.

"What is it?" Ari asked as soon as he had shut the door behind himself.

"Do you remember the journalist?" Aaron had mentioned Zack's existence and assignment on a few calls with his parents and emails home, but not in much detail. He definitely hadn't mentioned that he'd been crushing hard on him. But then, his family also knew how much he liked to flirt; they might have assumed.

"The one you were supposed to suck up to so he could write flattering things to make the skating powers that be like you more than you do?"

"Uh, yeah, that one," Aaron said, taking the stairs down to street level. His sister wasn't saying anything he hadn't said to her first, but it felt different hearing it now.

"And?"

"And I slept with him."

"That was stupid," Ari said without hesitation.

Aaron felt himself bristle. What did Ari know about Zack? Or his choices?

"No, it wasn't."

"Ohhhhh, that makes it sound like even more of a mistake."

"Look, do you want to know what's going on or not?" Aaron snapped, pushing open the door and stepping out into the muggy evening warmth. A mosquito immediately buzzed at his ear and he swatted it away.

"Is there more going on than that?" Ari asked.

"Kinda," Aaron said, then wondered why he was prevaricating. This was Ari. And he desperately wanted to talk about this with someone who wouldn't automatically see it through the lens of skating. "Yeah. There is. You'll like it," he joked. "It makes me look super irresponsible. Or something. Kind of. Anyway...." he trailed off, not sure, now that it came to it, how to say it. Of all the times for his blurting power to fail him.

"Let me guess, he's married," Ari said dryly.

"Divorced," he corrected.

"Aaron!"

"What? He's divorced. It's kosher." Of all the things about Zack that made a relationship with him complicated if not downright unwise, his former marriage didn't even make the list.

"What is wrong with you?" Ari moaned.

Aaron could imagine her, on the island, outside, somewhere in the dark, listening to the water and the seals and his own voice, an unwanted tether to the normal human world. He glanced up at the sky as he walked, taking the path that ran around the perimeter of the apartment complex, but it was overcast and there were no stars or moon to be seen.

"So I didn't google him, before... you know," he finally admitted.

"Oh nooooo. Aaron!" Ari sounded equal parts horrified and delighted. Aaron could only hope she would eventually choose to date someone so he could tease her in turn. "What is the terrible news?"

Aaron scrubbed a hand over his face and was glad that, this time at least, there was no one around to see him blushing. "There is no way to say this that isn't wildly embarrassing."

"All the better." Now she just sounded delighted.

"Don't tell Mom," Aaron pleaded

"Is he in porn?" Ari asked.

"No! I mean, not technically? Why did you ask that of all things?"

"Because I know you and it takes a lot to make you squirm?" Ari offered. "Now, spill."

"He's also a photographer, and Charlotte googled him when she decided to be disapproving earlier."

"Charlotte is correct."

"You've never met him!"

"She's still correct. And the google machine found?"

"Erotic bondage photos of his ex-husband?" There was no one around, so Aaron made his grimace of extreme embarrassment at a tree instead.

"Oh *noooooo*. No, no, no, Aaron, no! Come back to the island this instant. You don't know how to do *anything*!"

Aaron laughed, but not because Ari was necessarily wrong. That he had no idea what he was doing with his life was obvious. That Zack also had no idea what he was doing with his life, was also somewhat obvious, and at a given point Aaron would have to deal with that. That his sister, who had never dated anyone at all was the one pointing it out…. Well, that was exactly what he deserved.

"I'm trying to go to the Olympics," Aaron said in his defense. It was the only reason not to turn tail and run home. That, and that he actually liked Zack.

"And how is this helping make that happen?" Ari asked.

Aaron didn't have an answer yet, but he was pretty sure Ari had just accidentally shown him the direction in which to look.

✦

By the time he got off the phone with Ari it was late, not for civilians, but for skaters. Charlotte had gone to bed when he crept back inside their apartment, and he willed himself to head to his own room before he wound up marooned on the couch watching TV. He didn't have to be up too early on Sundays, but he still had to make it to the rink to help teach an introductory skating class.

Sleep didn't usually elude Aaron. He was almost always too tired – from the restaurant, from skating, from travel – to lay awake for long. But tonight, half an hour after he'd crawled into bed, he was still watching the lights from the cars outside play over his curtains. Even though he knew it was the worst for sleep, he grabbed his phone off the nightstand and thumbed through his contacts to Zack.

> Aaron: Hey. Last night was awesome. My roommate googled you - that's less awesome and we should discuss. Ask me out again

"Way to go, Aaron," he murmured to himself. He'd meant to be angry with Zack and ask why he hadn't told Aaron about the pictures before. Which he was, at least a little. Instead he'd been way too forward. *Oh well.* Zack deserved to be uncomfortable too.

> Zack: How pissed are you?

Aaron stared at the phone for a long moment before he replied.

> Aaron: I just told you to ask me out again. Clearly not pissed enough

> Zack: Ah.

Aaron: Helpful

Zack: You told Katie.

Aaron: And Katie told you

"For fuck's sake," Aaron muttered to himself as he watched the little dots that meant Zack was typing a reply. Triangulating any of this with Katie was not what he wanted to do right now. Also, while Aaron didn't have much shame, it was too much to consider Katie having any more information about this than she already did.

Zack: She doesn't want you to be distracted.

Aaron: Those photos were pretty distracting

Zack: Do you want to talk about this now?

Aaron: Nope. That's. Why. You're. Supposed. To. Ask. Me. Out. Again.

Aaron couldn't believe he was annoyed enough to bother with all that punctuation and yet *still* wanted to go out with Zack.

Zack: No three-day-play-it-cool-radio-silence thing first?

Aaron: No time, trying to get to the Olympics. Also do you know what people do at the Olympics other than win?

Zack: I'm going to assume the answer isn't 'lose.'

Aaron: The IOC provides a crapton of condoms and they've been known to run out

Zack: So you're saying you have plenty of options if my attention wavers.

Aaron: Or if you can't be bothered to mention things I shouldn't be finding out from my roommate five minutes before I'm supposed to be landing a bunch of quads, yeah

Zack: You get that there was no easy way to bring it up, right?

Aaron: They're on the internet under your real name!

Zack: Sometimes I forget what freaks other people out; my life has had a lot of adventures.

Aaron: Bondage and war zones?

Zack: Bondage and war zones. When do you not have ice before 8am so I can ask you out?

Aaron: I don't have to be anywhere before lunch tomorrow, but it's a little late

Zack: Are you in bed?

Aaron's breath caught in his throat.

Aaron: Yes

Zack: Do you want to do something for me?

Aaron: What can I do from here?

Zack: That's easy. What I tell you.

So Aaron did. Touching himself when Zack said he could. Stopping when Zack said to stop. And answering Zack's questions whenever he had them.

Zack: Do you wish I was in your mouth right now?

Aaron: Yes. Always

Zack: Always? Already?

Aaron: Like this, I don't feel like I was made for anything else

He'd think differently in the morning, but for now the things he was fumbling to type while his hard cock bobbed against his belly were true. It demanded more attention than Zack was quite willing to let him give.

Aaron: Please let me have more... I really need —

Zack: Next time, can I tie you up more? Properly?

Aaron: I want that more than anything

Even more than he wanted to get off right now, although he was determined to have both.

Zack: Can I tie your cock up too?

Aaron didn't know how that would feel. Would it hurt? Would it be the exquisite agony of being trapped in his clothes and Zack saying no? Would it be worse and therefore better?

Aaron: Yes. Are you touching yourself?

Zack: Fucking yes.

Aaron: Can I touch myself?

Zack: Please. I want you to come so I can picture you cleaning up your own hand with your perfect mouth.

That was all Aaron needed to tumble over the edge. Then, although Zack couldn't see it, and he hadn't asked him to do it, Aaron licked one hand clean, while he used the other to squeeze at his spent dick, so that it hurt, just a little.

14

August

Minneapolis and Saint Paul, MN

The adult hockey league information session that weekend brought out the most motley of crowds. On Saturday afternoon Zack found himself sitting on the benches by the ice with a couple of thirty-something guys in rental skates, two sixteen-year-olds complaining woefully about homework, and a woman with her own hockey skates featuring hot-pink laces.

Tasha, who was running the session, eventually chivvied everyone onto the ice to see if people could handle themselves at all. There was a clear split almost immediately between people who still needed to learn how to skate and people who just needed to learn how to play hockey. To Zack's immense surprise he was in the second group, although barely.

Hockey skates were a whole new experience. All in all, they were definitely an improvement for him. The blades felt steadier and the lack of a toe pick was an improvement, although not having it as a reminder of the danger of throwing his weight too far forward was odd. He felt a bit like a weeble, but since he couldn't fall down as easily, he felt willing to take a lot more risks. *Who knows, maybe I'll finally learn how to stop reliably.*

After the session Zack wound up in conversation with Matt, another guy from his group.

"What do you do?" Matt asked as they sat unlacing their skates. "In the real world, I mean."

"Uh, I'm a journalist," Zack said, bracing himself. People out in the wild could react strongly – positively or negatively – to that piece of information. He also wasn't sure why Matt wanted to know – or what he might want from Zack.

Matt looked intrigued. "Oh! That's awesome. Would I know your work?"

An award-winning book on some of the world's worst conflict spots and some erotic bondage photos, depending on your interests, Zack thought glumly. There was a reason his life was a mess.

"Maybe," Zack shrugged, hoping Matt wouldn't press. "I got sent here to do a piece on the figure skaters. You know, with the Olympics coming up." The TCI skaters – one of them in particular, at least – were more of a personal conversational minefield than either his conflict work or his photography, and yet, easier to talk around.

"You mean with how Luke Koval's injury shook up the U.S. men's field?"

"Um. Yes. Exactly." Zack didn't ask *how did you know that?* but Matt must have read it on his face.

"Figure skating is awesome, I've been following it since I was a kid. I thought about trying it myself, but." He held out his arms; like Zack, he was tall and broad and there was a bulk to his muscle. "I'm not made for it."

"Yeah, me neither," Zack said, happy to steer the conversation away from his own career. "Though I guess there's always pairs skating. Some of those guys are built."

"Eh, I'm trying to take a break from people. Not to say that you have to be dating your pairs partner or anything. But I'm trying to get my life in gear on my own before I take on any responsibilities to anyone else." Matt looked somewhat abashed. "Sorry, that was a lot. My divorc-iversary is next week and it's been on my mind."

Zack chuckled. "My divorce got finalized a couple of months ago. I didn't know divorc-iversaries were a thing."

"Oh yeah? I'm sorry, man. That shit sucks."

"It does indeed. But life is better for it. Now I'm trying to get out and do things."

"That's the spirit!" Matt gave Zack a manly – and nearly absurd – clap on the back as he dumped his skates into his bag. "Plus, it gets easier with time," he said, with an air of experience that would have been ridiculous if he hadn't seemed so earnest about it.

Zack, to his surprise, warmed to it. He hadn't had anyone to talk to about his ex since he'd left Miami, and in Miami it had been too complicated to talk to any of their shared friends about.

"That's what I hear," Zack said.

"Hey, are you doing anything after this?" Matt asked, shouldering his bag.

"Not really, no," Zack admitted. Matt was either coming on to him, or he had a new friend. The fact that he wasn't sure said less about Matt than it did about Zack and how woefully out of practice he was with humans in non-extreme circumstances.

"My shift doesn't start 'til six, want to get a smoothie or something?"

Zack's best alternate option was to go home and daydream about the next time he was going to see Aaron. And while that had its appeal, being obsessive wasn't going to help anyone.

"Yeah," he said. "Why not?"

✦

They got smoothies at a place down the street and sat in the nearby park to talk. Matt seemed equally happy to talk about hockey, his job as an aide at an assisted living facility, and his ex.

"She left me," he said, his tone philosophical. "Which sucked at the time but in retrospect I do not blame her one bit."

"Oh yeah?" Zack was equal parts amused and charmed by Matt's candor.

"Hell no. I was a crap husband. Never did stuff around the house, unless it was a badly done half-finished home improvement project we had to hire someone to fix, never talked about feelings and shit, you know."

"I do know, actually," Zack said. "Although it was my ex who was that type of crap husband, not me. I was awful in different ways."

"Gay?" Matt asked.

"Yeah," Zack said. It was always strange being out but having to come out to new people because of how their assumptions worked. He appreciated being asked head-on.

"Cool. Straight," Matt said pointing at himself. "Anyway. Came home one day to her ring on the table and a letter saying I was going to hear from her lawyer. Which was a hell of a wakeup call, although too late of course. There were a lot of other ones before that I should have heard. I've been trying to do better since, you know? Not to try to win her back. I'm not *that* shitty. But because I don't want to be that guy anymore. I started going to therapy, I learned how to cook, do my own laundry. It's been good."

Sitting in a park discussing past relationship woes and current plans for self-improvement was not what Zack had expected to get out of his first hockey practice. But, he thought, as he sipped his smoothie and asked Matt what sort of cooking he liked to do, it could have been much worse.

✦

Over the next couple of weeks Zack's life settled into a comfortable pattern. During the day he would clean, work out, and noodle around with his writing. He still wasn't sure *what* he was going to end up writing, but his agent had been enthusiastic about the rough personal essay he'd sent her. For now it was enough to get words on the page about his own life.

He ran errands for Marie and had coffee with her on her front porch occasionally. Twice a week he had practice with his adult league team, and on Thursdays he met Matt for an extra hour of work on their skating basics.

He kept his appointments with his therapist and worked with his realtor to get his condo on the market. At some point he was going to need to go back to Miami to deal with the last of his life there, especially closing on the condo once it sold, but there was enough to do in the meantime he didn't feel *too* guilty about kicking that particular can down the road.

And, of course, there was Aaron. While Zack definitely still needed lessons, he didn't need them from him anymore. Hockey wasn't Aaron's thing, and Zack was now learning with the rest of the hockey enthusiasts. This was for the best on multiple fronts. Aaron's training schedule was getting more crowded and tightly regulated, and he didn't have that type of spare time.

But that didn't mean Aaron didn't have other time for Zack. When they crossed paths at the rink Aaron would catch his eye and give him the most mischievous, knowing smile. It made Zack wildly happy, both to have Aaron in his life, and to have the shared, related passion of the ice.

Of course, the passion was not only on the ice. Whenever he had a free evening Aaron would invite himself over to Zack's place. Which meant Zack needed to stop half-assing things. Because Aaron loved being tied up, and Zack was starting to feel guilty about – and frustrated by – the level and limits of improvisation involved.

So eventually, he took himself off to the local big box home improvement store to grab some cotton rope in various lengths and thicknesses. He'd have to run them through the wash more than a few times to get them soft enough to comfortably use on Aaron, but other than coming up with a story for Marie about why he was doing so much laundry, that wouldn't be a problem. And now, someday, Aaron could stop looking wistfully at Zack's photos, and know what those images felt like and whether he liked it. But not yet; Aaron was too busy and Zack didn't want to distract him any more than he already was.

Right now, Zack's favorite nights were when he would hang around the rink after hockey practice to watch Aaron work before they went home together. On those nights they were often the only two at the rink, the rest of TCI quiet around them while Aaron's music played.

It didn't take Zack long to become familiar with his programs. And while Aaron's short was improving steadily, even Zack could tell something wasn't quite right with his free skate. He'd watched enough old competition videos of enough skaters at this point to know when something was great versus merely competent. While he didn't know enough about skating yet to be able to tell *what* was missing, it was clear enough to him that something was. Aaron's frustration with it was clearly growing, too, especially as the high-performance skating camp that kicked off each season drew closer and closer.

On one such night, bundled in the hockey box with his laptop perched on his lap so he could ostensibly write while Aaron skated, Zack watched him work through a sequence he didn't recognize. For once the sound system was silent; the only noises were those of Aaron's blades slicing through the ice.

"What're you working on?" Zack asked the next time Aaron stopped at the boards for water.

Aaron shrugged. "Just messing around." His cheeks were flushed and his curls were wildly tousled, a look that made Zack want to suggest going back to his place early, if he thought for a moment Aaron would leave before his work was done for the day.

"Something new?"

"Maybe."

Which was all Aaron would say about it until that night when they were in bed.

Zack was tempted to see if he was interested in trying out the newly acquired ropes and leaving him breathless until he answered Zack's questions about whatever he'd been working on at the rink, but that hardly seemed fair or kind. Besides, Aaron was a delight, kink or no kink, and he was so eager to get Zack horizontal, Zack couldn't mind letting him take the lead. Vanilla enthusiasm could be its own kind of amazing, he thought as he came with Aaron's tongue in his mouth and their dicks side by side in his fist.

"You," he said after he caught his breath, "are too much fun."

"I am not," Aaron corrected, sitting up and running his hands through his hair. "I am precisely the right amount of fun. Now do you want to know what I was working on at the rink or what?"

"Obviously."

"The long program Katie and Brendan have for me isn't working. I mean, it's fine. It's a good program, and I can do it, and the judges will like it. But, it's not me. And you've made me realize one of the things it lacks." Aaron said.

"What's that?" Zack couldn't imagine what that could be.

"Stillness," Aaron said.

The word hit Zack in waves. Because what Aaron meant, he was almost sure, was those moments where Zack made him be quiet and still, eyes closed and dutiful, in service to his pleasure.

"I don't know how that's going to translate to the ice," he said.

"Neither do it. But I need music with more space in it for those moments, for the breath between elements, and I hope Brendan lets me have it."

"I can't imagine how anyone could refuse you anything." Zack breathed.

15

A Week Before High Performance Camp

Twin Cities Ice

After his conversation with Zack, Aaron knew he didn't have any time to lose.

He had a meeting with both Katie and Brendan the next morning to review his training plan for the rest of the month and discuss travel logistics for camp and the upcoming Grand Prix series. They didn't often coach him on the ice at the same time, so his opportunities to talk to the two of them together were usually limited.

They met in the cramped little coach's office at the rink. Katie had evidently come from the farm; she hadn't yet changed into skating clothes and still had on mud-spattered boots. Aaron fidgeted, nervous, while Brendan gave him his ice times for the upcoming month and Katie queried him about which elements he felt he needed to focus on most.

"Anything else we need to cover?" Brendan asked as he clicked through a spreadsheet on his computer.

"Actually, yes. There was one thing," Aaron spoke up before he could lose his nerve. What if they said no? What if they were upset at his request? He'd already asked for so much from them this year.

"What's up?" Brendan asked.

Aaron took a breath. "I want to skate to a different song for my free skate," he blurted.

Katie and Brendan both looked at him. Brendan had on his mild-curiosity face that Aaron knew was his way of saying *What the hell?*

Katie said it out loud. "What the hell, Aaron?"

"You know I've been frustrated with the program as it is – and the music. It's not working."

"You have that music," Katie said, her voice studiously neutral, "Because you didn't have a strong vision for your program when we started."

"I know," Aaron said. "But I think I do now."

"Camp is two weeks away." Brendan looked pained. Aaron squirmed. Enthusiasm from either of them at this late notice…. He'd known he couldn't have expected that. And they hadn't said *no*. But still. That didn't make their reluctance fun.

"Then we better get started sooner rather than later, right? I mean. If you're okay with that."

Katie and Brendan often told their skaters to speak up and ask for whatever it was they felt they needed to succeed; even so, Aaron worried he was overstepping. Katie and Brendan had other skaters to worry about, and this was a change that was going to take up a good deal of time when that was never something any of them had in abundance.

His coaches exchanged wordless looks, which made Aaron squirm more. The way they seemed to be able to communicate without speaking was unsettling and, in this moment, didn't bode well.

"It wouldn't be a complete re-choreograph," he said, too antsy to let the silence sit and wanting this too much to not argue for it the best he could. "Just... disassembling and reassembling it to different music. With a different vibe."

"That's still a lot of work," Katie finally said. "Mostly for you and Brendan."

Aaron nodded. Brendan was, after all, in charge of most of the skaters' choreography. That was part of his and Katie's division of labor.

"Is this about what I think it's about?" Katie asked, narrowing her eyes at him.

"I don't know. What do you think it's about?" Aaron went for his best attempt at innocence.

For the first time, it occurred to him that whatever Katie knew of what was going on between him and Zack, Brendan knew as well. Which was fine, as far as it went, Aaron didn't expect Katie to keep secrets from her spouse, especially when they pertained to someone they both coached. But he didn't want to talk about Zack in front of Brendan. As much as Aaron trusted him, he was still closer to Katie.

Katie gave him a long, piercing look. Aaron made himself meet her eyes and reminded himself she couldn't actually read his mind.

Finally, she sighed, throwing up her hands as she stood.

"If you can work it out with Brendan, it's fine with me," she said. She seemed less annoyed than resigned, and Aaron drew a sigh of relief.

Once Katie had left for a session on the ice with Charlotte, Brendan turned to Aaron. "She's not upset with you, you know."

"I know," Aaron said. Now that the dread of the conversation was over – and he'd gotten what he wanted – he was thrumming with excited energy again.

"And I'm willing to put in the time with you, if this is what is going to make it happen for you," Brendan said. "But it is going to be a lot of work. More for you than for me – and you're going to have to bring this to camp like we haven't been making changes on short notice. The music you have is a safe choice."

"Safe never won any medals," Aaron pointed out.

"All right, safe isn't a guarantee," Brendan acceded. "But do you know how many *Swan Lake* routines have won gold? Or *Romeo and Juliet*. Or…"

Aaron cut Brendan off. "Okay, I take your point. But I've skated to warhorses for years and they haven't gotten me where I want to go." *Warhorse* was the term in the skating community for any piece of music frequently used – some said overused – by skaters at all levels. They were solid songs, and while Aaron never objected to a good *Tango de Roxanne,* he craved variety and the originality that could come with it.

"All right." Brendan seemed resigned. "What do you have in mind?"

Aaron pulled his phone out of his pocket. "Can I show you?"

✦

At the end of the song – it wasn't quite the right length for a long program and would need edits, but what didn't – Brendan narrowed his eyes at Aaron. Aaron was used to scrutiny, but he still had to ball his fists to keep himself from squirming under Brendan's assessing gaze. He was pretty sure this song had just told Brendan everything there was to know about his deal with Zack regardless of what he already knew from Katie.

"This?" Brendan asked.

Aaron nodded. "Yeah." He felt exposed – though, he reminded himself, if he was going to skate to his song all season, that was a feeling he was going to have to get used to.

"You're sure?" Brendan's face and voice were studiously neutral. Aaron tried not to freak out at the lack of reaction from him.

"Yeah." Then again, nodding firmly. "Yes. I'm sure."

"All right," Brendan said, a smile breaking out on his face. "This song is *incredible*. Let's get to work."

✦

Fitting in time for developing a new program – even one that was mostly, as Aaron had said, pieces of his previous program rearranged – was a challenge. He and Brendan met late that same night, in the time Aaron would usually be working at the rink by himself if he wasn't home doing books for the restaurant. Or with Zack.

To Aaron's surprise, Katie arrived partway through their session. As she had been that morning, she was dressed for the farm; she must have come after her evening rounds with the cows.

"Getting closer," she said, watching Aaron finish a step sequence. "But –"

"Yeah, I see it," Brendan said, without her needing to finish the sentence. He did a little pivot on the ice, then launched into another set of turns and steps that took him from one end of the sheet to the other. Aaron's calves burned just watching it.

"Do you think you can do that?" Brendan called from the other side of the rink.

"Uh. Sure." Aaron, in fact, thought no such thing. All the individual elements were items he was perfectly capable of executing, but in that combination, with the deep edges and flair that Brendan always brought to step sequences... not so much. That was where the hard work, and the magic, would have to be.

"Also, Aaron," Katie chimed in. "Please fix your arms, if you're not gonna skate to a warhorse don't skate like you're a warhorse."

"Got it." Aaron rolled his shoulders to loosen some of the tension. Katie was right – his posture and carriage needed grace and flow. Even if his legs felt like they were going to fall off.

"Ready? And – go," Katie and Brendan said at the exact same time.

Aaron chuckled to himself at them as he took a crack at the footwork. The steps were challenging and the speed with the music would be brutal, but it sang.

Yes, Aaron thought as his blades carved patterns on the ice. *This is what it's supposed to feel like.*

He couldn't wait for Zack to see it.

✦

The next few days were relentless, unending work. His free skate, to his dismay, got worse, not better. His technical elements were solid, the artistry was there, but the emotion, after those first brilliant days, was a mess – sometimes. Sometimes it was brilliant. Consistency had never been Aaron's strongest attribute, but that had always been about jumps, not the rest of it. Whatever was going on, it was driving Aaron up a wall. And frustration, as it turned out, did not help him skate any better.

One night, only a few days before camp, Katie reminded him he could go back to his old program. Whereupon he freaked out at her completely about needing to show his true self and broke down in tears in the middle of the ice.

"Break time," Katie declared promptly, and steered him to the door.

Once he was seated on the bench in the hockey box, Katie got him tissues and his water bottle and sat beside him.

"I've noticed a pattern," she said. "And I'm curious if you have."

"I have noticed nothing except the rapidly diminishing number of days before I have to show this program off at camp."

"Your footwork is strong, your jumps are solid, and I have nothing to say against your artistry."

Aaron nodded. Praise, welcome as it was, didn't make him feel any better when it still wasn't *working*. And after he'd asked for and gotten a new program…. He sank his head into his hands.

Katie rubbed a gentle hand across his back. "All of which means it's your emotion that isn't working."

"Sometimes it works." Aaron tried to cling to that. If he could get it to work when he needed to… but no. People could win a medal by luck, if all the stars aligned. But he couldn't have the kind of season he needed to get to the Olympics solely on luck.

"It works when it's me here with you," Katie said. "And I've walked by a few times when it's just you and Zack. It works then too."

"You've seen that?" For a moment, Aaron was startled out of his misery.

"I work stranger hours than you know. But anyway. It works for me and it works for Zack. Not –" Katie gestured to the rink, where a handful of other skaters were on the ice and another handful were working on off-ice drills on the mats. "When anyone else is around."

Aaron pondered that for a moment. "Huh. I guess I hadn't noticed."

"Which tells me something. If this is the program in which you want to showcase your true self."

"That I'm only comfortable being that self around you and Zack?"

"Bingo."

"How do I fix that?" Aaron asked plaintively. He hoped she had the answer. Katie came closest to understanding what it was like to be from a world so different from what anyone else came from. If anyone knew how to deal with this problem, she did.

"No idea," Katie said. "I've been retired for years and still struggle with it. But," she said, standing and offering him her hand to pull him to his feet. "Now that you know what the problem is, maybe you can work the solution out for yourself."

✦

Working out the solution himself probably should have meant spending time alone either with meditation or journaling to try to crack the problem that Katie had raised. And Aaron did, dutifully try that for a couple of days. But while he could see the problem clearly he didn't see a solution to it, at least not one that was anything other than practice.

Dealing with fear – physical or emotional – was mostly about desensitization. At a given point he had to believe the problem would solve itself through time.

And time, of course, dictated every aspect of his life. Eventually, on the night before camp, he had to accept he had done all he could to prepare for it and allow himself, instead, some time to relax, whether that meant thinking about something else or thinking about nothing at all.

He went over to Zack's place knowing this was his last chance to see him not just before camp but before the season and its pressures truly got underway. Unfortunately, the challenges of having any sort of personal life while competing were already making themselves known, at least in Aaron's head. He'd have to talk to Zack at some point about all the rules around food and sleep he was going to have to follow to be at his competitive best.

He didn't think it would be a big deal, but he still felt strange talking about it. What was normal for a competitive athlete could easily seem – and perhaps was – disordered to a normal person.

Zack asked questions where he was curious, but shrugged most of it off. Aaron recognized this not as indifference, but as someone accepting him at face value. *No wonder I feel uncertain around nearly everyone else.*

"I have a question," Zack said after dinner. "Which you can totally say no to, as I realize the timing is either bad or romantic… in a pervy way."

Aaron barked with laughter. "What is it?"

"You seem to like the bondage thing," Zack said.

Understatement. "I do, but that's not a question."

"I bought some proper rope for doing some proper work with it. If you're interested. I mean, it's right before camp, so if you're not or not *now* I super understand…."

Zack was babbling, and Aaron was aware he found it quite cute. He was also aware that his whole body suddenly felt pulled towards Zack with a force he couldn't control.

"Yes," he said.

Zack blinked at him, startled.

"Did you think I was going to say no?" Aaron asked.

"I didn't… I wasn't thinking at all," Zack said. "Most of the people I've dated, if we were doing stuff like this, I met them in spaces where it was a given they shared the interest. Which means you're exciting and new and I am out of practice."

Aaron smiled. He liked the idea that Zack sometimes felt as out of place as he did. He found it reassuring and flattering.

"I like being exciting and new," Aaron said. "Now tell me what's next."

✦

Aaron got undressed as Zack laid out the different lengths of rope and explained how they could make this about art or sex or some of both.

This is why I like you, Aaron thought as he stretched – that was the reality of skating. Every moment that he moved, he was either looking for more mobility or to work out some stiffness from his training.

Zack stared him, clearly fascinated.

"What?" Aaron asked, coming up from a standing backbend.

"How long can you keep your back arched like that?" Zack asked.

Aaron squinted at him. "With my head upside down, not that long."

"But if you were lying on the ground?"

"You mean like this?" Aaron said. He dropped onto his stomach and reached back to grab his ankles in a yoga bow position. "Pretty much indefinitely. Why?"

"Can I tie you up like that?" Zack asked. "You would be so beautiful and strange."

✦

Zack made Aaron get up on the bed for the actual project.

"If my idea works," he said, "it will be more convenient later, trust me. For now, close your eyes."

Aaron did as he was told. He felt himself drop out of the world as soft rope was looped around his ankles with a knot tied sharply between them. The ropes then found his wrists, and Zack wove and coiled and knotted them up his arms, explaining softly about the different types of rope bondage that existed in different cultures and how he had taken what he had learned in terms of art and pleasure and safety but was also making things up as he went.

Aaron, trapped now in the bow until Zack released him, absorbed maybe half his words.

Zack seemed to sense how far away he was and ran his fingers through Aaron's hair and across his face. Aaron whimpered slightly, and stretched to capture one in his mouth. He could feel his cock getting hard under him, which felt good now and was going to be torture later. He would surely struggle against his bonds and the bed to get release, and would no doubt only obtain it when Zack said he could.

Zack touched his hands. "Can you feel this?"

"Yes."

"No tingles, all normal?"

"All good," Aaron said impatiently, annoyed to have to deal with the world again for the moment.

Zacks hands moved to his feet. "And here?"

"They're fine," Aaron nearly snapped. He understood the concern, truly he did. But his circulation felt fine. He'd had pairs of skates that were worse for him than this.

"Good. Then, I'm going to add more rope."

Aaron hummed and dropped his head forward, as Zack laced rope through the harp-shape formed by his legs, hands, and back. He tried to picture it, like the cables of a suspension bridge, and while the image pleased him, he still wished he could see it for himself.

"Take a picture?" he asked, breathless. He needed to know and to see what this thing was that he had fallen into with this man.

"Are you sure? I can't imagine you want anything like this floating around."

"I trust you," Aaron said, "and we can delete it later."

Zack tied a final knot and tucked in a tail of rope. As he stepped away from the bed to get his camera, Aaron felt a moment of desperate fear, not that he would be abandoned like this, but that he would be made to wait further for his pleasure.

But Zack was back in a moment, caressing his back and his face and his ass, gentling him, the wild animal he was.

Zack's hands left again, but then there was the click of the camera – once, twice, another handful of times as Aaron threw his head back to make the position look perfect.

The motion sent him rocking on the bed, forward and back over his hard dick that was pressed into the mattress under him. He groaned.

Zack chuckled.

"You're very clever," Aaron managed.

"You have not," Zack said, "seen anything yet."

Aaron heard the sound of the snap and zip on Zack's jeans and opened his eyes to Zack pulling his cock free and jerking himself off.

"Yes, please," Aaron breathed.

"Oh good."

Zack stepped closed to the bed. He placed one hand along Aaron's throat and under his chin to coax him into lifting his head. Immediately, Aaron opened his mouth to take him in. He needed this – the taste, the smell, the thickness on his tongue and the way it drove all the rest of his life away.

Zack placed one hand in Aaron's hair and tightened his fingers quickly. It didn't quite hurt, but Aaron gasped around his cock as more nerve endings came alive.

But the trick of it all was yet to come. Zack tugged softly on Aaron's hair and the bow of his body rocked forward – over his own hard, miserable cock – as he took Zack in further. Under no control of his own, back and forth he went, trapped, as he fucked his own cock into the mattress while Zack stood there, letting his dick fuck Aaron's mouth in turn.

16

The Morning After the Thing with the Ropes

Zack's Apartment

In the end, Zack had cut Aaron out of the ropes. Not because he needed to – Aaron's circulation was fine, and the position, as he had said, posed no obstacles. But they were both so terribly overwhelmed – Zack had come over Aaron's face and then Aaron had found his own release against the mattress – and Zack's fingers were shaking too much to fiddle with knots. He just wanted Aaron, held and safe and bundled up in his arms.

Which he was, now that Zack had dealt with all the clean up their little adventure had demanded. Against his side, with his head on his shoulder, Aaron was now quiet and no longer full of the little whimpers he had made as he was coming back to himself.

"That," he said eventually into the long silence, "was exactly what I needed."

"Are you nervous about camp tomorrow?" Zack asked.

"Yes and no," he said. "It's both a very big deal and not. I'm still having trouble with the program."

Zack frowned. He couldn't figure that one out. "It's looked great every time I've seen it."

"That's exactly it," Aaron said, rolling onto his back. "It's apparently great if you or Katie are watching it. Anyone else, and it's as if I don't want them to see it."

"Do you know why?"

"It feels too revelatory. I'm not used to trusting that people want to see who I really am."

"I wish I could fix that for you," Zack said and meant every word of it. But this was, he knew, beyond his power. Aaron would simply have to make a choice; that was the nature of fear, unfair as it was.

"I know. I appreciate it. I wish I could fix it for me too," he said with a little laugh. "Hey, can I see the pictures?"

Zack leaned over the side of the bed to grab his camera so that Aaron could page through the photos on the little screen on its back. He watched as Aaron touched the screen.

"The ropes are pretty," he said, looking up at Zack. "That's cool. Can you send me these?"

"Sure," Zack said. "They're your photos to control entirely."

◆

Aaron had just left Zack's apartment when his phone rang. Zack glanced at the screen and swore. Sammy. Whatever this was going to be – which was probably that Sammy had read his incomplete draft and wanted to kill him – he didn't want to deal with it while not fully dressed and not remotely awake.

Hastily he pulled on pajama pants and a t-shirt and hit the answer button before the call rolled to voicemail.

"Sammy. Hi."

"Zack! Good morning."

"What is it?" Zack scrubbed a hand through his hair and wished he could be getting in the shower right now. Or, better yet, going back to bed.

"We're starting to edit your piece. Which is full of holes."

"I know, I told you it was."

"Well, the holes haven't filled themselves. There's barely anything in here about the other kid. Sauer. It's not balanced."

"He won't answer my calls! Nor will his coach or anyone else at that place. I don't know if that's me or them or –"

"Try again."

"I can't right now, because he's currently on the way to some high-performance camp with the *other major contender for the U.S. Olympic Team who I am currently sleeping with!*"

"Oh, fuck." Sammy sounded despairing. "Zack, you're the worst."

"I am aware!"

"What were you thinking?"

"That I sent you my draft and that he's extremely cute and anything else I am thinking about this situation is absolutely something you don't want to know." Zack knew he sounded panicked but he didn't know what to do or say or how to fix any of this.

"I hate you," Sammy said in the voice of the long-suffering.

"I know that too!" Zack tried to take deep breaths. There were going to be consequences to this mess and he didn't want to face any of them.

"Since you're already violating all journalistic ethics in every way possible anyway, maybe get your boyfriend to get Sauer to talk to you since they're going to be in the same room."

"That's a wretched idea." Zack was appalled at the notion. Aaron was already wound up beyond belief about camp, and it was more than obvious Sauer was not his favorite person.

"So is sleeping with your subject. Or former subject, or however you're justifying it to yourself. And you'll notice that while I'm mad about it, the only thing I want here is to get this piece finished and in my magazine so everyone involved can get paid and famous as appropriate, so maybe a little thanks would be appropriate here."

Zack deflated. The truth was, he had no better or even any other ideas for how to get the material he needed for the article. If he had, he never would have considered this.

"Fine," he told Sammy. "I'll ask him."

"Good."

✦

Zack sat down with his laptop on his bed. The sheets were still rumpled and, if he closed his eyes, he could imagine he still felt Aaron's warmth in them. Aaron probably wasn't at the airport yet, much less at camp, but Zack wanted to get this done with.

Hey,

Hope your flight goes well. Or went well. I know this is crossing several boundaries and that's why I'm not including any emotions or compliments in this email. You can absolutely say no and it changes nothing between us, but if you're willing, I have a favor I need to ask you...

He laid out what he needed to Aaron, read it over once to make sure everything was spelled correctly and then again to make sure it made sense.

He hit send.

17

U.S. High Performance Figure Skating Camp

Sacramento, CA

The first day of camp was always the worst. Checking in. Seeing everyone he wanted to, and everyone he didn't. Cayden Sauer topped Aaron's list of people he wanted to spend as little time with as possible. Not because they were the ostensible rivals for an Olympic spot; Aaron had good friends he competed with all the time. But because Cayden was a jerk and seemed to like making people feel small. In the constant jockeying for some sort of position, both in the social order and the psychological game, he was always an instigator in the unpleasant thick of it.

At least Aaron could sit on the other side of the room and ignore him during endless meetings that involved people reading aloud from schedules and rules Aaron could read himself. He had Zack's email, asking him to ask Cayden to talk to him, but he could deal with that later.

The skaters at camp might have been on the same team, but they weren't, not really. There weren't any other U.S. men's singles skaters from TCI that Aaron could hang out with. Angel and Nikolai were in juniors, and Sam and Morgan were a pair. They all had their own schedules and their paths rarely crossed. Sure, being here was about preparing for the first half of the season, but it was also about starting to see who would manage to make the second half of the season and the Olympics. Which was the only reason anyone would put themselves through all this.

✦

Aaron skated a few laps around the rink as he warmed up to show off his free skate program for the federation officials. He tried a few jumps to test how the ice responded. Although the ice itself was fine, Aaron disliked pretty much everything else about the situation. The arena was mostly unpopulated, with empty seats stretching out on all sides. The panel of officials were seated behind their table, frowning and – it felt from the ice, at least – soulless.

Rightly or wrongly, Aaron was sure, any number of other people, including Cayden, were lurking somewhere, watching him and waiting for him to fail.

Don't fail, Aaron told himself when he got the signal to begin. *Just skate.*

His first run-through felt bumpy. He had no falls or major wobbles, but he didn't feel like his blades were fully in the ice or his head was fully in the game. He didn't love that, but he knew he wasn't alone in that. Camp was all the hardest parts of competition with none of the fun bits.

He was happy to watch the rest of his – Teammates? Competitors? Both, really – skate their programs before he had to go again. Technically, it felt better immediately. But after insisting to Zack and Brendan and Katie that he needed music with more space in it for stillness and expression, he now wasn't filling up that space in the music. He was, simply, scared.

"Sixty second pep talk?" Brendan asked as Aaron got off the ice.

What Aaron wanted was to go take a nap until he had to skate again. "Yeah, sure."

Brendan drew him off to the side away from the boards. "You're here," he told him, concern clearly showing on his face, "to solve their problems. And you better figure out how only you can do that, because everyone here can do a triple axel, so that's not the issue."

"Sometimes it's the issue," Aaron noted.

"Okay, sometimes it's the problem, but let's pretend it's not. What makes you special?"

Aaron was afraid he might have been gaping. He was probably gaping.

"Don't tell me you don't know."

"I don't know."

"Okay," Brendan said, "If I had to take a guess, it has something to do with that place you're from."

"All it does is make me sort of awkward."

"You're from the hidden world, Aaron. Time to stop hiding it."

✦

Close your eyes, Zack had said. *I don't want you to think or feel or be anything else right now.*

Zack had meant one thing when he had said that, but Aaron had trusted him, in circumstances far outside his experience, and it had been wildly worth it. Nothing that had happened since had made him regret that choice or mistrust his instincts. Now, he needed to take that advice and make it about skating.

As the music for his program started, Aaron closed his eyes. Hardly remarkable in itself; many skaters did, to find some sort of internal reset. But then he kept them closed. He'd trained a million elements that way since he was a kid; he knew where his body was on the ice; he knew how fast he was going; he knew what to do; he just had to trust. Himself or Zack or his whole messed up life.

He came around one end of the rink into his triple axel. If he was going to die doing this, this would be it. But his entry was on a circle, not a line, and he was pretty sure he was cutting in away from the wall. Glide on the right back outside edge, step onto the left forward outside edge, and *jump*.

He came down clean, smiled, and still didn't open his eyes until he was sure he was right in front of the people serving as judges today.

He snapped his gaze up to look at them as he went by. He made eye contact with one of them, by accident, as he did it. And she gasped.

What a good trick.

What a good boy, Zack had said.

Aaron knew Brendan might kill him later, especially if the powers that be weren't impressed by this little experiment, but right now he was having the time of his goddamn life.

✦

Brendan was waiting for him as he got off the ice at the end of the program.

"What *was* that?" he demanded as Aaron slipped on his guards. He wasn't yelling – Brendan never yelled – but there was definitely an edge to his voice. Which put a bit of a damper on Aaron's elation.

"I decided to try something." Aaron said. He was breathing hard and had to scrub sweat off his forehead with his sleeve.

"Half your run-through with your eyes closed?"

"It wasn't *half*," Aaron protested, shifting from foot to foot. He still felt jittery with the thrill of the performance.

Brendan slung an arm around his shoulders and steered him away from the ice toward a quiet corner. And that was like Brendan too, not to scold where he might be overheard. Which was what made Aaron suddenly nervous. He'd taken a wild risk, and he had no idea yet if it would pay off. What if the officials hated it? What if Brendan was pissed at him? What would the other skaters who had seen it think – and say?

"If you'd hit the boards and hadn't seen it coming, come *on*," Brendan said, once they were away from everyone else. "You could have injured yourself. Badly. When we have you do elements with your eyes closed it's not at speed or under pressure for a reason. What were you thinking?"

"You were the one saying I should trust myself more."

"Yourself! Not the physical constraints of the time-space continuum!"

"But did it work? Was it good?" Aaron had to ask. Not to prove a point to Brendan, but because he wanted to know.

Brendan gave him a disbelieving look. "It was *frightening*."

"Katie is frightening."

Brendan looked stunned. "Do you say that to her?"

"No. She says that to me. Like she says we're alike."

"Oh God." Brendan sank his head into his hands. He ran his hands back through his hair, then looked up at Aaron. "Where is Katie when I need her? This is not my forte."

"Um."

"Aaron?" Both Aaron and Brendan looked up with a start. One of the officials was hovering nearby, notebook in hand. She gave Brendan's spiky hair an amused look. "If you're ready, we have the feedback on your long program now."

✦

The officials, as it turned out, *loved* Aaron's new presentation of himself. They had reams of notes and things they wanted him to change and improve – hell would freeze over before the camp officials saw anything they *didn't* want to improve, except maybe Jack Palumbo's skating, but it was a resounding nod of approval.

Aaron felt like he was walking on air as he left the rink for the day. Outside he found Cayden, evidently waiting for the shuttle bus back to the hotel – and for once, not surrounded by his clique of skater friends. Now was surely the perfect time to fulfil Zack's request.

"Hi!" he said brightly.

Cayden barely glanced up from his phone. "Hi?" he said.

How does he make even that sound mean? Aaron wondered. Like Cayden was some lofty skating god and Aaron was someone far beneath his notice. But he persevered.

"I have a favor to ask. Not for me. For my – for someone else."

"Yeah?"

"So you know there's a journalist who's doing a piece on the people competing for –"

"For Koval's space, yeah," Cayden said. "I know. He called me and my coaches about fifty times. I hear he spent a lot of time at Twin Cities." He gave Aaron a suspicious look that Aaron did not like at all.

"Why didn't you answer?" he asked.

Cayden scowled. "Because I don't do shit like that. If it's not in my schedule, it's a waste of my time."

"That sounds excessively rigid," Aaron couldn't help but point out.

"What it is, is successful. Because that journalist dude is right about one thing: Only one of us gets that spot. And it's going to be me. Because I spend my time working. Because I want to win. You, you just want attention."

Aaron considered himself a fairly laid-back human being. High-stress competitive athletic career aside, he liked people and liked being friendly with them. But with Cayden's words, he saw red.

"Sure I do. Why the fuck else am I an elite athlete?"

"Elite doesn't mean scrambling for a spot on someone else's misfortune," Cayden said.

"My only competition is myself," Aaron said. *I work. I have worked* so hard. *And I will not let you drag me down.*

Cayden gave a vague shrug. "That'll certainly be true when I'm in Almaty and you're... not."

Wow, Aaron thought. *I actually hate you.* He tried to reign his temper in before he got in trouble for being unsportsmanlike. "You do you. It was just a question."

"Not a very bright one."

"Whatever," Aaron said, already walking away. He could catch the next shuttle.

"See you at Nationals!" Cayden called after him.

Aaron couldn't fucking wait.

18

In the Middle of Camp

Minneapolis and Saint Paul, MN

Midway through the week Aaron was away at camp, Zack sat in the booth at one of the several sports bars in downtown Saint Paul. He and his hockey team had just lost a game spectacularly, and were now out for a beer and commiseration. Matt and the girl with the pink-laced skates – Emily – were reminiscing about the Miracle on Ice, and Zack was trying to figure out if either of them had been alive in 1980, when a commotion broke out at the other end of the bar.

Everyone at the table, including Zack, turned to look. Two men, big burly guys he didn't recognize, were shouting in each other's faces. What they were shouting about wasn't clear, but that hardly mattered. Especially when one of the dudes shoved the other one in the chest – hard.

"You going over there?" Matt asked.

Zack hadn't realized he had stood up until Matt spoke. "Yeah," he said.

"You want help?"

"Sure."

Together they hurried over to the bar. Briefly, Zack thought of Aaron, and his days as a bouncer in his parents' restaurant. This didn't seem like the kind of place that would have a bouncer on staff, and the kid working the bar was shrinking back from the brewing brawl, looking terrified.

Getting between the screaming men was not difficult. They were drunk enough that their aim was bad, and Zack and Matt were both bigger than either of them. Still, it was a crowded space, and more than one chair got knocked over in the process of wrestling the combatants apart.

"Really," Zack heard Matt say to the guy he was corralling, who had stopped insulting his barfight counterpart and was now cursing out Matt. "If you want to hurt my feelings, you need to get more creative than *that*."

Zack chuckled grimly to himself. Then backup arrived, in the form of what seemed like the entire staff of the bar at once, and Zack and Matt could fall back and let the professionals take over.

The brawlers were escorted out, and Zack and Matt returned to the rest of the hockey guys – where they were met by cheers.

"Our heroes!" somebody shouted, while someone else bounded over to the bar to order more drinks for everyone.

Matt gave Zack a high five. "We are awesome!"

"Yeah we are!" Zack dropped back into the seat he'd abandoned. He gratefully accepted a beer from the kid who had been behind the bar when the fight started.

"Thank you, you guys," he said, his cheeks flushed. "You guys get beer on the house *forever*."

"It's no problem." Zack couldn't help grinning. The entire thing had happened so quickly, and was so very absurd, and would surely make for a wonderful 'ridiculous things that have happened to me' story.

"Yeah, anytime." Matt raised his own glass. "To independent bouncing!"

"To independent bouncing." Zack picked up his own glass – or tried to. It slipped out of his hand and rolled off the edge of the table onto the floor where it shattered, spilling beer everywhere.

"Oh shit, I'm so sorry," Zack jumped up, or tried to; exiting the booth was awkward, and he was mortified. The bartender, however, took it in stride; evidently this was the kind of crisis he knew how to deal with.

"Hey, no worries, be right back with a mop and stuff!" He darted off, and Zack was left to shuffle out of the booth while avoiding the puddle of spilled drink and broken glass.

"Are you okay?" Matt asked suddenly.

"Yeah, why?"

"You're not breathing quite right," Matt said.

"Oh." Zack tried to assess his own state of being and came up blank. His focus had narrowed strangely, and his heart was pounding deafeningly in his ears.

"Um," he said. "I think I should go sit down somewhere."

He started to stagger off in the direction of the bathrooms with a vague idea of achieving privacy, but Matt caught him by the arm and helped steer him to a quiet back corner instead.

"Sit here," he said, pushing Zack gently down into a chair. "I'll be right back."

He returned in a moment with two glasses of ice water, both of which he pushed at Zack.

"Drink," he said.

Zack's hands were shaking badly, but he managed to down half of one of the glasses in one go. "I'm not drunk," he said.

"I know. Panic attack?" Matt asked, brisk and almost clinical. Without judgment.

The wild pounding in his ears didn't stop, but something loosened in Zack's chest.

"Yeah," he admitted. "Something like that."

"All right," Matt said, calm and with an air of unflappability Zack hadn't seen from him before. "You need anything?"

"Um." It was hard to think in this state, but Zack tried. "I don't think so."

"Cool. I've got nowhere to be and the staff loves us now, so we can chill out here a while, okay?"

"Yeah. Okay."

Matt sat with him while Zack sipped water and tried to take mindful breaths the way his therapist had walked him through. He wasn't sure how long it had been by the time his breathing had finally returned to normal of its own accord and his heart was no longer doing a tap dance in his chest.

"Thanks," he said.

Matt looked up from his phone, where Zack had been watching him play some kind of off-brand scrabble game. Badly.

"It's nothing. You okay?"

Zack shrugged. "Better, at least. It's been a while since I've had that happen. That bad, at least."

"Don't worry about it." Matt set down his phone. "My brother was in the service; I've seen what that can do to somebody."

"I wasn't in the military," Zack felt compelled to clarify for some reason. He realized he'd never told Matt what he did, beyond journalism generally. "I was a war correspondent."

"That's intense," Matt said. Again with that neutrality; he wasn't judging or impressed, which was a relief. Zack could barely manage his own emotions right now, much less someone else's.

"Yeah." Zack looked at his hands. Steady, now, thankfully. "Thanks," he said again. For sitting with me."

"It's no problem. You want to go home and get some rest? You okay to drive?"

"Yeah, I should be. I definitely wasn't before, but now, yeah, I got it."

"Any word from Aaron?" Matt asked as they walked out to the parking lot together.

"Not much. He's been busy with camp."

"You should give him a call, say hi. Hear a friendly voice."

"You're a friendly voice."

"Yeah, but I'm not your cute skater boyfriend."

Zack sputtered. "You said you were straight!" was his knee-jerk and not particularly useful reply. He wasn't jealous, but he was confused.

"I am, but I am also progressive and have good aesthetic sense. He's a great skater. *And* very attractive. Tell him I hope he leaves that Sauer kid in the dust."

"Will do," Zack said. He was still amused, but the mention of Sauer only reminded him of all the ethical lapses he was flirting with in regards to Aaron.

By now they had reached their cars. Matt unlocked his with his key fob, and it beeped in the still night air.

"If you need anything," his friend said solemnly. "I don't care what time it is. Call me, okay?"

Zack nodded and unlocked his own car. The night had been a mess, but Matt's reaction had reinforced how much he had going on here in the Twin Cities even aside from Aaron.

I should write Sammy a thank you note, he thought to himself as he drove home. *Because this is all, somehow, his fault.*

✦

Aaron's name appeared on Zack's caller ID as he let himself into his apartment. Zack toed off his shoes and hit the answer button as he flopped down on the couch.

"Hi, you," he answered it. On his screen blurry chunks of pixels coalesced into Aaron's face. Visible behind him was a headboard and some unmistakably bland North American hotel room art.

"Zack! Hi! Angel went out so I wanted to call and say hi."

"Hello," Zack said warmly.

"How are you?" Aaron asked.

Zack thought about telling Aaron about the bar fight he and Matt had broken up – and the panic attack that had followed – but instantly dismissed it. Aaron didn't need the distraction. And right now, Zack wanted to forget it had happened.

"Good," he lied instead. "I had a hockey game tonight and went out for drinks with the guys."

"Cool! How'd you do?"

"Wretchedly," Zack said, then changed the subject. "How's camp?" No matter how much Zack had immersed himself in figure skating culture and knew how sports worked, calling the training and evaluation thing Aaron was at 'camp' was still weird. He kept picturing him in the woods somewhere, trying to start a fire with sticks and a magnifying glass.

"It's, well, it sucks. I mean, I'm doing great! Skating, that is."

"Oh?" Zack said, inviting elaboration on either point.

"Yeah. My free skate – I tried something new. I kept my eyes closed, the way you had me do when we had sex. The energy of the whole thing, my energy, changed. I – I finally found the stillness I'd been looking for. And the judges *loved* it. So, thank you."

"You're welcome," was all Zack could manage. The magnitude of what Aaron was giving him credit for was too great for him to be able to say more. He was relieved when Aaron kept talking, evidently not expecting more of a response from him.

"Otherwise," Aaron said, "camp is pretty terrible. I was gonna email you, but... I tried talking to Cayden. He was a huge dick to me, and now all his friends are being dicks to me, and I'm pissed at them all."

Zack's conscience, pushed and nudged and sometimes outright shoved to the side since this thing with Aaron had started, came roaring back to him with a force that took the breath out of him. *I asked him to get Sauer to talk to me. He did what I asked. And now he's dealing with shitty consequences because of that. Because of me.*

I went too far, was the painful and overwhelming conclusion. *And it's already hurt Aaron.*

"I'm sorry to hear that," he said mechanically, when he realized Aaron was probably waiting for a response from him. *I can't do this anymore.*

19

Returning from Camp

Minneapolis and Saint Paul, MN

Aaron got back to the Twin Cities late, because he, Brendan, Sam, Morgan, Angel and Nikolai all agreed that getting home at midnight and getting a few hours of sleep in their own beds was infinitely preferable to flying in the morning and still having to do a full day of training. Not that Aaron was sure he'd be able to sleep in any case. He was still riding the high of his achievements at camp, still pissed at Cayden for being a jerk, and impatient to see Zack and talk it all over in person with him. He was used to there being a lot of chatter going on in his head as he managed his time and his feelings, but right now it was louder than ever.

Aaron: Just got in!

He texted Zack with one hand, rolling his bag out to the airport parking garage with the other. He'd texted Charlotte as soon as the plane landed, but he wanted space from his teammates before he reached out to his boyfriend.

Zack's reply came while Aaron was getting in the car.

Zack: Glad you got in safe.

Aaron: What are you doing tomorrow?

Aaron waited to start the car until the reply came in.

Zack: Dealing with some work stuff, but can meet you at four for coffee. That new place on the corner near Marie's?

Aaron: I'll be there

Aaron turned the key in his ignition and was glad there was no one around he had to school his ridiculous grin for.

✦

Despite his worries, Aaron fell asleep the moment his head touched his pillow and woke up before his alarm went off. Apparently his body was as eager to get to work as the rest of him was.

The sky as he drove to the rink was noticeably darker than it had been a few weeks ago. The days were getting shorter, one more reminder for Aaron that fall – and the competition season – was coming. He had ice time with Katie, ostensibly to start implementing the reams of notes and feedback from camp. But as he walked through the front doors, he couldn't help but worry she would be less than impressed with the risk he'd taken at camp. She'd have good reason to be displeased, as Brendan had. But she'd always felt like his closest ally when it came to that program, along with Zack, and he didn't want to lose her support... or his comfort with her.

There was no one else on the ice yet, and the cavernous space echoed with the slightest of noises while Aaron put his skates on. The door from the lobby banged as he was stepping out onto the ice. He glanced over his shoulder to see Katie, her skates already on, striding towards him.

Aaron braced himself, but when she joined him on the ice she was smiling broadly.

"Tell me *everything*," she said as they skated laps to warm up. She didn't need to be with him for this, but chatting was part of their ritual together.

Aaron felt some of the tension he'd been holding dissipate. She wasn't pissed. Probably.

"It was amazing. The skating, at least."

"It was, I saw it. Brendan sent me video and all your feedback. But I want you to tell me why. You were like a different creature out there. What changed?"

Aaron braced himself. "Before I say anything to incriminate myself, I want to be sure. You're not mad at me?"

"No, not mad. You freaked Brendan out, though, so if I have to go to camp next year with you all, I am going to blame you."

Aaron laughed. "That's fair." Though he didn't think he'd put Brendan off *that* much.

"Now spill," Katie told him.

"Brendan told me I should stop hiding the fact that I'm from somewhere strange."

"Brendan was right," Katie agreed.

"So I had to figure out how to do that. Or not do that, I guess," Aaron said. "And the first thing I tried was the thing with my eyes closed." If she wanted him to, he would talk about Zack and how he'd come to that decision. But in the past few days he'd spent so many hours workshopping his program that that particular impetus had, if not faded, at least evolved.

"To be clear, I'm not mad, but if you *ever* do that again in a non-training situation I'm putting you on zamboni duty for the rest of the season," Katie said firmly.

"I'm not trained on the zamboni," Aaron protested.

"That can be remedied," she said crisply, but it was more funny than it was an admonishment.

Aaron giggled. "Okay, yes, I know that was risky. But it worked! And if I can do it in practice, I should be able to do it in competition."

"*Should*," Katie emphasized.

"Anyway, it worked. It shut out the *noise* of everyone else – not their actual noise, but the space they were taking up in my head. I felt real. And solid, you know?"

Katie nodded. "I do."

"Then, by a fluke, I freaked out the judges. That one in particular, the one I made eye contact with, but all of them really. I could feel it in the room. I've never been able to make an audience feel like that before. It was incredible."

"It is. When it works. And it wasn't a fluke." Katie sounded a little wistful. "The thing going on in your head, can you keep making it happen? And can you keep feeling good about it even if you don't get quite that lucky in catching a judge's eye?"

"I think so. I did for the rest of the week at least. In between Cayden being a jerk and contradictory instructions to tone it down and turn it up and also snark about the unreliability of my quad loop."

"Your quad loop is unreliable."

"I'm aware of that! Why do people think I'm not aware of that?"

"You haven't fixed it."

"If I could, don't you think I would have by now?"

Katie gave a vague shrug of acceptance. "No matter how good you get people aren't going to stop being who they are. And they're not going to stop having ideas about how you should make it better. Now, let's get to work."

✦

After Aaron finished his training for the day – and after he'd gone home to shower and change – he drove to the café to meet Zack with the windows down and his free skate song blasting on the car's sound system. Aaron wasn't usually one of the skaters who listened to their own music constantly. But this season was different, in so many ways – and *he* was different. Surrounding himself with the song he had chosen and Zack had inspired seemed eminently right.

Zack's rental car was already in the lot. Aaron parked next to it and hopped out, still humming to himself. He found Zack inside at a little table in the corner, his laptop and an iced tea on the table in front of him. When he saw Aaron he quickly closed the laptop and put it away, and stood to enfold Aaron in a hug.

It was brief and entirely appropriate for a public space where people recognizing Aaron wasn't a possibility so much as an inevitability. Still, Aaron sat down across from Zack with the scent of his aftershave and the memory of his warmth wrapped around him.

"How was camp?" Zack asked as he slid back into his seat.

"It was good. Did you watch the video?"

"Many, many times."

"Did you like it?" Aaron jiggled his leg under the table, too full of energy to be able to sit still.

Zack tapped his fingertips against his lips thoughtfully. "Yes. Of course I did. It was you. But it also didn't seem to matter whether I did or not. The thing you did, that frightened the judges... I could feel that even on a screen."

Aaron smiled. "Good."

"I also think," Zack said slowly, glancing at Aaron as he spoke, "that maybe you weren't so much skating the way you have sex with me, but – skating as if you weren't trying to hide anything about yourself."

Something on the back of Aaron's neck prickled.

"Brendan said something similar, with less information, of course. Katie did too. But I think it's both – where I'm from, and who I'm learning to be when I'm with you. And that's good. It means I'll have a lot to draw from. Camp is only the beginning, you know. But now people are talking about me, not because I'm one of a handful of contenders but because I was *interesting*. All because of you." Aaron had to stop talking to draw a breath, which was when he realized he'd been babbling. Kind of intensely. He felt his cheeks grow warm.

Zack, thankfully, seemed amused. "I am not what makes you interesting, and my dick did not make you a better skater," he said with a gentle laugh.

"You're right. But you have given me a new way to think about how I use my body."

Zack's face smoothed out into a mask of calm consideration, and something in his eyes shuttered.

Aaron's stomach clenched instantly. He made himself breathe while Zack collected his thoughts, the way he had to wait for his scores to come in. He didn't know what was coming, but every nerve in his body was suddenly on alert.

"Aaron," Zack said quietly.

And Aaron knew in that moment that the answer – to a question he hadn't even asked – was no.

"Yeah?" The word came out as more of a croak. He cleared his throat. Part of him wanted to run before Zack could say whatever he was about to say, but Aaron had never run from bad news or bad scores before and he wasn't about to start now.

Zack looked at his hands on the table, then up at Aaron again. "We can't keep doing this."

"You mean the bondage? Did Katie freak out at you? Because it doesn't –" Now Aaron was really babbling, but Zack cut him off.

"Not the bondage, Aaron," Zack's voice was soft, only for his ears. "Any of it. All of it."

"Okay." Aaron blinked and found he was blinking back tears. He screwed his hands into fists under the table, suddenly desperate to keep his feelings in check. The fall had been both unexpected and painful, but he had to pick himself and keep skating. "Can I ask why?" he said when he thought he could control his voice again.

Zack sighed. "Because I'm in the middle of a divorce and you're going to the Olympics."

"Trying to go," Aaron said reflexively. "And you said the divorce was final."

"Yes, both those things are true." Zack said firmly. "You don't need the distraction. I need to not let you into the blast radius of my life. For both our sakes. I do not have my shit together. And I should have never asked you to speak to Sauer for me."

"You don't get to dump me because Cayden's an asshole," Aaron said. Of course, Zack could dump him for any reason he wanted, but that was such a useless terrible one.

"It's not because of Cayden. But that situation was evidence of me not being ready to look after anyone's wellbeing but my own."

"I can handle myself."

"You can. You also deserve every bit of consideration. Honestly, I need to spend some time with myself before I try to date anyone else. You're lovely, and you deserve better than to be a rebound for someone who's made some pretty questionable ethical choices."

"So after the Olympics…." There were limits, Aaron knew, to what you could fight for, in skating and in life. There was no arguing with a judge's scores. Or a federation's decisions. But everything else – he hadn't gotten this far in the sport by not *trying*. And he wasn't going to give up now. "Whether I make the team or not. And once you have your shit together, you and I can do this again. Right?" he asked.

Zack shook his head, and Aaron, feeling stunned, felt the last of his hope drain away.

"No. I'm sorry Aaron. I really am. But me being your boyfriend while not actually dating you is more irresponsible than what we're doing now."

"What if I don't care?"

"I do, though." Zack's face still wore that mask of practiced coolness, but his voice was sad. "Very much."

Aaron realized he had two choices: Stay and beg, or go. As much as he wanted to be loved, Aaron had enough pride not to want to take the first option. Even if he had thought more entreaties might make an impression on Zack's firmness. Which he definitely did not.

"Okay. I get it." He put enough coldness in his voice to have the satisfaction – small as it was – of seeing Zack flinch a little. He stood, his chair scraping roughly on the floor as he did. "I'll see you around, since you moved up here for some reason, I guess."

Aaron had been broken up with enough times in enough places – bedrooms, living rooms, restaurants, and, on one particularly memorable occasion, halfway through the Trophée de France – that trudging out to his car alone and miserable was unpleasant, yes, but not unfamiliar. Breakups had a routine the way loss at a competition did. He'd always recovered relatively quickly from them, but, this time, something felt different.

He started his car, and his short program song blasted on the speakers as he did. He slammed the off button on the dashboard, then sat there with only the sound of the engine for company. Heartbreak had possessed a routine until he'd had the genius idea to skate to a song that was, in his mind at least, about fucking the guy who now had broken up with him.

He let his head fall back against the headrest. "It's gonna be a long season," he said out loud.

✦

Aaron arrived home to find Charlotte sprawled out in the middle of the living room with one leg up on a chair, practicing her over-splits. In the background, a French soap opera blaring from the television. Sometimes Aaron tried to piece together what was going on with his extremely limited French vocabulary; sometimes, he made up random plots in his head. This time, Aaron stopped directly in front of the TV, blocking her view. He was being a jerk, but right now he was upset enough not to care.

"Eeeeeey," Charlotte hissed. "I can't see anything."

"Congratulate me. I got dumped. Again."

She fumbled behind her for her laptop and paused the stream. "Good," she said.

"It's not good!" Aaron said, failing to resist the urge to stamp a foot. This was not the sympathy he wanted right now.

"No. It is." Charlotte was firm. "Now you'll go to the Olympics, and he can feel foolish."

"Is there any chance you can be sympathetic about this?" Aaron asked.

Charlotte pursed her lips and thought about it. "No. Not so much. Go whine to Huy."

"Because complaining to my ex about my other ex –" Of course, Huy was Aaron's friend more than he was an ex, but Aaron was going to be funny where he could.

"Is exactly your speed, no?"

Aaron peered down at her and her flexibility that was excessive even for a figure skater. "You know I hate you, right?"

Charlotte shook her head and smiled. For that, Aaron was glad.

"I know you lie," she said with a laugh and hit play on her computer.

Aaron could recognize a dismissal when he saw it, and as much as he wanted to go sulk in his room, he did really want to whine to someone. He also wanted to make sure he could still skate his damn program with the same magic he'd summoned at camp and without feeling absolutely miserable about Zack.

There was nothing for it. He had to go back to the rink.

✦

During the school year, the rink at this time of night would have been busy. Hockey practice on one sheet, club ice on another, both packed with school-age skaters while more kids, their parents, and coaches filled the hallways and spectator spaces. But it was summer and there were a hundred other things to do in places where it wasn't cold all the time, so the place was quiet.

Brendan was working with some of the pairs on the sheet the elite figure skaters usually used, but there was only a desultory scrimmage happening on the hockey rink and a few skaters on the sheet earmarked for general freestyle practice. The fourth was entirely empty.

In the midst of college-age women practicing some serious doubles and an older couple doing a very stately Viennese Waltz to the maddeningly repetitive accordion music being piped over the sound system (not their fault, or Vienna's, Aaron knew, but did the ice dance test songs always have to be so… so?) was Huy. Huy was one of those skaters who had *it*, that ineffable quality that allowed him to command an entire arena. Right now, all he was doing was practicing compulsory figures in one of the hockey circles, occasionally moving to give way to a lefty jumper practicing her lutz. Figures weren't required in competition anymore, in part because they were dead-ass boring to watch for ninety-nine percent of the audience. Yet the precision and flow of Huy's skating as he traced the same patterns over and over still made Aaron stop and stare.

Aaron couldn't resent the fact that Huy would medal ahead of him at any international competition they were ever at together. One, they were friends, even aside from the ex thing, and two, he was just so *good*. Technique and expression. Aaron would kill to have his lines, and all he was doing right now was paragraph loops.

Huy gave him a nod when Aaron stepped onto the ice, but otherwise left him to his own work. Aaron shoved in his earbuds, hit play on his phone, and started skating the program that existed because of Zack.

Sure, he had to steer around the other skaters and mark the jumps because it was late and he was tired – tonight was not the night to get hurt. But he could still do it. Not as bad as it might have been. Not as good as it needed to be. But it wasn't gone, and that was something. Eventually, maybe it wouldn't break his heart.

When the song in his ears ended, he skated over to the boards for water. Huy was there already, fiddling with his own water bottle and watching him.

"I heard you were quite the sensation at camp," Huy said.

"Who'd you hear that from?" Aaron felt like it was important, to know if it was from Katie or Brendan or gossip from Cayden and his cronies.

"Does it matter?"

"It might."

Huy shook his head. "Nah. It doesn't. Good is good."

"Says the person who is always effortlessly great."

"No, says the person who comes here in his off hours to do misery-making exercises that people hate so much they removed them from competition decades ago. But sure. Think it's effortless if you want."

Aaron shook his head. "Sorry. I didn't mean that." Still, he was pretty sure that even if he gave up everything in his life besides the ice he still wouldn't skate like Huy. But since that wasn't possible – the restaurant and his family would always need him – the point was moot.

"It's cool." Huy shrugged and changed the subject. "I like the new program. It suits you. In a way that I don't think people are going to expect. Which is great." He set down his water and reached for his box of tissues. On the cold rink, everyone's nose ran constantly. "You needed something new."

"Zack broke up with me," Aaron blurted.

Huy stopped with his hands raised to his face, the tissue over his nose, his eyes wide. "Oh lord."

"You don't need to sound like that!" Aaron protested.

"Yes. I do." Huy blew his nose, balled up the tissue, and chucked it into the bin on the other side of the boards. "I didn't even know you guys were together," he said, looking affronted. "How did I not know you guys were together?"

"Because you spend your off hours busting your ass doing figures?" Huy, of course, also had his own life and relationships which kept him plenty busy outside of skating, but Aaron tried not to dwell on that.

"Mm." Huy leaned back against the boards. "Were you into Zack because Zack, or were you into Zack because you're desperate to be monogamous with every pretty person who walks into a room?"

"I'm not desperate," Aaron protested, although he wasn't sure Huy was wrong.

"You do a pretty good imitation," Huy said.

"Ow!"

"It's not inherently a bad thing. None of us do what we do here because we're quite all right."

"Even you?" Aaron kicked his toe pick into the ice. Huy was doing his best to cheer him up, but he did not at all want to be cheered up.

"I'm doing figures in my free time. What do you think?" Huy sighed. "Look, we all want what we want. But if we make choices that definitely aren't going to give us that... that's what's messed up. I want to win, so I show up and do figures."

"I don't want to win, I just want a chance *to* win," Aaron clarified. He knew where he stood, and he knew how fragile and tenuous that position was.

"There's your first problem. You need to believe you can do what no one else thinks you can. Trying to scrape into your dream by a hair's breadth is not how you make that happen."

"Okay. But realism."

"Sure. But I'm telling you to aim higher. You're going to have to podium at a lot of things to be at the Olympics. Grand Prix events. And U.S. Nationals."

"You think I don't know that?"

"Sometimes I wonder."

"Now you sound like Katie."

"I'm not saying you're not focused. Or driven. Or anything like that," Huy said. "Because you are. I don't know if I'd keep hammering at stuff as long as you have from where you are."

Aaron grimaced. It was not a flattering assessment. It also wasn't necessarily wrong. He felt his mood sink further.

"You're certainly persistent," Huy went on. "But you don't give yourself enough credit for how far you've come to be *here*."

That, admittedly, made Aaron feel a little better.

Huy nodded around at the ice sheet, almost empty now except for them. "But I see the way you want so much to be somebody's one-and-only and yet don't direct that energy at people where that's likely to happen. So it makes me wonder if you know how to win anything – on or off the ice. Most importantly, it makes me question your choices. About everything. A lot."

"Is this the polyamory as resource management lecture again?" Aaron asked. Suddenly, more than anything, he felt tired. He wanted to go home and sleep for about a week.

"Maybe. I don't know," Huy said. "That analogy never seems to work for you. But the sooner you figure out how to stop wasting time keeping various parts of your life as separate drains on your emotional and creative resources, the better. I know we all have to compartmentalize in this sport all the time, but you need to figure out how to use everything you have to get everything you want."

"My free skate is about my now-ex and I fucking. I don't think I'm compartmentalizing here."

Huy, who was rarely phased by anything, and certainly not the romantic and sexual adventures of his fellow skaters, was clearly phased now. But he took a deep breath and continued on as if Aaron hadn't been appalling.

"No. But I know you. You're going to want to either put your head down and focus on the work, or go out and find somebody else to fall for, for the rest of the season. When what you need to do is lean into the thing where you feel heartbroken and pissed off and lonely and put it all in the performance. And when you make the team and get to the Olympics, you and me and my boyfriend will have a threesome, yeah?"

"Why am I friends with you?" Aaron asked. Because good advice aside, Huy never ceased to be Huy – always generous, and never quite in the way Aaron wanted or needed.

PART II

20

Autumn

Minnesota and Florida

Breakups were miserable, and Zack second-guessed himself about Aaron more than once. But Aaron did not need more inconsistency from him, and Zack needed to focus on having a life that wasn't about constantly running to and from distractions that ranged from inappropriate to dangerous. So he stayed in Saint Paul and kept playing hockey because it didn't make sense to do or go anywhere else. He played in more games for the rec league, and he was happy to be perfectly adequate. Maybe one day, he'd manage to score a goal, but that seemed far away.

He told Sammy about Aaron's failed attempt to get Sauer to call him, and about the breakup which had been partially precipitated by Zack's inability to handle that mess. Sammy had no sympathy to offer and no interest in absolving Zack of his journalistic sins, which was fair. After all, it didn't matter that he had broken up with Aaron; it didn't erase their past or the way it had compromised Zack's objectivity. The only solace he was given was that

Sauer would be yanked out of the article completely, allowing Zack to rework his initial swiss cheese draft into a truly compelling profile of Aaron and life at TCI.

Zack knew as he worked on it that it was a love letter, but he was grateful that it was as much a love letter to a place and a sport, as it was to his first post-divorce ex.

Who he did, of course, still see around the rink. They'd nod to each other – tight and miserable – when they passed at the front desk or by the vending machines. Matt, at least, remained a steadfast friend amongst that chaos, offering sympathy, conversation, and ongoing instruction in the art of hockey trash talk. All further bar fights were avoided, and Tasha drilled him ruthlessly in edge control.

But while skating and friends and the legacy of his own mistakes continued to exist, so too, unfortunately, did Florida. As the calendar ticked towards Thanksgiving, Zack didn't know what he wanted to deal with less – his ex and the condo that was now under contract to sell or his parents who now expected to see him for the occasion since he wasn't in another country.

Either way, he had to get on a plane. This time, when the adrenaline and the panic started, he felt entirely justified.

✦

The condo, when he visited it for the last time, felt remarkably alien. His ex had finally taken his things, as well as all manner of things that Zack hadn't necessarily expected to go missing. Gone was all of their cookware, the chaise lounge that they had only bought for the living room because the realtor had thought it would make the place sell faster, and most of their art. The photo of his ex's hands coiled with rope remained, as did boxes that Zack had never bothered to unpack when they had moved into this place originally.

He couldn't wait to purge all of it. Except the photo. Art was art, and he'd sell the damn thing on the internet to some collector who wanted something vaguely sexy for their guest bedroom. Beyond that, he did not care. So much so, he was willing to spend the Thanksgiving holiday at his parents' house, rather than sleep a single night in that apartment again.

His parents lived in a gated community up in Jupiter, which was only the first of many reasons he didn't usually visit them. His parents had never been his biggest fans, and there was no winning with them. Going into conflict zones hadn't been heroic to them; just foolish. On that point, they'd quite possibly been right. But when he had stopped, they had thought him a coward. They'd treated his book deal much the same: like it was a waste of time until it wasn't enough. Their opinions on his marriage and divorce were equally as skeptical and unhelpful, but Zack had the sense to know that a stopped clock was right twice a day. Which didn't make it less infuriating, but did make it not matter.

"How's Wisconsin?" his father asked, pouring them both a cup of coffee.

"Minnesota," Zack corrected.

"What? Oh yes. Of course," his father said vaguely, as if anywhere not in Florida simply wasn't worth distinguishing from anywhere else.

"It's fine," Zack said. The same answer he'd given when asked about his day when he was in high school or his last trip to a combat zone. "I'm going to move there."

"For good?" his father asked. He seemed startled, which was at least a victory.

"For now. I like it there."

"Ah," his father said. "Well, good luck with all that." Then he started talking about politics.

Zack tuned him out. He was too unsurprised by his father's indifference to be hurt by it.

I'm done with all of it, he realized. Not only the condo, but Florida. His family's bullshit. The feeling that his failures were innate, versus being ordinary messed up stuff he could deal with and fix, like anyone else.

The problem with him and Aaron had been bad choices, yes. But mostly, Zack realized now, it had been timing. Aaron had said as much, and Zack hadn't wanted to listen. Because then he would have had to be patient and deal with his mistakes, and face the possibility that what he wanted wasn't nearly as important as what Aaron was working towards.

Oh well. Insight was great, but it couldn't overcome circumstances any more than it could overcome twenty-four hours and a turkey dinner with family that was going through the motions all the way around. They even had to be difficult with him about hockey – of all things! – when he was just trying to do what all men were expected to do on national holidays, which was talk about sports.

His choice to stick around the Twin Cities may not have made sense initially, and he may have been thinking with his dick. But now he was all in. Permanently. Simply because it wasn't this, which felt like not only a relic of a life he had never wanted, but also a relic of a life he had never had.

21

The Grand Prix Season

Sapporo, Japan and Montreal, Canada

As the days in the Twin Cities grew shorter, the hours Aaron spent at the rink – and the gym – grew longer. There was constant strengthening, conditioning, and artistic polishing. His programs would never be perfect in the first half of the season, maybe not even until he got to the Olympics, assuming he did. But the work of improving it, and himself, was constant either way. That was the nature of competitive skating and what he loved about it: Every day was a challenge to get up and do better than he had the day before. And in the process become, somehow, more himself.

The work was, at its core, lonely. Sure, he trained alongside Charlotte and Huy and all the others. They shared ice for part of most days, did warm-up routines together, went to pilates classes together, played board games on Friday nights, and hung out at the farm when they needed a break or the opportunity to do hard work that wasn't about the Olympic dream.

But still, when Aaron skated his programs, he was alone on the ice. And at night, falling asleep before nine because he was exhausted and sore, he was alone in his bed, too. No one could understand what those things felt like for him, even if they lived their own version of them. He did his best to do what Huy had recommended, and he leaned into his own sadness and sense of isolation to let them be fodder for the program. It worked, at least as far as his skating went – in the last few weeks of the pre-season Katie had no complaints about the emotionality of his programs – but it wasn't a fun mental place in which to live.

Aaron missed Zack, sometimes so much it startled him. In a different year he might have found someone else to have some fun and blow off some steam with. But he had no time, and even if he had... nobody was like Zack. And Aaron, who had loved variety in his happily-ever-after one-and-only fantasies, now only wanted him.

The feelings of loneliness and missing Zack only fueled each other, and they grew more and more acute as Aaron's first Grand Prix assignment ,the NHK Trophy, drew closer. He couldn't shake them as he boarded the flight; his only relief was that some of the juniors had a competition the same weekend and, since Brendan was going with them, Katie was travelling with him.

Maybe it was her presence, at turns soothing and prickly as his own mental state needed. Maybe he was tired enough of feeling sad that he pushed away the rest of his own mental chatter while he skated and focused solely on *being* on the ice. Whatever it was, to his own surprise, Aaron was in fourth at the end of the short program and managed to climb to second in the free skate.

Aaron had never been so thrilled with a second-place finish as he was that night, taking a victory lap with Philippe Chastain and Yin Jae-Sun. Nothing was guaranteed until he was named to the team, and everything depended on how well Cayden did at his own Grand Prix events, but this was the best placement he'd ever had in an international event. He got off the ice at the end of the medal ceremony and fell into a massive hug from Katie and about a thousand notifications on his phone, most of them texts from his family.

Still, something didn't feel right. Aaron tried to explain it to Katie on their way home, while they waited in Warsaw's Chopin Airport on an unexpected stop due to a storm. In his luggage was the silver medal, which had turned out to be oddly challenging to airport security.

Halfway through what was, he thought, a very eloquent discourse on skating and loneliness Katie interrupted him with a gentle nudge to his shin.

"You want the guy who dumped you in order to, very reasonably, sort out his life and issues. I didn't eat ice cream for three years so I could go to the Olympics. You just won a silver medal at an important event. I think you can deal."

Aaron slumped back against the uncomfortable airport seating. "I feel like it gets harder the closer I get. And you always had Brendan."

"Mmm." Kate hummed thoughtfully. "'Had' is a word with a vast shade of meanings. He broke my heart all the time. I guess, more importantly, I broke his all the time too. We were a mess until way after we won."

"I know, I've seen videos."

Katie made a dismayed noise.

Aaron continued. "I believe you when you say it was rough between you two. But you still had somebody, you know? I'm busting my ass and getting on a ridiculous number of planes and not seeing my family for months and it's *only me*. I don't think you get how hard it is to be a singles skater."

"If you want to try pairs, I can hook you up," Katie said dryly.

Aaron laughed despite his frustration. "I don't want to try pairs!"

"Didn't think so." Katie smiled. "And I'm afraid loneliness is the price you're going to have to pay for a while."

"I miss home," Aaron admitted. "I'm lonely, and I feel like I don't belong here. On the ice it's all good, but for everything else… I feel like I'm masquerading as an actual person."

"Because you're a skater?" Katie asked.

"No. Or, yes, but not just that." Aaron fiddled with the strap of his carryon. "Because of the island. The rest of you are all mainlanders and you don't know how different it is here. How…strange I find all of you." Saying it aloud made Aaron feel even more different than usual.

"I had to pretend too, you know," Katie said. "Brendan's from the world and had money and was easygoing and fit in with the other skaters. I wasn't and I didn't. Still don't, really. You're from a place that's hard."

"I'm from a place that's strange," Aaron corrected. "I don't know how to explain what it's like, that we're all waiting to go back to the water. I know people are afraid of you when you skate, sometimes, but have you ever scared somebody because of where you were from?"

"Oh, Aaron." Katie's voice was unusually tender. Which somehow made it all that much worse.

Aaron slouched lower in his seat.

Katie uncrossed and recrossed her legs. "I know I've scared Brendan a whole bunch of times."

"That's different," Aaron said.

"Is it?" Katie asked. "I don't think Zack was scared of you. He's just doing something else. He got divorced six months ago and he's selling a house in another state. He is also, may I remind you, a war reporter, and you, my sweet island child, are not the scariest thing he's had to deal with. If he's into you, he has your best interests at heart and you'll see him again when that's right for both of you."

"I know." Aaron sighed plaintively. "But I got silver at the NHK. That's a big deal. And I want someone to celebrate with."

Katie leaned her chin on her hand. "You mean other than on the phone to your family? And sitting here with me?"

Aaron felt guilty for thinking it, after all the support they had all given him, but it was true. "Yeah. More or less," he said.

Katie seemed unbothered. "Fair. But there's a bar on the other side of the terminal called Business Shark. If you want to have one brief terrible toast to your victory…"

Aaron appreciated the offer more than he knew how to express. But it wasn't what he wanted. Even with Katie, with whom he cherished such a kinship.

"Thank you," he said softly. "But I think I'll hold out for the ice cream."

✦

The Grand Prix season was a marathon not only of skating, but of travel. A few short weeks after the NHK was Aaron's second Grand Prix event, Skate Canada in Montreal. With his strong performance at his first event Aaron had high hopes for his second, no matter how unlikely they were to manifest in anything. He still couldn't quite believe he'd gotten a silver in Sapporo, but now corners of sports media were humming quietly about him.

That said, this was not an event where he had a chance of pulling off an unexpected but not totally shocking silver. For one thing, Huy was competing for Canada. For another, so was Aizat Beysenov for Kazakhstan. That they'd take gold and silver in one order or the other was a given. Beyond that, everyone from the major network broadcasters to the fans in the stands knew it was a race to bronze which Aaron, frankly, did not expect to be in.

He also knew that there was no chance he'd place high enough to be able to advance to the Grand Prix Final. That was okay; U.S. Nationals was where it counted for what he needed to make happen. All he had to do here was keep doing the work and place respectably.

In Montreal, Aaron found it harder to mire himself in loneliness the way he had in Sapporo. Charlotte as well as Huy was competing, which meant he had hotel rooms to hang out in and companions for 5 a.m. wakeup times for practice. Brendan also wound up leading late-night yoga sessions to manage their collective nerves and insomnia.

The men's short program was on Friday; both Huy and Aaron had skated relatively early and were hanging out together backstage watching on the monitor when Aizat popped what should have been a quad lutz.

Huy winced, presumably in empathy for a fellow competitor, but Aaron – rightly or wrongly – started rapidly calculating points margins. When the night ended, the leaderboard confirmed what he already knew: Aizat was lagging, badly, and the door to something other than third place cracked open.

Saturday morning, as Aaron he got dressed for his practice session, his phone barked with an incoming text.

Katie: Skate for your life.

He took Katie as literally as he could and attacked his long program as if it were his last chance to see ice in a dying world. It felt terrifying and reckless and electric and if he couldn't keep the barest edge of control over it, he knew he'd wipe out and into last place.

But he held on, because he had to, and when his scores were announced and he realized he was in second place behind Huy with a personal best. In the kiss and cry he screamed with delight and then buried his face in Brendan's shoulder.

Brendan closed his hand around the back of Aaron's neck. "You just won a ticket to the Grand Prix Final."

For the first time ever. *Eat that*, Aaron couldn't help thinking in the general direction of Cayden. Who had all but qualified for the Final with a gold and a silver at his own Grand Prix events, but had already announced he'd be skipping that competition to 'focus on preparing for Almaty.' As if he'd already been named to the Olympic team.

Jerk.

In Aaron's bag at their feet, his phone barked with incoming messages of congratulation. Huy tackled him in a hug on their victory lap, and Aizat, who'd managed bronze, shook his hand warmly. Backstage Charlotte, with her own gold medal from the ladies' event around her neck, hugged him and kissed both his cheeks. Aaron let himself enjoy the moment and the night; starting tomorrow, there was a hell of a lot of work to do. He'd been good and he'd been lucky, but the GPF was a whole new level and something he had never experienced before.

When the plane's wheels touched down on the tarmac at Minneapolis-Saint Paul he had exactly eleven days until he'd be wheels up on his way to Saint Petersburg for the Grand Prix Final. Nothing and no one else could exist. Aaron barely had time to empty his suitcase, do his laundry, and repack it in between training sessions, food, and sleep. If he passed anyone coming or going at the rink, he didn't notice them.

Medaling in Saint Petersburg wasn't likely for him. This time, truly only bronze would be open, and Aaron would be lucky to not come in last of the six. If he screwed this up or had a bad day, he wouldn't have a chance at the U.S. Olympic team. And he'd never forgive himself.

22

The Grand Prix Final Men's Short Program

Miami International Airport

The monitor at the gate read *Minneapolis-Saint Paul — Delayed,* so rather than sit and check the departure time obsessively for the next however long it took, Zack decided to take a walk.

He ambled around the terminal for a while, taking refuge in people-watching rather than thinking about anything. His parents sucked, his ex sucked, and flying sucked. All he wanted was to be home, which was now far away and cold. He stepped to the side of the concourse as a flood of passengers disembarked from a plane. It was then he noticed one of the TV screens in the bar across the way. Figure skating, especially men's, was the last sport he'd expect to encounter in a bar in Florida, and yet there was an ice rink with a lone figure standing in the middle of it.

Zack squinted to see better. It couldn't possibly be... and yet. Aaron's black costume for the short program, studded with silver and rhinestones, shone out across the concourse.

Zack made his way through the crowd of tourists and reachedthe TV in time to see Aaron close his eyes and start to skate. The volume was way down, but Zack could hear the music in his head anyway. He'd watched Aaron practice often enough.

Whatever this broadcast lacked in sound, it made up for in close-up shots. Zack hadn't ever been able to see Aaron's face like this before, when he'd been watching him from the other side of the boards. He was as utterly mesmerizing as when Zack had had him in his own bed; more, perhaps, because Aaron was making himself this vulnerable, this expressive, this *himself* not only for Zack but for anyone who might be watching. And this wasn't even the program that was – according to Aaron – about the two of them.

Aaron closed his eyes again on what Zack knew was his final spin. He struck his ending pose and the crowd, after a moment's hush, exploded in applause. Zack still couldn't hear them, but he could read it in their faces and in the way they jumped out of their seats.

Aaron was thousands of miles away, but when he opened his eyes again, they landed on the camera and – Zack was absolutely sure – on him.

Zack was spellbound. The broadcast was, somehow, live – *who here cares that much about figure skating to turn this on?* – and he had to stay and watch. Aaron took his bows and skated to the edge of the ice where he was instantly pulled into a massive hug by Brendan. Sitting in the kiss and cry, Aaron's leg jiggled with nervous energy while Brendan chatted animatedly with him, clearly trying to distract him from the interminable wait.

When the scores came up, Zack still wasn't well-versed enough in the intricacies of the scoring system to be able to understand what it all meant, but he did understand the big "Current Standing - 2nd" beside Aaron's name.

Zack had been trying so hard to stay away from everything figure skating; hockey was so much safer for his heart. So he had no idea how many skaters were left or when the free skate was. And oh, how he wished he did. Before he could find any of that out, though, a boarding announcement crackled over the airport's PA. "Final call for flight to Minneapolis-Saint Paul, final call – "

He had to sprint back through the concourse to get on the plane before the doors shut.

✦

Zack heaved a sigh of relief as he pulled into the driveway of Marie's house, already feeling more at ease here than he had anywhere in Miami.

When he stepped out of the car the air was crisp with the promise of winter. Even that was welcome, in its way; cold was an indelible part here of life in the Twin Cities. Marie was in the front yard, raking the last of the leaves, though she stopped to return his wave.

"Welcome back," she said as Zack unloaded his bags from the trunk of the car – another rental; his own car wouldn't arrive from Florida for another few days.

"It's good to be back," Zack said.

"Wonderful. I'm glad you made it in one piece," Marie said. "But now that you're here," she gestured with the hand not holding her rake. "I can tell you, it's time for you to find a new place."

"I…." Zack rocked back on his heels, stunned. He'd just spent a week closing out his life in Miami, and he'd landed back in the Twin Cities not an hour ago. He knew his three-month lease extension with Marie was almost up, but he'd been vaguely hoping she'd let him stay on longer again.

"Why?" He couldn't help asking.

"Because if you're going to be hanging around here for a while longer, and I suspect you are, you need a more permanent place than my in-law apartment," Marie said. "I need that space for actual visiting skaters who are not functional adults who should be allowed to be totally on their own."

Which Zack could surely appreciate, and yet…. "I'm not sure I'm a functional adult who should be allowed to be totally on my own," Zack said, trying to lighten a moment that was wildly unbalancing.

Marie put a hand on her hip and looked him over. "That makes two of us. But my understanding is that you've been trying to fix that?"

"Yeah?" That much, at bare minimum, was true.

"Great," Marie nodded firmly, like that settled the matter. "You get to make room for some competitive skater or other who has never lived entirely in the real world."

"Okay." he said. There was the direct communication his therapist was always trying to encourage. And then there was this. "Did I do something wrong?"

"No. Stop looking guilty like that. And this has nothing to do with the fact you were seeing Aaron Sheftall. To be clear."

Zack hadn't known he was capable of blushing; apparently, in front Marie at least, he totally was. "You knew about that? You never said."

"Pretty sure I heavily implied I knew, but say anything? Why would I? You're both adults. It's none of my business."

"Even for the gossip?" Off-kilter as he felt, Zack couldn't help teasing.

Marie winked at him; the gesture felt oddly anchoring. "Even for the gossip. Your secrets are safe with me."

"All right. So like… now, or?"

Marie scowled at him. "Would I kick you out like that? No. But you'll thank yourself if you're in a place of your own by the new year. If you need help looking, you know where you can find me."

And with that, Marie went back to her raking, leaving Zack feeling more discombobulated than ever.

✦

At hockey practice the next morning Zack was pleased to find that he hadn't lost too much ground. He'd only been in Florida a week, but that had been the longest he'd been off the ice since he'd started. He even remembered not to keep looking over his shoulder to see if Aaron was passing by on his way to his own practice; after all, Aaron was still in Russia.

"Hey, glad to have you back!" Matt said cheerily as they eased off their padding and unlaced their skates in the locker room. "How was Miami?"

"Complicated," Zack replied honestly.

"You did a lot of hard work there. You should be proud of yourself," Matt said earnestly.

"Calling 1-800-Got-Junk and also telling my parents off wasn't exactly hard work. Unpleasant, but."

"Still. You did it and you should feel good about that."

"Maybe once I get caught up on sleep." At the very mention of it, Zack had to stifle a yawn. "But I'm glad to be done. Finally. But when I got back here Marie told me I needed to find my own place."

"You should!" Matt said enthusiastically. "A whole new start and all that. Do you know where you want to be? My building might have an opening; I can ask. And we'll all help you move," Matt said, speaking to the team at large.

He was met by various nods and verbal assents. Zack was touched and little overwhelmed by the support. He cleared his throat as he packed his skates back in his bag.

"Thanks. All of you. I don't have a plan yet, I haven't had a chance to think about it. But I'll take apartment leads if you have them."

"Great!" Matt stood up, hefting his own hockey bag, and slapped Zack on the shoulder. "We're all going out for drinks tomorrow night, you're gonna come, right?"

"Definitely." Maybe it was how the Twin Cities treated all comers in need of a home, but Zack was folding back into the pleasant routine of life here as if he'd never left. After the ordeal of the holiday, it was a balm to his soul.

Zack had every intention of getting back to his car, driving back to Marie's house, and sleeping for several more hours before he embarked on work of any sort. But as he made his way down the hallway between rinks, he passed the conference room with the door ajar. Glancing in he saw Nikolai, one of the junior men's skaters, fiddling with a laptop projecting something on a screen at the side of the room. Katie was beside him scrolling through something on her phone.

Nikolai glanced up and, catching Zack's eye, waved. Katie looked up and gave him a nod. Zack waved back, ready to keep walking and get back to his car – and his bed – as soon as possible, but then he noticed what was playing on the screen: A figure skating competition.

He stopped; he couldn't help himself. "Is that the Grand Prix Final?" he asked from the doorway.

"It is!" Nikolai said brightly. "The ladies finished about an hour ago. Charlotte came in third! Chiemi Maeda won, of course. Men's free skate is about to start."

Katie gave a terse nod of acknowledgement, now typing rapidly on her phone. Zack had no idea who Chiemi Maeda was, and made a mental note to read up on skaters from other disciplines.

Nikolai bounced on the balls of his feet, evidently excited. "Do you want to stay and watch?"

Zack had already stepped inside the room without consciously realizing it. "If I'm not intruding."

"Not at all!"

A few more people trickled into the room as the zamboni on the screen finished its resurfacing. Evidently they'd been here to watch the women skate as well and had been off taking a break; bags and coats were piled in the back of the room, which Zack noticed when he went to set down his own gear.

"They're starting, they're starting!" Nikolai called, and all at once the volume of chatter in the room dropped as people gathered around the screen.

For all the time Zack had spent around elite competitive figure skaters, he hadn't yet watched a competition alongside them. Saint Petersburg was on the other side of the planet, but Zack felt like he was experiencing the tension and excitement firsthand, channeled through the other skaters.

Katie kept herself slightly separate from the rest of the group, phone now clenched tightly in her hand. Between skaters, she paced the length of the room. When someone was on the ice, she stood as if transfixed, her eyes glued to the screen. Zack could feel the tension rolling off of her. She was, without a doubt, freaking out.

Zack couldn't blame her. Some of the kids in the room talked in between skaters, comparing rankings and season's best scores and how much room there was or wasn't for the remaining skaters to medal. He wished they wouldn't; he was nervous enough for Aaron without the ongoing reminders that his most likely placement was fifth or sixth... in a field of six.

"Katie," he called between skaters.

She whipped around sharply, as if displeased to have her pacing interrupted.

"Do you want to sit with me?" he asked on a whim. He tried to make his voice as gentle as possible. "We can do breathing exercises together."

"He's not your problem anymore," she said sharply, though she did draw closer to him. "But he's still mine."

"I know. I'm not making it about him. I'm making it about you."

She looked at him quizzically.

"I know it feels like you're going to die," he said softly. He didn't know why this was suddenly so important to him, but it seemed like the right thing to do. He was entangled with these people whether any of them liked it or not. "And I know you can't change that. But come on, I have experience with this type of misery. We can be panic buddies. Just for right now."

"Okay," she said, grudgingly, taking a seat next to him on the floor. "Just for right now."

23

The Grand Prix Final Men's Free Skate

Saint Petersburg, Russia

Aaron *hated* skating last. Skating last meant more time waiting, stressing out, and exerting every possible effort to keep his nerves under control. Skating last at the Grand Prix Final was even worse. Huy and Aizat were top-five world skaters; Aaron had never made it to the Final before and didn't feel like he was in the same league as them. No one had travelled all the way to Saint Petersburg to see him skate. Half the audience, he suspected, was here for Huy alone. And no one, after seeing Aizat's show-stopping program, would care what Team USA's Aaron Sheftall had to offer.

Then you've got nothing to lose, he told himself as he got ready to take the ice. He unzipped his jacket and handed it to Brendan, then slid off his skate guards. *No title to defend. No reason not to show them all of who you are.*

Aaron's nerves evaporated as soon as his blades met the ice. Maybe it was his own cliched pep talk; more likely it was the feel of the ice under his blades. This was where he was meant to be. This was what he had trained for. This was what he was meant to do.

Aaron took his starting position, took a breath and – as if he was readying himself to jump off the dock on Whisker Island into the waves – closed his eyes. The music started.

Halfway through Aaron knew this was the best he'd skated this program all season. The audience to whom he'd been nothing but a vague name a few minutes ago were now at the edge of their seats, clapping to keep time with the music and exhaling in relief every time he landed a jump. The applause, when he finished, sounded like the roar of the waves on the shore in a storm.

✦

It took forever for Aaron to get out of there. After he'd placed third and cried – but only a little and into Brendan's shoulder so nobody saw – there was the medal ceremony and testing and the press conference and the gala and so many interviews, because this was Russia and people very much cared about skating here.

Katie sent a congratulatory text, and he was grateful to be able to respond in kind. He wasn't up for a verbal conversation right now. His family has blown up his phone too, of course, and he texted back and forth with them on the ride back to the hotel with Brendan, Charlotte, and Huy.

Huy invited Aaron to grab food with him and a bunch of other people, but Aaron begged off. After the whirlwind of the day he wanted to be alone to process. So while Huy and Charlotte ran off to enjoy the city, Aaron dumped his gear in his room and slipped back outside as quick as he could, before he was waylaid by other skaters or their fans.

He turned up his collar as he went; used as he was to the cold in general, December in Saint Petersburg was no joke. The wind was biting and only a few other adventurous souls were out on the streets. He walked along the Neva, up past the Winter Palace and the Summer Garden – a whole year in less than a mile. It seemed fitting under the circumstances.

As Aaron passed beyond those most central tourist locations, his legs somehow unwilling to give up this day, he heard a bark. He reached on instinct for his phone. But his volume was still off the way he always had it at competition. Keeping his phone silent was common courtesy to the other skaters, and also, no one needed to hear his seal alert. Besides – The notes? The words? The sounds? – of the barking weren't quite right. Like a sensible person, Aaron looked around expecting a dog. He didn't see one.

As he continued to walk, the barking seemed to follow, and Aaron checked his phone more than once; perhaps he had turned it back on by accident after the time he had checked before. But he had not, and the sound was most assuredly coming from the river.

It continued to propel him forward along the embankment until he came to a set of steps that led towards the water. Aaron started down them. He took the first few too quickly, then slowed considerably when he realized they were slick. Falling into an icy river in Russia was not the headline he wanted on the night of his greatest triumph.

He took another cautious step down and squinted into the dark. Something bobbed in the water below. *Please don't be a dead body, please don't be a dead body, please don't be a dead body*, Aaron's brain unhelpfully supplied. He fished in his pocket for his phone once more, turned the flashlight on, and held it up. Below, in the water that he was now far too close to, a pair of large brown eyes blinked back at him before dipping beneath the water.

He took another step down, his free hand trailing along the wall. The rough stone was icy under his fingers. Suddenly the eyes reappeared and the whole of the creature he'd seen rose out of the water and up onto the steps.

It was a seal. Because of course it was.

It and Aaron regarded each other for a moment before the seal barked, jerking its head.

Come closer, come closer.

Aaron did, offering a hand to sniff the way he would to a nervous dog. "I don't think you're supposed to be here, buddy," he said softly.

The seal barked, launched itself from the step to the water – smooth and splashless – then clambered back up again, this time touching its nose briefly to Aaron's hand.

"What do you want? I don't have any food. Is that what you do... lure people down here to feed you?"

The seal seemed indignant at Aaron's suggestion, and repeated its leap into the water and return to the step.

"Are you lost?" Aaron crouched lower. He didn't dare take another step down, unless he wanted to lose his shoes in the water.

The seal, which was massive, butted its head against Aaron's hand as he stared out into the dark wondering from which direction it had come. The seal continued its contact, seeking affection, Aaron presumed, in a manner very similar to a dog. He wondered if he should call a wildlife rescue, assuming that was the sort of thing one did here.

But then his eyes adjusted and his heart, which had already had the strain of so much joy and victory – nearly stopped. For his friend pressing its head against Aaron's hand was not alone. Out in the river beyond the steps, the sleek domes of two dozen or more seal heads bobbed. And their eyes, benign and gentle, watched him to a one.

A part of Aaron – the part of him that no longer lived on the island that he was from – understood the moment like a horror movie. Any mainlander would have run at this point, slipped on the stone steps, hit their head, and sunk beneath the murky water forever. But he was, for all his best efforts of pretending, no mainlander.

He looked down at his friend, who no longer pressed up into his hand, but watched him, knowing he knew, finally, its question.

Aaron shook his head. "I can't go with you," he said. "Not yet."

The seal bounced up and down on the step, a sort of nod as its flippers slapped against the water. Then, with one last press of its head to Aaron's fingers, it was gone. So too were its friends when Aaron looked out into the water.

Only then did his legs start shaking. Terror or a long night of pushing his body to the limit on the ice, he didn't know, but he needed to get back. Carefully, he turned around on the steps and climbed them, up to the normal world of the embankment. Had anyone seen the seals? Or heard them?

An older man leaned against the safety rail smoking a cigarette. Against his judgement, Aaron summoned what little Russian he had from being a figure skater in general – it was always good in this profession to have what Russian and Japanese there was time to learn.

"Ty videl?" Aaron asked in his clumsy Russian. *Did you see?*

The man looked at him, nodded, and replied in English. "They came for you."

✦

Aaron ran all the way back to the hotel, half-convinced he had imagined the whole thing by the time he slammed the door to his room. But he had half-a-dozen strange and urgent messages on his phone from his sister and his hands smelled like the river. He pulled off his clothes and practically flung himself into the shower. He was so happy for the heat and the soap and the very clear view of his perfectly human legs that he sat down on the floor to marvel at them.

"Oh my God, what is wrong with you?" Aaron muttered to himself as he thunked his head back against the tiled wall. Then he laughed. He'd just had the most important and successful performance of his competitive career to date and he'd responded by wandering around a city he didn't know petting errant wildlife? For that alone he deserved every peculiar thing that would ever happen to him.

"All right, Aaron Sheftall, time to get your shit together."

He climbed to his feet, turned the shower off, and wrapped himself in the hotel-provided bathrobe before dealing with his messages. The ones about the competition could wait.

He texted Katie first.

Aaron: When you do things that scare people — off the ice — is that generally a good sign or a bad sign?

Then, his sister:

Aaron: Sorry. I was taking a walk and met a friend, that's all. You need to recalibrate your nonsense.

Not that Aaron necessarily believed that. He didn't know *what* he believed right now. But he knew it was the rational thing to think.

Katie replied first.

Katie: Good. For me at least. What's going on?

Aaron felt some of the tension loosen in his gut.

Aaron: I'll tell you when I get back. Still thinking about it. How messed up is it if I text Zack?

Katie: Depends on what you want from that choice.

Aaron: Fair answer.

He flopped onto the hotel bed, folding his arms under his chin and looking out at the lights of the city below. He could see the dark, unlit line of the river, compelling even as he was warm and content and *human* here in his room.

Aaron turned his thoughts firmly to Zack. What *did* he want from Zack? What could he say to him? What response was he at all likely to get back? He was trying to figure that out when his sister decided to weigh in.

Ari: Liar.

Aaron stared at the message, wanting to be annoyed. But he couldn't be, because that was the answer: To his skating, to the mess with Zack, to the encounter with the seal.

Aaron: True.

Ari: Are you going to explain?

Aaron: Not now, no.

He'd always been a liar hiding in plain sight. He was always trying desperately to fit into a skin that was not his own. As a skater, as a boyfriend, and as whatever singular creature the mythology of the place he was from insisted he must be. But enough. He thumbed through his phone for Zack's number.

Aaron: Thank you for making me see myself. I know that's on me more than on you, but I may have changed my world

at this comp, and since you started this story I wanted you
to know how I'm finishing it.

Aaron tossed the phone aside onto the pillows next to him.
Before he knew it, he was asleep.

24

After Aaron's Free Skate

Zack's Apartment

After he had sat with Katie and watched Aaron's incredible skate – and his astonishing third-place finish – Zack went home and slept for hours. The early-morning hockey practice plus the emotion of watching the Grand Prix Final had worn him out entirely

He woke in the late afternoon to the insistent chirp of his phone. He groped for it on his nightstand, expecting something from Matt perhaps. Instead, a text from Aaron flashed on the screen. *What time is it in Saint Petersburg?* Zack did mental time zone math. Midnight, or thereabouts.

Aaron's message was thoughtful and clear and asked for nothing even as it left one hell of an opening. Zack knew it deserved a reply of some sort. But he was going to need some time to figure out both what he was feeling and what he wanted to say about it.

He silenced his phone and tossed it down on the bed, then made himself get up and get something to eat. He'd skipped lunch, and his body was suddenly remembering that he was starving.

By the time he'd finished eating leftover takeout from the day before, he decided that a text back to Aaron wasn't sufficient. Aaron reaching out, in the moment of such a triumph, deserved more than that. Even if they weren't holding a space for the other for later. Maybe especially because of that. Aaron never hesitated in asking for what he wanted, and he wasn't asking for anything here except to be listened to and be seen. Zack could give him that.

He hit *call* on Aaron's number. The phone rang... and rang... and rang. At about the eighth ring Zack realized that it was now about two in the morning in Saint Petersburg. Aaron was probably asleep. And if his phone hadn't rolled him over to voicemail yet, for whatever reason, it probably wasn't going to. Which was annoying, for his purposes. He had to settle for a text, lest Aaron think that Zack had misdialed or been upset at his message. Upset was the last thing Zack was.

Zack: Hey. Hope I didn't wake you. You did great today. Which you know, but I want you to know that I saw you. If I don't talk to you before, safe travels home.

He hoped, desperately, that his words would leave some sort of opening for a reply and that they weren't just going through the motions of some peculiar closure.

25

Mid-December

Katie and Brendan's Farm

Aaron awoke from a dream about swimming in a warm summer sea to a blaring alarm, a sky that was still dark, and about a hundred more notifications on his phone. Levering himself out of bed, *everything* hurt. The exertion and excitement of the last few days was finally taking its toll.

He couldn't stop thinking about the seals. As he packed up his things and got ready to meet everyone downstairs for the ride to the airport he could still see their gleaming eyes peering at him through the darkness and feel the warmth of the one he had – wildly unwisely – pet. The images were almost enough to drive out the memory of the cheering crowd and the weight of the bronze medal around his neck.

Almost, but not quite. He'd won the most important medal of his life. He had and was continuing to blow away everyone's expectations. All that was left now was Nationals, and he knew now that he could do there what he needed to do.

Plus, even if he *did* make the Olympic team, it wasn't likely he'd ever have a day like the one he'd just had. Seals in Boston, after all, would be much less remarkable than in Saint Petersburg.

He wished, as he took the elevator downstairs to the lobby to meet everyone else, that he could find a way to say goodbye to the ones here.

Aaron didn't look through his notifications until they were at the airport waiting to board. Most of it was excitement from his family and friends, but there was one name that leapt out at him. *Zack.*

He read Zack's text at least three times before he was able to absorb any of its meaning; his feelings were too intense. Katie had asked him what he'd wanted out of a potential exchange with Zack. What he wanted was, he now realized, this. Exactly this. To be seen by him, and to have their connection not be wholly severed. In all, it was a *lot* for ten in the morning at Pulkovo Airport with his bronze medal in his pocket and the memory of the seals.

Their flight was called, and in the flurry of gathering bags and boarding passes Aaron didn't have a chance to reply. Not until he'd settled into his seat between Charlotte and Brendan did he pull his phone back out to type.

Aaron: Thank you :) About to get on an intercontinental flight and my coach is right next to me so I can't call you back rn. Also training is gonna be a lot when I get home. There's a dinner at the farm next week. Come with me, we'll hang out

Zack: What's the occasion?

Aaron: Trying to be people as well as skaters

Inviting Zack to the farm for dinner when they hadn't so much as spoken in months was probably a lot and the kind of thing Aaron should have spent more time thinking about first. *Oh well*. He was currently feeling too much to have much brain power left for thinking. Besides, what was the worst that could happen?

> Zack: Are other not-skating people going to be there?
>
> Aaron: Probably. There will be people in from out of town and stuff. There's a whole crew. It's fine
>
> Zack: Okay. I'll go. On one condition.
>
> Aaron: What's that?
>
> Zack: Tell Katie first. For real this time.

Charlotte paused in tucking her things in the seatback pocket. "Why are you laughing?" she demanded.

✦

The next week was a haze of gym time, ice time, and time spent reviewing the footage Katie shot of him at practice, looking for places to improve. The Christmas break was coming up, but in an Olympic year that meant maybe a handful of days off to visit family, which for Aaron was more complicated than not. Winter weather meant the risk of getting trapped on the island if he were to go home. Which was terrifying with Nationals in the first week of January; when it came to selecting the U.S. Olympic team, Nationals was everything.

The work, when it could be, was a pleasure. But much of it was hard, unpleasant, and boring. But that was the price of excellence, of getting to compete, and of taking a whole audience along with him. Aaron came home every night bruised, sore, and so hungry that he went through what felt like twice as many groceries as usual.

When the night of the dinner at Katie and Brendan's came, he spent ten minutes looking for a clean shirt that wasn't practice wear before giving up and throwing on a t-shirt from a junior training camp. It was the farm, after all, and even if Zack was going to be there, well. He'd seen Aaron looking rougher than this. Plus, they'd all probably wind up visiting the cows anyway.

His phone barked in his pocket as he walked out to his car.

Ari: You still haven't told me.

Aaron: Busy now!

Ari: Stop ignoring me.

Aaron: I'm getting in the car, can't talk right now!

He left his phone in the back seat as he drove so he wouldn't have the least bit of temptation to glance at it. Which turned out to be the right choice, because it barked at him the whole drive to the farm.

What the fuck am I doing? Aaron wondered as he took the highway out into the country. He'd had very little time in the last week to form a strategy for tonight or even think much about it.

His phone barked as if in reply. If the seals were trying to give him an answer, Aaron couldn't interpret it.

"Thanks, guys," he said aloud. "Real helpful."

Arf!

His phone was such a menace.

When he parked at the farm he surveyed the other cars, but he didn't know what Zack was renting these days and thus had no idea if he'd arrived yet or not. Finally, Aaron snatched his phone off the backseat once he had parked. One of the very many texts from Ari was:

Ari: I know something happened.

"I'm an elite athlete. Something's always happening, Ari," Aaron muttered as he stalked up the walk to the front porch. His life was plenty weird enough without his sister making it weirder.

He let himself in, the squeak and slam of the screen door announcing his arrival. It sounded like summer, never mind that it was December and seven degrees out. He kicked his shoes off, tossed his coat on top of the others already piled on the stair railing, and joined the group gathered in the living room.

There was a small crowd of people already there. Sam, Morgan and Charlotte were deep in conversation with Shane, who coached jumps, and Haruka, who taught dance and artistry. A flurry of French drifted from a corner where Fitz, Gabe, and Huy were together talking about something too quickly for Aaron to be able to decipher it.

And there was Zack, sitting on the couch next to Angel, chatting with him and looking as if he'd always belonged in the group. Aaron took a moment to imagine a life where that was really the case, as if they could always be part of the same universe together. The idea took his breath away.

Zack, as if feeling Aaron's eyes on him, looked up. He wore a fleece jacket, zipped all the way up despite the wood-burning stove next to him throwing out its cheery warmth. Aaron wanted to throw himself into his arms.

Before he could tell himself to think better of it, he did precisely that, bouncing across the room and hugging Zack.

At least, he tried to. Zack was still sitting down, which meant that Aaron landed on his lap with his arms around his neck and his face, for a brief moment, in the fleece-covered warmth of his shoulder.

Zack chuckled, and Aaron could feel it reverberate between their bodies. His arms tightened around Aaron's back; Aaron had, somehow, forgotten how strong he was and how secure he felt in his embrace.

"Hello, Aaron."

"Hi."

From behind him came a cough, he wasn't sure from who. Zack dropped his arms, Aaron peeled himself away and stood up again, feeling sheepish.

"Er. Hi everybody." Gossipy as skaters were, not everyone here was from TCI or knew his history with Zack. He'd just given everyone a lot to talk about. Which he didn't mind for his own sake, but was a lot to put on Zack, who he'd barely spoken to in months.

"Excellent boundaries, Sheftall," Katie said, walking into the room.

"Sorry," Aaron muttered. *I should have thought this through better.*

Zack touched his fingertips to Aaron's wrist. "It's fine," he said softly, in a manner that was far more for Aaron's ears than theirs.

Aaron wished he had worn long sleeves; they would have hidden the goosebumps that broke out up and down his arms.

At that moment, Brendan appeared in the doorway to announce that dinner was ready.

✦

Be chill, Aaron told himself as he made his way to the dining room. *Be chill. Be* way *more chill than that.* He hadn't talked to Zack face-to-face in months. He'd invited him to dinner at Katie and Brendan's because he'd been having feelings about Zack, seals, and winning, not necessarily in that order. At some point he wanted to have a conversation with him, about all of that, but really about anything at all. And for that to happen he should probably not break his streak of, somehow, managing to not freak Zack out.

He could totally manage a meal sitting next to Zack. He could chat with Katie about the cows, practice his Japanese with Haruka, and wish his French were better so he could eavesdrop more effectively on Fitz and Huy. *Ugh. Canadians.* But he didn't know what to do about Zack. He'd gotten himself into this situation by winging it, but he probably shouldn't try to get himself out the same way. So he relied, perhaps too much, on gracious small talk and other people occupying Zack's attention.

As Aaron was helping to clear the table, his phone barked in his back pocket. Yet again. Loudly, and repeatedly. He set the dishes he was carrying on the counter next to where Brendan was rinsing things at the sink and frowned as he dug out his phone.

Ari was calling him. Again.

"Not *now*," he complained aloud.

Katie set down another stack of plates next to him. "What is it?" she asked.

"My sister," Aaron said. He went back to the table for more dishes. Katie went with him.

"Is something wrong?" she asked.

Aaron sighed as he gathered up dirty silverware. With everything else going on in his head tonight he didn't have the bandwidth for Ari.

"She thinks there is."

Katie grabbed a dishcloth and began wiping crumbs off the table. "With reason?"

If there was, I'd know how to talk to her about it. "Maybe. I don't know. She's been wanting to chat about some stuff since I was in Saint Petersburg, and I haven't wanted to deal."

"You've also been busy," Katie pointed out.

"Yeah."

"But right now," Katie continued, a glint that some might call mischievous in her eye. "You have the evening off and nothing on your schedule before noon tomorrow. Go call your sister back, okay?"

"*Ugh.*" It was possibly the last thing Aaron wanted to do. Among other things, he wanted to spend time with Zack tonight. Though since he hadn't figured out how to do that like a chill human being, perhaps he should take the out for now.

His gaze fell on Zack, who was helping Angel set up a board game on the freshly-cleared table.

"Don't worry," Katie said softly. "I won't let him leave before you're done." She nodded at Aaron's phone. "I don't think that's going to get any easier the longer you wait."

✦

Aaron went out onto the screened-in porch to call Ari. It was the same place – and the same time of day – he and Zack had hung out the first time Zack had come to the farm, back in June, but it was hard to believe that. Instead of a marvelous sunset sky and warm summer breezes, there were dark fields and a wind that nipped in through the screen. The night was clear, and stars shone brightly in the sky. Not as brightly as they did at home, where there really was no human habitation around for miles, but still much more brightly than in the city. The landscape was quieter than the island was, though. On the island there was the constant sound of wind and water. Here, the profound silence was punctuated only by the occasional sound of a car on the far-off highway or a burst of laughter from inside. The quiet felt lonely, and Aaron was struck by a sudden burst of homesickness.

He opened his text messages, didn't bother to read Ari's most recent volley, and hit call.

"Finally." His twin answered immediately. "I was starting to get worried."

"If you'd been really worried, you would have called Brendan."

"Maybe I did."

"Ari!" Fuck, was that why Katie had told him to call? But no. She and Brendan didn't do triangulation like that. For that matter, neither did Ari.

"What? I know something happened. And you're not telling me what it was," Ari said.

"How's home?" he asked. Aaron tried to picture her there. Was she outside by the water, looking up at the same stars he could see? Or was she inside, warming up in front of the cobblestone fireplace in the living room?

"Very, very cold. Now. What happened?"

Aaron sighed, resigning himself. "Has it ever occurred to you that my life is plenty eventful simply because I have a life that involves a lot of events?"

"We both know that's not what I mean," Ari said.

Aaron wondered if she had told their parents about any of this. "Fine. I was in Saint Petersburg, this was the last day, after the gala – "

"Yes, whatever, skip to the thing."

So Aaron did, and, in as few words as possible, told her about the seals in the Neva. When he was done – including the exchange he'd had with the man on the street – Ari made an irritated sound in her throat.

"When things happen like this, *you have to tell me.*"

"Why? It was one of those things that happens sometimes when wildlife and humans share a habitat. I wouldn't call you if I found a raccoon by my apartment, which, by the way, happens all the time."

Aaron was still annoyed, but more than that, he felt unnerved. Being out here, in the dark, on Katie's farm – it wasn't as wild as the island, but there was still a strange sort of energy here. The same energy, in fact, that he'd felt that night in Saint Petersburg. The kind that made him feel like anything could happen.

In the distance, a dog – an *actual* dog, the farm that adjoined Katie and Brendan's had two of them, Aaron had met them – barked. Which didn't help.

"There are so few of us," Ari finally said.

"There's exactly two of us. We're twins."

"You know that's not what I meant, and you don't act like it sometimes," Ari said sharply.

The blow, Aaron knew, was calculated to hurt, and it did; he hunched in on himself and tried to take deep breaths of the cold winter air to dispel the hot wash of guilt and shame he still felt for leaving the island in the summer. But he'd given up so much already. He couldn't make up the time he'd decided to give to skating instead. That had been true for years and years now, so long it was nearly his whole life. If he lost his focus now, none of it would have been worth it anyway.

"I don't have time for this," he snapped. "I'm trying to go to the Olympics. The seals are just seals, and I'm just a man. But I have to focus." *No matter how weird my life is.*

"I'm not trying to get you to not go to the Olympics." Ari's voice rose in frustration. "I'm trying to make sure you come home again."

"I am coming home! Next week," Aaron said.

"For a few days." Ari sounded sullen.

"That's all I have time for," Aaron said, all but pleading. "Can't it be enough?"

"I think that," Ari said, "is up to you."

✦

The call was not as unsettling as what had happened in Saint Petersburg, but Aaron still felt the need to gather himself once it was over.

He was so tired. He'd spent so many months working to bring his true self – his island self – onto the ice. He had two Grand Prix silvers and a Grand Prix Final bronze to show for it now. He was a force the federation wouldn't be able to ignore when it came time to pick the U.S. team. Nationals would be the final determining factor there, but he'd done the work he needed to so far this season and done it well.

And now Ari wanted him to swear he would one day return to their island for good. Which he should have been able to give an immediate and unqualified yes to, but the idea of it made him tremble. His life was global, expansive, and public. The island was essential to him... and such a small, private place. Could he exist on that island without the rest of the world – and all the ways it, too, had formed him?

He glanced through the window into Katie and Brendan's living room. Zack was there, in the center of everyone, playing board games. He laughed at something someone else said, his eyes sparkling. Zack, somehow, had been folded into his extended skating family. Zack, who Aaron had fallen so hard for in so many ways, who'd seen Aaron skate his heart out but still knew almost nothing about Ari, about his family, about the life he had come from.

And now Aaron, wrung out with guilt and uncertainty, had to go back inside and pretend everything in his head was fine to everyone he was closest to – or, in the case of Zack, the person he wanted to be closest to. It felt like too much, but what else could he do?

Zack and Katie both glanced up at him when he slipped back inside. Katie gave him the look she'd given him across the boards a hundred times at practices that had gotten too hard, too weird, too emotional. It meant: *Are you okay?*

He nodded. He wasn't really, but it was nothing she could do anything about.

"Aren't you freezing?" Zack asked, looking him over with a concern that made warmth bloom in Aaron's chest.

"I never get cold. You know that," he said.

"I know you never get cold at the rink," Zack corrected with a hint of a smile. Aaron blushed; he knew he had hogged the blankets every time he had shared a bed with Zack, how he had complained that he was freezing, and insisted that Zack hold him closer.

"Dude, you're making me cold just looking at you," Huy piped up from his corner of the couch.

"Do you want to play?" Zack asked, resetting the board for whatever they'd been playing. That teasing look was still in his eyes.

"Yeah, sure, all right."

Zack shifted in his own seat, making room for Aaron if he wanted it. Aaron very much did. Their shoulders pressed against each other as he sat down, and he let himself bask in the warmth. He still wanted to get Zack alone for a conversation – he owed him that, after inviting him here in the first place – but Aaron still didn't know what he'd say when he did. In the meantime, proximity was nice.

The idea to invite Zack to the island occurred to him as he hopped his piece around the board. It was so patently absurd that he shook his head at himself and told himself to forget it immediately. But apparently he'd left all his mental discipline at the rink, because he couldn't stop thinking about it.

He'd spent the season bringing more of his island self to the world. Maybe, just maybe, the path needed to go both ways. If he could show Ari more of who he was on the mainland, maybe he could be that person and her twin. And he could show Zack the island in person – he had asked how to make that happen from almost the moment Aaron had told him about it.

In the end, impulse control lost to feeling.

"Question," Aaron said during a break in the game while the others chatted together. He jiggled his foot as Zack glanced over at him.

"Yeah?" Zack said.

"What are you doing for your winter holiday of choice?" *Well, here we go.*

A faint crease appeared on Zack's forehead. "Um. I'm not sure," he said. "Avoiding my family and their opinions about my life choices, probably."

Aaron couldn't imagine being estranged from his family like that. The idea of Zack being alone over the holidays was wretched, which seemed to make inviting him to the island make slightly more sense.

"Do you want to come home with me?" he asked.

Zack stammered for a moment. Aaron tried not to giggle even as he realized he should have phrased his question more precisely.

"I mean to the island," he clarified. "For the holidays. You can't stay here by yourself!"

"I absolutely can." Zack looked somewhere between horrified and amused, which was not precisely the reaction Aaron had been hoping for. Though was the reaction he knew he deserved.

Zack went on. "I also probably shouldn't impose for several days, including a major holiday, on people I've never met."

"Oh! Don't worry about that." Aaron shook his head, glad to be able to put that uneasiness to rest. "We don't do Christmas. Except for the Chanukah bush."

Zack frowned. "What the fuck is a Chanukah bush?"

"It's what you call a Christmas tree when you're the only Jewish family in an ice-bound island community." *It's a way of seeming normal,* Aaron thought somewhat glumly, *when you're different from the twelve other people you live around.*

Zack looked baffled. But the frown was gone, replaced by a look of caution and curiosity. The look was one Aaron had seen on his face before, usually right before Zack suggested they do something involving rope and very little clothing. Aaron *loved* that look. Even now when they definitely weren't together at all, and he was probably starting a giant mess when he did not have the time to deal with anything of the sort.

"You should come," he urged. "I mean, except, of course, if you don't want to," he added. *I have weird boundaries, not bad boundaries*, he told himself. "We hardly ever get visitors in the winter, you'd be a hit."

"This feels strange and ill-advised," Zack said, looking around nervously.

Aaron followed his gaze. Katie, seated in the armchair diagonally from them, was clearly following every word while ineffectively pretending to ignore them.

"Everything about me is strange and ill-advised," he said, dropping his voice and leaning into Zack's shoulder so Katie, or anyone else, couldn't hear. "And no pressure or assumptions or expectations. I get where we're at, which is basically nowhere, but I don't know. Your job when you showed up here was to find out who I am. Come find out who I am."

"Yeah." Zack took a breath. "Yeah, okay."

✦

At the end of the night they were among the last to leave. After shouting their goodbyes and see-you-tomorrows to everyone, they lingered next to Aaron's car, their breath rising toward the distant stars. Aaron wondered if anyone still in the house was watching them; he hoped not, but knew better than to assume.

As the hubbub of departing guests subsided and the quiet of the country night rose around them, Zack leaned sideways against Aaron's car, his arms folded across his chest, presumably for warmth. Aaron resisted the urge to step forward and be wrapped up in those arms.

"I feel like there are a lot of logistical questions I should be asking you," Zack said. "If I'm going to your island with you."

Aaron still couldn't believe he'd asked Zack to go – or that Zack had said yes. He leaned against his car too, mirroring Zack's posture.

"I meant what I said. no expectations, no implications, no strategy. You're important to me, even if we're not together." Aaron felt his cheeks burn as he admitted it. "I just… feel like I'll be happier if you know who I am. And the island – not the ice, or your bed – is the only way. And really, you can't spend the holidays by yourself," he finished.

"Everything you've told me about it sounds so remote," Zack said, a note of cautiousness in his voice.

"Are you nervous?" Aaron asked.

"Maybe."

"It's fine," Aaron said firmly, in a burst of the same confidence with which he'd led Zack through so many skating lessons. As if Zack's nerves were about how they were going to get to the island and not the foolishness of the plan to begin with. "You'll be with me. We'll fly to Cleveland, then get a plane to Put-In-Bay. I've already got my flight scheduled. We can add you to it. Someone will meet us there to get us back to our island… boat or snowmobile, depending on how frozen the lake is. Though if the cold keeps up like this, definitely snowmobile."

Zack blinked at him. "That's a lot of steps."

"Like you just said, it's remote. Have you not been paying attention?" Aaron said dryly.

"Of course I have. But I wasn't expecting an invitation there. I wasn't expecting another invitation *here*," Zack added, looking around the quiet farm.

"I know it's a lot," Aaron said, softening his tone and trying not to feel guilty for being impulsive and also so very much. "I'm sorry. If you don't want to come you don't have to. Really."

"I do want to," Zack said, with a fervor that was both surprising and highly gratifying. "And if you want me to see where you're from, don't ever apologize for it."

"Well, then. So many steps it is." Aaron cleared his throat. Zack was so close, so warm, so real, and right in front of him. They were going to be on the island for days together.

"One more question," Zack said.

"Anything."

"Where am I going to stay?" Zack finally blurted.

"Oh! In my parents' house." Aaron realized, belatedly, that he probably should have led with that piece of information. "We don't have hotels or anything, not in the winter. We have ice, rocks, extreme proximity to the Canadian border, and… some very specific wildlife."

"That sounds a lot like some of my assignment locations. Minus Canada. And the cold."

"Yeah, you'll want to pack layers."

"You'll tell your people I'm coming, right?"

Aaron huffed. "I pulled that stunt one time and you're still holding it over me," he complained to the sky.

"It was a memorable time." Zack looked like he was about to say something more, but he stopped himself, looking intently at Aaron.

Aaron felt himself flush under the heat of his gaze. "I should go," he said.

Zack drew closer to Aaron. "Early ice?" he asked with a sympathetic face.

"No. I mean, yes, I do." Aaron shook his head. He was so close – he could lean up and kiss Zack if he wanted to. And he wanted to. However. Zack had been the one to break up with *him*, and Aaron needed to not impose on whatever boundaries that had created between them. "I've already made enough impulsive choices for the night."

Zack looked Aaron over with a gaze that warmed Aaron to his core. "I have self-control," he said.

"Well," Aaron replied. He fumbled for his keys and unlocked his car before he could do any one of a number of very un-chill things to Zack. As much as he hated to leave, his heart thrummed with anticipation. "Congratulations to you."

26

Horrifying Plane Travel

Lake Erie Islands

A few short days after dinner at the farm, Zack packed his bags with all the layers he'd accumulated living in the Twin Cities and waited outside Marie's house at an inhospitable hour for Aaron to pick him up and drive them to the airport.

Perhaps the atmosphere between them shouldn't have felt so comfortable, so natural, as they spent the drive in companionable silence. After all, they were exes, embarking on an absurd holiday visit Zack would have judged any of his friends for taking. Matt had seemed enthusiastic about the trip, at least, but Zack suspected Matt would be enthusiastic about anything someone thought would bring them happiness. The trait made him a valuable friend, but a questionable source of advice.

Still, here Zack was. With Aaron, who was as compelling as ever. And Zack knew himself well enough to recognize that the element of adventure and dubious choices only made this trip more appealing, not less. He'd been a war reporter for a reason, after all.

A war reporter who'd wound up with a fear of flying as just one of several mental souvenirs from that work. And while there weren't that many miles between the Twin Cities and Aaron's family's home, getting there was anything straightforward.

The first leg, from Minneapolis-Saint Paul to Cleveland, was fine. Suboptimal, because Zack hated planes, but it was nothing beyond his expectations. There was a normal plane with normal jet engines, and Aaron kept up a lively stream of chatter that didn't require much of Zack beyond listening to it. Deep breathing exercises and a constant reminder to himself that he wasn't flying into danger was enough.

But then they landed at Hopkins. Zack followed Aaron as he navigated his way through the terminal and finally out onto the tarmac itself. Where sat the smallest plane Zack had ever seen at an actual commercial airport.

"You're joking," he said.

Aaron dropped the handle of his roller bag and waved, presumably at the pilot.

"We're going somewhere with fewer than a hundred people," he said. He sounded amused. "Did you think the plane needed more than ten seats?"

"That plane doesn't have ten seats," Zack protested.

"Correct. And they won't all be full!"

Zack took a deep breath. Then another. Here he stood on the tarmac, with his backpack on one shoulder and his camera slung over the other, about to board a plane. It was the sexy reporter self-image he secretly kind of loved, except for the part where he was in the American Midwest trying not to have a panic attack.

Aaron evidently knew the pilot, a woman wearing a heavy winter coat and a ski hat emblazoned with a Canadian maple leaf. Aaron greeted her warmly and introduced her to Zack – her name was Stephanie – and they stood chatting for a few moments while Zack tried to collect himself.

Eventually Aaron collapsed the handle of his roller bag and hefted it up to climb the less-than-a-handful of steps to the plane. He must have sensed Zack's hesitation, because he stopped with one foot on the first step.

"You okay?" he asked with a frown.

"I have friends with trucks bigger than this plane." Zack tried to joke, but the words came out panicked. Which he was. He didn't want to talk about this.

Aaron smiled encouragingly. "It's going to be fine. I promise. There's no weather today."

"Good," Zack muttered. He pulled himself together as best he could and followed Aaron up the stairs. "because this thing is going to crumple if a stiff breeze looks at it."

"You don't like flying?" Aaron asked as they tucked themselves into the two front seats. Of which there were only six. In total.

Zack hesitated. He hated admitting this. But he was here, on this minuscule flying death tube, because Aaron had invited him. Aaron who wanted Zack, who had dumped him, to come to his island to see his true self. That was a gesture of trust and vulnerability of immense proportions, and Zack would be repaying it poorly if he didn't tell the truth now.

"I really don't," he said.

"Really? I thought you flew a lot. For reporting and stuff."

"Oh, I do. Or did. Usually in planes like this. Which is why I don't like it." Zack had a story, about the time the door on the Cessna he was in opened when they were three thousand feet up. It was fine, in the sense that no one died and they didn't even lose any luggage, but it was one of his least favorite memories that didn't involve being shot at. So much so that any attempt to articulate the story caught in his throat. Even now, for Aaron, he couldn't manage it.

"Ah." Aaron looked at him keenly. "Bad experience? Or experiences?"

"Yeah." Zack nodded and breathed a little easier. Even if he hadn't been able to tell the story, still Aaron knew something at least.

Aaron reached across the narrow aisle between them and grabbed Zack's hand. "Don't worry. I won't let you fall."

Zack was about to retort that flying was not like skating and that Aaron could definitely not catch him if anything went awry, but at that moment the plane's engine kicked in and the whole of it started to vibrate as the propeller picked up speed. His heart leapt into his throat and stayed there.

For the next hour, he was aware of only three things: that his body and brain did not want him on this plane, the light outside the window changing from gray to blinding white, and Aaron's hand clasped in his own.

Aaron talked the entire flight. Zack couldn't take in most of what he was saying, much less respond to it, but Aaron kept on talking all the same. Part of Zack's brain wanted Aaron to shut up, so it could focus on their imminent demise. The rest of him was grateful for Aaron's efforts and that he wasn't minimizing Zack's distress.

He had no idea how he was going to do this flight again in a few days. Maybe they could snowmobile all the way back to the mainland. Although he didn't know how he felt about snowmobiles yet either.

"We're almost there," Aaron said. His voice sounded as if it was coming from a very great distance as they passed, closer than Zack would have preferred, a large Doric column. Which was kind of a strange thing to pass, considering it wasn't attached to a building. It was just standing there at the end of a bit of island in the middle of the lake.

Zack braced himself as the plane began its descent. He kept his eyes screwed tightly shut while it shuddered and bumped it way through the windy sky, before its wheels finally bounced on the tarmac as it touched down.

They taxied briefly, before coming to a stop between two other planes in a manner more like a mall parking lot than an airport.

Somehow, Zack got off the plane – or Aaron got Zack off the plane – because the next thing Zack was aware of, he was standing in front of the trailer that held the airport's small office. His jangled nerves aside, it was a far cry from a war zone. He raised his hand to shade his eyes from a world white with snow, which was when he realized he still had Aaron's hand in a death grip.

"Sorry," he muttered.

Aaron shrugged. "Don't worry about it," he said, like holding people's hands for traumatic tiny plane flights was something he did every day. No more or less remarkable than picking the little kids up when they fell all over themselves trying to march on the ice.

The thought was somehow comforting, though Zack still had no idea what they were doing. The cold air that whipped across his face and made him wish he'd put on a scarf before getting off the plane made it somehow easier to breathe more deeply.

Aaron turned to say goodbye to Stephanie the pilot. "Say hi to Sue and the girls for me, yeah?"

"Of course." Stephanie pulled him into a warm hug. "Say hi to your folks for us, too." She offered Zack a hand, which he shook on autopilot, and gave them both a cheery wave before turning to deal with something on the plane.

"You with me?" Aaron asked quietly.

"Barely," Zack said. He felt queasy as his brain and his body tried to catch up with each other and also solid land.

"Okay. That's the war of 1812 monument," Aaron said pointing at the ridiculous Doric column that Zack had noticed from the air. He spun around. "That way is where the tourists go and my parents' restaurant." He jerked a thumb to one side. "Nature preserve... Canada is over there. America is back there."

"Where's home?" Zack asked.

"That way. Across the ice. See the island with the ruined castle looking thing?" Aaron said.

"Yeah? You didn't tell me you have a castle."

Aaron shook his head. "We don't. We're on an island behind that island."

Apparently Zack had misjudged the size of the chip on Aaron's shoulder about this place. Everything was, he was quite sure, about to get very weird. And he couldn't wait.

Aaron led Zack the short distance to the little trailer and held the door for him. Once they got inside Aaron waved at someone; it took Zack's eyes a moment to adjust but when they did, he could make out two figures, bundled up in coats and hats.

Aaron launched himself at the larger of the two and got a bear hug in return; Aaron's father, Zack assumed. He held Aaron tight, his eyes closed. Zack wondered, wistfully, what it was like to have a family that welcomed you back like this. Even when he and his family had been on speaking terms, he'd never had a moment like this.

His gaze fell on the other person who had come to meet them, who had to be Aaron's twin. Same cheekbones and sharp chin, same curly brown hair, though hers was longer; a braid trailed over her shoulder. And the same warm brown eyes, although hers were narrowed at him right now, clearly calculating.

Aaron's father finally let him go and stepped forward to shake Zack's hand, then pulled him in for a hug too, one of those one-armed ones the guys on the hockey team sometimes exchanged.

"Glad you boys made it," Aaron's dad said warmly, as if Zack were some lifelong friend of Aaron's returning to the island for the hundredth time.

"Thanks for having me," Zack said sincerely.

"Of course. Now. Zack," Mr. Sheftall said, gesturing toward the door of the airport that led out to a snow-covered parking lot. "Have you ever been on a snowmobile?"

Zack had, in fact, never been on a snowmobile. He considered volunteering his past in various war zones as if his once-upon-a-time vague competence in one type of extreme environment translated to the same in another, but he knew – and he was sure these people also knew – that it did not. Instead, he stood around feeling useless while Aaron helped his father and sister secure their luggage on two different vehicles parked in the lot.

"You're with me," Ari told Zack, the first she'd spoken to him. She handed him a helmet.

"Okay?" Zack said, but he couldn't help throwing a questioning glance at Aaron.

"Weight limits," Aaron said, matter-of-factly, settling in on the other snowmobile behind his dad. He pulled on his own helmet. "Hold on, and you'll be fine."

✦

After the whole *thing* with the plane, Zack was not anticipating enjoying a snowmobile ride across a frozen lake to a speck of an island. And yet, as the two snowmobiles raced out onto the vast expanse of ice, Zack felt his unease melt away. There were no sounds other than the engines, and no people other than the four of them. It was all so bizarre that Zack didn't have brain space left to feel awkward about the fact that he was clinging to Aaron's sister.

This was, frankly, too damn much fun. Zooming across the blindingly-white landscape reminded him of adventure, the kind he thought he'd have back when he was a kid and dreaming of being an adult who could do whatever he wanted anywhere in the wide, wide world. Zack whooped when the snowmobile hit a bump, sending up a shower of snow. Ari glanced back over her shoulder at him, and while he couldn't make out her face through the visor of her helmet, he was pretty sure she was smiling too.

✦

The sense of adventure didn't fade when they finally reached Aaron's family's house, a low, snug-looking building tucked between a sheltering rock face on one side and a bunch of evergreens which effectively encircled it. The side of the house facing the lake had the best view, but the smallest windows, presumably to block the effects of the wind from the water. Smoke rose invitingly from a chimney.

Aaron grazed his fingers over the mezuzah on the door post as his mother greeted them, and there was another round of greetings and hugs in which Zack was included as if he was a lifelong friend.

"Let me show you your room," Aaron said once they'd shed their coats and boots.

He led the way through the kitchen, down a flight of wooden steps that creaked pleasantly, and through a door that stuck so stubbornly he had to lean into it with his shoulder to get it open. The room itself was pleasantly bright, with light coming in from the windows high up in the walls and, to Zack's more specific relief, warm. There was a hot water heater in one corner, and the room evidently hadn't been updated since the eighties if the fake wood paneling and deep shag carpet were anything to go to. But there was a bed, a bathroom, and even a coffee maker set up on top of a dresser.

"It's a bit weird," Aaron said, his back to Zack as he tugged open the curtains flanking the windows a little further. There was more a note of challenge in his voice than apology, as if he were daring Zack to be judgmental about his home. "But everything here is a bit weird."

Zack dropped his bags by the door. "I love it," he said honestly. "I love weird, generally." He tried not to think too hard, or at least too consciously, about whether and how Aaron fit under either of those words in his head.

"If you hear banging in the middle of the night, it's just the pipes."

"Duly noted."

"And I had my folks bring down another space heater," he said, pointing to the thing in the corner. "It should be warm enough, snow is a great insulator, but I know how you feel about the cold."

"Thanks," Zack said sincerely, touched.

"We're gonna eat lunch soon, but if you want to get yourself settled…." Aaron's voice trailed off and he drifted back toward the door. "Yell if you need anything."

There wasn't much Zack needed to do in the way of unpacking, but he was grateful for a few moments to himself to shake off the last of the plane nerves and recalibrate to his new surroundings.

As he sat down on the bed to take off his wet socks and put on dry ones, the scent of the same laundry detergent Aaron used rose around him. Zack let himself breathe deep and smiled.

✦

After lunch Aaron offered to take him on a tour of the island, and once they'd put all their layers back on they tromped back outside.

Aaron led the way down to the shore, or where the shore would have been had the lake not been frozen and the beach not covered in snow. The sound of pebbles crunching beneath their feet was the only sign they were so close to the water. Aaron, who had been so chatty on their journey, was silent as they walked side-by-side. The snow wasn't very deep, barely past their ankles, but the path hadn't been cleared and the walk took more effort than Zack had expected.

"How big is this place?" he asked eventually.

"Not big. Maybe a couple miles around."

"And it's just your family here?"

"What? No." Aaron laughed. "I'm not James Bond, my family doesn't own a private island. There's like four other families. You'll see their houses as we go."

"Still, four other families is not a lot of people."

"It's not. But there's forty or so that stay year-round on the main island. So by comparison."

"Mind if I take some pictures?"

"Knock yourself out."

Zack was glad he'd brought his camera. There wasn't much to see, to be sure, but what was there was rich in shape and texture: The bare branches of trees silhouetted against the sky, the mossy roof of one of the neighbor's houses, a tiny frozen waterfall where a stream ran down to the shore.

Aaron perched on a rock by the edge of the ice to watch him. "I didn't know you did nature pictures too."

There was a slight emphasis on the 'too' that made Zack immediately think of the last time he'd had his camera out with Aaron: The night before Aaron had left for the Grand Prix Final. He wondered if Aaron still had the picture Zack had taken of him then.

"I don't usually get the chance. But it's beautiful here."

"Beautiful and strange," Aaron said.

"Like you," Zack said, before he could stop himself.

Perched on his rock, his cheeks already red from the cold, he was pretty sure Aaron blushed.

✦

By the time they returned to the house from their walk, the sky was already growing dark, which meant the whole snowy landscape was slowly fading into dusty purple twilight.

They ate dinner together with Aaron's family, where they caught Aaron up on all the local news that hadn't gotten covered at lunch. After dinner Ari went out to the garage with Mrs. Sheftall to work on a recalcitrant motor of some sort, and Aaron went off with his dad to his parents' office to deal with some of the accounting he did for them, leaving Zack to his own devices.

He sank into one of the overstuffed armchairs near windows that peered out towards the lake. Behind him was a hearth in which a fire crackled merrily, throwing warm light around the room. Beside it was a waist-high synthetic tree decorated with twinkling lights and an assortment of blue and white plastic dreydls, and topped with a silver-painted wooden menorah that looked a bit like a high school shop class project gone awry. *And that,* Zack told himself, *must be the Hanukkah bush.* He wondered if it was Aaron or Ari that had made the topper.

By now it was fully dark outside, and far on the horizon he could see lights glimmering faintly. The distant signs of human habitation, invisible during the day, somehow made this little house seem even more remote.

It had been a long time since Zack had sat and done nothing, and he found himself zoning out peacefully, watching the lights blink on the horizon. In the distance, he could hear a dog barking.

✦

Zack came to some time later to the touch of a hand on his arm. He jerked awake, his heart pounding, but it was only Aaron crouched in front of him, a look of concern on his face.

"You okay?"

"Yeah, I'm fine." Zack scrubbed a hand over his face. "I didn't mean to fall asleep."

"You've had a busy day," Aaron said, without a trace of sarcasm. "Here you go." He set down a mug of hot chocolate on the arm of Zack's chair, then dropped into the opposite chair, curling up in it around his own cup of tea.

"Thank you," Zack said, sitting up properly and wrapping his hands around the mug. It steamed gently.

"It's no problem."

Zack became aware of the utter silence of the rest of the house, aside from the crackle of the fire which someone must have built up again while he dozed. In other places and times in his life, silence like this would have been eerie. Here it felt strange, to be sure, but comfortable nonetheless.

"Where's everyone else?" he asked.

"Gone to bed. It's late." Aaron took a sip of his tea. "For here, at least."

"You always keep skaters' hours, don't you," Zack guessed.

"Pretty much. Someday I'll take a vacation and sleep 'til ten in the morning *every day*," Aaron said, looking off into the distance with exaggerated wistfulness.

Zack laughed. "Sounds decadent."

Aaron smiled. "You have no idea."

Zack could have said he had some idea; how many mornings had Aaron had to peel himself out of his bed to get to the rink? But he hesitated. Unlike Aaron, he could rarely blurt what he was feeling.

He realized, as he and Aaron sat and just… looked at each other, that this was the first time they had been alone together in months. The hours in transit today decidedly did not count. Zack should probably ask Aaron what his plan was, or if he even had one, but he decided he didn't care. Being here with him right now was enough.

Aaron broke the silence first, tucking his knees up under his chin and wrapping his arms around them. "How do you like it here?"

"This place is – haunting, I think, is the word," Zack said.

Aaron cracked a smile. "I've been telling you. And you can see why I don't say more than that."

Zack nodded. "I guess it's the sort of thing you need to see to believe."

"Do you regret coming?" Aaron asked.

"No. God. Not at all," Zack said, with a vehemence that surprised himself. "I love it here," he admitted.

"Yeah? You haven't been here a whole day, yet." Still, Aaron looked pleased at Zack's declaration.

"Yeah," Zack said firmly. "Don't get me wrong, that plane ride in was fucking terrifying. But once we got here...." he trailed off, thinking about it. "Since I stopped going out on assignment, I've spent a lot of time and a lot of hours in therapy trying to figure out how to exist. But here is... out of the world. There's no crowds, no loud noises, nothing happening. I get to just be and be curious about something that's not going to kill anyone. It's great."

"Is it that hard for you? To – be, in the world?"

"I don't know. Honestly? I know I don't work in the way most people do. Even without the PTSD. I'm an adrenaline junkie."

"Which is how you got the PTSD," Aaron said.

Zack shook his head. "I have PTSD because I was in multiple war zones. If I'd been more reasonable, I could have gotten my thrills from, I dunno, bungee jumping."

Aaron tilted his head consideringly. "You don't seem like the bungee jumping type. Although I didn't think you'd be the hockey bro type either, and look how that turned out."

"Thank you?" Zack wasn't sure if that was a compliment.

Aaron smiled. "I've watched some of your games. You're not half bad."

Zack was startled. "I didn't know that. That you'd watched any of the games."

Aaron shrugged. "Hard to keep an eye on the audience when you've got a helmet and everything on. Anyway. I never hung around long. Just wanted to see you. I was surprised you stuck around, actually. After... everything."

"You mean with us?"

"Well, yeah. You finished your article, right? Or at least the part that was about me. Then you broke up with me. I know you said you were going to move to Saint Paul, but I still sort of figured you'd disappear after that."

"I didn't move to the Twin Cities for you, you know," Zack said, careful to keep his tone light. Teasing.

"Really? Why not?" Aaron put on a look of exaggerated feigned offence. "But I'm so cute!"

Zack laughed. "I won't deny that. But I like it there. I can get work done. And I feel like I have a community, with the hockey guys and Marie. Although Marie is kicking me out, so I need to find a new place of my own when we get back there."

"You're really gonna stay? Aaron asked.

"For now, at least." Zack looked down at the hot chocolate he still held cupped between his palms. He swirled the cup gently, watching the melted whipped cream marble the surface. "Which is probably the most I can say about any place at any point. I probably needed to say that about Florida, but didn't realize it at the time. And like I said... I can get work done there, in Saint Paul. Which has value."

"What are you working on?"

"A book," Zack admitted.

"Oh. Like the one you won those awards for? That I still haven't read and definitely need to some day?"

"It's fine," Zack said. "It's not exactly easy reading." Truth be told, he couldn't quite square Aaron existing in the same universe in which he'd written that book. Some part of him, problematic as it was, wanted to protect Aaron from that world.

"Well, I'm not an easy reader. Come on, what's your book about? You spent all those weeks watching me work, it's payback time."

Aaron had a point, but still, Zack hesitated. He hadn't told anyone what, exactly, he was working on yet. Saying it out loud made him feel too vulnerable. But Aaron made him want to try.

He fortified himself with a sip of the hot chocolate. "It's a memoir."

Aaron frowned. "Aren't you a little young to be writing your memoirs?"

Zack chuckled. "A memoir is not an autobiography. It's just a story that I happen to be in."

"And what story are you in?" Aaron asked, too keenly for Zack's comfort. "Your war zone stuff?"

"Not really. I mean… that's there, that's where it starts. But it's more about figuring out how not to live that life anymore."

Aaron seemed to ponder that. "Is that why Saint Paul?" he said thoughtfully. "We're your new life?"

"Something like that."

Aaron frowned. "Are you being evasive because you don't want to talk about it or because you don't know how to talk about it?"

Zack sighed. He was pinned to the wall on this one. "Some of both. You know, I took this gig, the article about you, because I was broke and a mess. And it didn't upend my life because my life was already upended. But it did give me something to latch onto in a way that's either me being mentally healthy… or really mentally not. I don't know." A log popped in the fireplace, sending out a cloud of sparks and making him jump.

"I'm trying to figure it out," he went on, adrenaline prickling unpleasantly under his skin. "What I've learned about telling stories is that you can tell when they are going to make sense, even if they don't entirely hang together yet. That's how I feel about this project. But it's strange to talk about. And most certainly to you."

"Oh," Aaron said. "You mean I'm in the book."

"Yeah."

"Isn't that sketchy?"

"In a journalistic ethics way? No, because it's not journalism." *And because this time I'm actually going to tell the truth about it*, Zack thought. "But are we two people who are going to have to talk about this at some point and we might not enjoy it? Yeah. You bet." Zack watched Aaron's face carefully, looking for his reaction.

"Don't stop there." Aaron looked, if anything, more intrigued.

"For what it's worth," Zack said, "The person who comes off looking poorly in memoirs is usually just the author. So… unless you're like 'No don't do that at all ever or I will cut an ice fishing hole and throw your body in it,' you probably don't have a lot to worry about."

Aaron gave an awkward laugh. "Well, I didn't until that speech."

"Sorry. I'm not used to talking to people about my shit."

Aaron shrugged. "It's all good. I'm not used to letting people see my island."

27

Aaron's House

Whisker Island

Aaron, Ari, and Zack spent most of the next day outside. Snowmobiling, snowshoeing, and even skating, once they'd shoveled off a big enough patch of the lake and thrown hot water on it to get a smooth surface.

"This seems counterintuitive," Zack said, dubiously, holding a giant soup pot they'd taken off the stove and eyeing the ice in front of him.

"How do you think zambonis work?" Aaron countered, plopping down beside him in the snow to put on an old pair of skates. He'd dug out another pair for Zack; there were always plenty of extras here, and no one needed anything fancy for lake skating.

"Much more efficiently," Zack said drily.

"I checked it this morning," Ari piped up from where she was lacing up her own skates. "It's ten inches thick."

"I have no frame of reference for what that means."

"Don't go on ice that's less than four inches thick," Ari said, in the exact same tone Aaron had used on Zack when he told him not to use his hands to stand up, lest someone skate over his fingers. "Five and up can hold a snowmobile... probably. Eight and up can hold a car."

"Probably?" Zack finished.

Ari nodded. "Ice is fickle. And you have to check it every day. Just because it was thick enough yesterday doesn't mean it's thick enough today."

"I can't believe you have three days off from figure skating training, and you come home and do... this," Zack said, finally resigning himself and dumping out the water. It splashed on the ice, the faintest wisps of steam curling in the air, before it cooled and re-froze in a beautifully smooth surface.

"Then you've forgotten one very important thing about me," Aaron said, testing out the feel of the ice with a few crossovers. Not as perfect as freshly-resurfaced ice in an arena – it was brittle in places, and would chip if he tried any jumps – but it had the indescribable feel of real, *live* ice, instead of water frozen over some compressors in a rink.

"What's that?" Zack asked.

"I love skating." *And I love you,* he thought.

✦

They returned to the house only briefly for lunch, and by the time the sun had set and dusk was falling, Aaron was tired, sore, and blissfully happy. These were the sorts of days he loved best. Having Zack there with him to share it all made it even better.

Zack had offered to cook dinner tonight, and Aaron helped out, enjoying the companionableness of sharing a kitchen. When they'd been dating there hadn't been a lot of time for cooking together, and he still had very fond memories of their first date when Zack had made dinner for him.

He stole sidelong glances at Zack as he chopped vegetables and dumped spices together with little regard for measuring. Spending so much time together had done nothing to lessen Aaron's desire to grab him, kiss him, and drag him off to bed. That Zack was interested, he was in no doubt of; whenever they spoke, Zack's gaze kept dropping to his mouth, and Aaron had looked up from enough conversational pauses to see Zack staring at him. What, if anything, Zack planned to do about that, Aaron wasn't sure. Which was all right. After all, Aaron had told him this was a no-pressure trip, and he'd meant it.

Zack seemed to fit in here on the island as effortlessly as he did with the group at TCI. Aaron wondered if that was because those groups were particularly welcoming, or because Zack had such a way with people. He suspected it was the latter. If either the people at TCI, or his own family, had found someone not up to their standards, they would certainly not hesitate in making those feelings known. Their acceptance of Zack was a strong stamp of approval. *I wonder if Zack knows that*, Aaron mused

✦.

"Do you want to take a walk?" Aaron asked Zack once they'd finished dinner and the two of them had cleaned the kitchen.

Zack looked dubious. "How cold is it out there?"

"Colder than it was when the sun was up."

"You're not natural," Zack complained, but he headed for the closet for his coat anyway.

Aaron said nothing. It wasn't the sort of sentence it was worth getting prickly about, not when they were both queer and living lives that could most generously be described as odd. But if his sister had heard it… that would have been one way to have a conversation about the mythology of this place.

Aaron knew he wasn't obligated to bring up the children's stories that were only extremely local knowledge – even the year rounders on the bigger islands didn't necessarily know them, not if they didn't regularly deal with the lake's furthest, smallest outpost. But those that did didn't trade on them. Aaron always thought that was notable, that the seals weren't featured on kitschy t-shirts and souvenir shot glasses. It was why he took Ari seriously – at least some of the time and against his better judgement. If the stories weren't true, wouldn't people be freer with them?

Zack sucked in a sharp breath as they stepped outside again, but Aaron drew in a more leisurely lungful, relishing the way the cold stung this throat and made his eyes water. The night sky was clear, and the stars spilled above them, making the world around them glow faintly. Aaron led the way down to the shore.

"What's that sound?" Zack asked, suddenly tensing beside him.

"Which?" Aaron stopped walking and cocked his head to listen. The wind blew through the trees. Somewhere, a dog whined, protesting perhaps a late-night walk. Probably on one of the Bass islands. Sound travelled oddly in the still night air.

Zack stopped, too. "The…." His voice trailed off. "I don't know how to describe it. Clapping? Something snapping."

"Ohhhhhhhhh." Aaron hadn't been aware of it until Zack pointed it out. In winter the sound was as familiar to him as his own heartbeat. But now that he was, he had a problem. Because there were two different answers he could give Zack, one sensible and practical, one much less so. The latter was a critical part of Aaron's own sense of self, but it might scare Zack off for good.

You invited him here, Aaron reminded himself. *Because you wanted him to know you, as you exist here. Tell him.*

Still, Zack at least deserved some kind of choice in the matter. Aaron started walking again. "Do you want the creepy answer or the real answer?"

Zack fell into step beside him. "Why would I want the creepy answer?"

Aaron smiled into the dark. "Because I offered you a creepy answer, and you're a journalist and that should interest you."

"I want to know if I should be alarmed by it," Zack said cautiously.

Aaron shook his head. "You shouldn't." *Probably*.

"Okay. Fine," Zack said. "But tell me the real answer first."

Aaron nodded. "Water expands when it freezes. And we're surrounded by it. There isn't always room for all the ice. So it breaks and buckles on the lake."

"That makes sense," Zack said, but Aaron wasn't done.

Ice was a part of the life of the island, as much as it ever was at TCI, just in a different way. "It pushes up against people's wooden docks," he went on. "It gets in the eaves and the pipes and the drains of the people who aren't here year-round. They hire some of us sometimes, to go check on their houses on the other islands. A lot of us won't do it. We're not lackeys to the summer people. They can pay to fix their damage from not knowing this place." He wasn't used to speaking to people other than his family about that; no one else understood. *Because you don't let anyone else know*, he thought.

"Okay," Zack said slowly. "That is, actually, almost a little creepy." He didn't sound bothered by the prospect, though. More intrigued. "What's the actual creepy answer?"

Aaron drew a steadying breath of the sharp, cold air. "Seals."

Zack stopped walking again to turn toward Aaron. "Excuse me?"

"The animals? Like my ringtone?" Aaron tried to imitate the sound to make the point, like a dog barking through a wheezing inhale.

Zack flinched. "*That* was creepy."

"I warned you!"

"But seals are ocean animals?" Zack asked.

"Yes. Mostly," Aaron said. "That's what makes it weird. There's a legend up here, about a lost colony of them. They swam in via the Saint Lawrence, before it was called that, and got stuck. Some of them, when they realized they couldn't make their way back to the sea, moved onto the land... for good. Not just to rest or sun but to grow tall and walk and become people."

"But not all of them?"

"No. Not all of them" Aaron said softly. "They're calling for us to return to the water, so we can go back once again and find the sea."

"Us?" Zack asked.

"Us," Aaron confirmed. "My family has been here for years. Generations. I'm not sure we know since when. One story goes that we got the land as a prize after the war."

"The column... 1812?"

"That's the one. There was no one living out here. They've done digs... found some hunting and fishing camps but otherwise, nothing. The indigenous people didn't want it. Neither did us more recent arrivals. Everyone more or less agreed it was good for the occasional bit of hunting and not much more. So I guess it was the cheapest thing anyone could think of. I mean if you're gonna reward people for service in a war you lost, why not dump them in the middle of a lake?"

"But you don't know if that's true?"

Aaron shrugged. "There's no paperwork, and I come from storytellers."

"Surely there's a deed?"

Aaron shrugged. He honestly didn't know. He knew deeds to houses were things people had. But people also usually came from places that weren't like this.

"My dad grew up here, and his father before him, and his father before him," he said. "Everyone he remembers always said everyone they remembered before them was from here too. So that's all any of us have. Stories fade in and out of truth, and all sorts of people are always making up tales about where they're from. Maybe the story about the war is true. Maybe the story about the seals is true. Maybe it's both or neither. Maybe it's worse."

Zack shuddered. It might have been the cold, but Aaron wondered if he'd made a mistake telling him. Especially when Zack had no way of escaping and was stuck with Aaron's probably-not-the-descendants-of-seals family for the next few days.

"Like I said," Aaron repeated firmly. "It's just the ice."

"Do you believe that?" Zack asked.

"Which?"

"Any of it."

Aaron shrugged. "The seals. Sometimes. Maybe. Ari takes it seriously. It's why she's never left, not even to go to college. But in the end, does it matter? We are who we are. Everyone has something that calls them home. Whatever home means for them."

By now they'd reached the end of his family's dock. Aaron stopped and tipped his head back, looking up at the sky. Zack did the same.

"I know in all the selkie stories it's the human who wants to catch the seal and keep them on land with them forever. But I'd rather be the one who stays here with you."

Aaron looked sharply at Zack, his heart suddenly pounding in his chest. He was as shocked by the heat in Zack's gaze as much as by his words. An entire life trying to exist in two worlds, a season struggling to bring his hidden home to light, and now – after everything that had happened, and then hadn't happened, between them – Zack accepted everything about Aaron, everything he was and might be, so easily.

"Really?" Aaron asked.

"Yes," Zack said firmly.

Aaron kissed him.

Even in the dark, even after he'd been so terribly strange, Zack accepted him easily into his arms. After all this time Aaron felt calm and giddy and like he was going to fly out of his skin all at once.

Aaron loved the play between the heat of his mouth and the terrible cold of the outdoors, but if he wanted this to go anywhere they needed to go inside.

"Can I stay with you tonight?" he asked.

"I don't know," Zack said. "What will your parents think?"

Aaron laughed. "That's not the problem," he said, although he didn't know the answer to the question. "Last I checked, we were broken up, and I told you this wasn't about anything. No expectations. And yet, here we are."

"The best, least surprising surprise," Zack replied. "Yes, of course you can."

✦

They slipped back into the house as quietly as they could, which wasn't very between the whispering and the boots and other layers that had to be discarded right in the entrance way.

Downstairs in Zack's room, Aaron got undressed as quick as he could before diving under the blankets on Zack's bed. He remembered the first time they slept together and how he had curled up under the covers on the bed in Zack's Saint Paul apartment, simply holding his cock in his mouth. It had been so strange, and soothing, and intimate, but this – his parents' house, their peculiar reunion with still unexamined consequences – was not the time for anything of the sort. And there were plenty of ways to make their bodies bright with the simpleness of hands.

✦

"What happens when we get back to Minnesota?" Aaron asked. His head was pillowed on Zack's chest, and Zack was lazily combing his fingers through his hair. The room was dark around them, lit only by the glow of the bedside lamp. The pilot light on the water heater hissed quietly, and in the distance he could still hear the snapping of the ice. *Or the seals.*

"What do you want to happen?" Zack asked.

Aaron didn't miss the note of caution in his voice, and hoped he wasn't about to get dumped again. Among other things, he could hardly storm out of his own house.

Evasion seemed safest. "You mean besides making the Olympic team?"

"I figured that was a given," Zack said. Aaron could hear the smile in his voice. "I don't want to mess up your deal. I also don't want to assume that I know what you want... or what's best for you."

"Thank you for that lovely change of pace," Aaron said sarcastically. Then he tried to be realistic. Which was difficult, with Zack's skin lovely and warm against his. "I can't... I shouldn't. Take my eye off the ball for the next few weeks. Nationals is everything when it comes to team placement. Besides which, I won't have time. It's a logistical question as much as a focus one."

Zack nodded. "That's more than fair."

"But," Aaron said. "When that's all done and the team assignment is out, for better or for worse, I'll have the bandwidth for things off the ice. And once I'm done with, or know I don't have to worry about, the Olympics, you should feel free to tie me up and have ridiculously hot sex with me as much as you want."

"Provided I ask first. And you say yes," Zack said.

"Yes, yes, of course," Aaron said.

Zack gave him a teasing smile. "You say that like I don't know you get off on my asking permission."

Aaron wanted to lean in, to kiss the smile off Zack's mouth and return to what they'd been doing, but there was something else he needed to do. He'd told Zack about the seals, he'd gone to bed with him again, but there was one more thing he wanted to share. One more thing he hadn't told another soul, except Ari.

"Speaking of permission," he said, rolling the edge of the sheet between his fingers. "There's something else I want to tell you. If that's okay with you."

"Of course," Zack said, without hesitation, and Aaron loved him for it.

"So, something peculiar happened while I was in Saint Petersburg...."

He told Zack the story of his surprise placement and the excitement and his subsequent walk around the city to work through his energy. Of the barking he'd heard in the water, of the dark eyes that had watched him. The soft, warm muzzle against his fingers. The man he'd met on the promenade after, not knowing if what had just happened had been real or a dream: *They came for you.*

Aaron knew it was a lot. Especially coming on the heels of his story about the origins of Whisker Island's inhabitants – his ancestors. Perhaps. But he'd invited Zack here because he'd wanted to bring his two worlds together, and for that to happen, he needed Zack to understand all of him. Even the parts he didn't entirely understand himself. And Zack didn't recoil, didn't frown, didn't dismiss anything Aaron told him.

Which, somehow, made Aaron feel more secure in his own skin. Like maybe stories could be true without having to be hidden, like maybe they could be true without destroying him.

Zack dragged a hand up and down Aaron's back while he talked, the sensation soothing. When he'd finally finished, worn out by the day and the sex and the stories, he closed his eyes, intending only to rest.

He fell asleep before he knew it, Zack's heart pounding beneath his ear like the surf on the shore.

28

A Winter Storm

Whisker Island

Zack crawled slowly back to consciousness to the sound of footsteps and voices from overhead. Aaron was curled up against him, a warm lump of unconscious boy, and for a moment the world seemed normal again. He worried about what Aaron's parents might think if they came down here and how awkward breakfast might be. But those were small, halfway familiar concerns, and unimportant in the face of this place.

He couldn't keep what Aaron had told him last night out of his head. The local legend about the origin of the island's inhabitants, Zack might have been able to rationalize or dismiss. There was no reason to take it any more or less seriously than any other bit of folklore he'd ever heard on his travels. Aaron's encounter with the seals in Saint Petersburg would have been easy to dismiss if it had happened to anyone not from this place. As it stood, having happened to Aaron, it was much harder to push aside.

Certainly Aaron hadn't invented the story out of whole cloth; it was simply too strange. And if he had encountered seals in a river in the middle of Russia, seals who had apparently been looking for him.... Were the Lake Erie seals real too, and was Aaron truly related to them?

Get a grip, Zack told himself. Aaron had had an incredibly exciting and emotional day. It had been dark, in a city he didn't know. Zack had been in enough high-stress situations to know that the night and adrenaline often combined to make people think they'd seen, heard and done things they couldn't possibly have. A seal was far from the strangest thing he'd known someone to imagine. Surely, that's all it had been, the Saint Petersburg seals and the island's selkie inhabitants both: A product of the imagination.

But his train of thought was interrupted by a chorus of barking seals, and he jumped, every hair standing on end.

In his arms, Aaron grumbled sleepily and reached for his phone on the nightstand.

That goddamn phone, Zack thought, thoroughly unnerved.

Aaron cracked open an eye to look over the notifications, and a frown creased his forehead.

"What is it?" Zack asked. In his current frame of mind, he thoroughly expected the answer to be calamitous.

"A front is moving through," Aaron said, scrolling. His hair was tousled from their activities the previous night, the curls falling into his eyes.

Zack gave into the urge to push Aaron's hair back off his forehead. "Is that bad news?"

"It might be. All weather here is risky. And we need to be able to fly to get out of here." His frown deepened. "There's not a lot of wiggle room in my training schedule right now. I really need to get back on time."

"What do we do, then?" Zack asked.

Aaron set the phone back on the nightstand with one last worried look. "Watch and wait."

✦

Later that morning a storm blew in. Zack watched the clouds pile up on the horizon. With nothing in between but miles of water, there wasn't anything to slow the storm down. The world seemed to shrink as it approached, the far-distant line of the horizon fading as a wall of grey swept across the lake. Aaron watched it and kept checking the weather radar.

Zack felt his unease rise. He could – and did – tell himself that the seals were just a story. But as the world outside disappeared, he couldn't help but wonder if the island, or the seals out beyond the ice, were trying to keep Aaron there. Where they thought he belonged.

Any outside pursuits were out of the question for the day. Everyone else sat down to play cards. Aaron invited Zack to join, but he demurred. Aaron should have some time with his family, and he needed some time to himself.

He settled himself by the fireplace, in the same overstuffed armchair he'd dozed off in his first night here, and pulled out his laptop. He wanted to check in with the outside world, especially if they were about to get stuck here or if the internet was about to go out. He needed a reminder that people and places outside this island existed.

A check of his email provided exactly that. It was ostensibly the Christmas holiday, so his inbox was relatively empty, but there was a message from Sammy. His article, about Aaron and TCI, had come back to him for one last round of edits before it got sent for publication. Zack skimmed through it, mostly checking to make sure his previous edits had found their way into the piece and nothing particularly egregious had happened in editorial.

When he got to the end of it, though, he couldn't help feeling like something was missing. This article was about skating, but at its core it was about Aaron and the story of his year. As Zack had learned in the last forty-eight hours, that story wasn't complete without a sense of this place, the island from which Aaron came and would always, Zack was sure, return.

He dashed off a last addition to the piece, a brief paragraph describing the island, its isolation, its peace, its mysteries. Though he knew better than to mention the seals as Aaron had told the story about them last night, he couldn't help but mention their possibility. Not something strange and supernatural like what Aaron had described, but the idea of a lost colony come inland. There were cases of such dotting the far northern hemisphere on multiple continents.

He had to find things elsewhere in the piece to cut to make the word count fit, but that turned out to be easy: He trimmed what little remained of the content he had about Cayden. In the end, he was pleased. It brought the piece together in a way that showcased Aaron as he truly was – the Aaron that he knew – to the world.

For the hell of it, before he sent it back, he grabbed the memory card out of his camera and paged through his recent photos from the island. Without checking first, he wouldn't dare send one that included Aaron for both legal reasons and a general sense of human decency. But he had some good shots of the landscape and the horizon that showed how desolate it was here and how far from everything.

He attached two to the email with his final edits on the story. *In case you need them*, he wrote.

He hoped Sammy decided they did.

✦

As the rest of the day went on, Zack could feel it in the air as Aaron got more and more wound. Or maybe that was the effect of shifting atmospheric pressure, as the storm continued to roar around them. Zack tried to breathe through it, but it was hard to relax. He could hardly imagine how Aaron must feel, with his entire season riding on being able to get off the island on time.

As they were getting ready for dinner, the world outside already gone dark, Aaron's phone barked with an incoming call.

"It's Stephanie," he said as he picked it up. "The pilot," he added, as if Zack could have forgotten the hero who had landed them safely on the slightly larger landmass to the south.

He took the call into the next room; Zack exchanged worried looks with Aaron's parents. The likelihood that Stephanie was calling to tell Aaron she wasn't going to be able to fly out on schedule seemed high.

Aaron, however, burst back into the kitchen with a whoop. "It's going to clear!" he called. He grabbed Zack around the neck for a hug, while his parents exclaimed with relief.

"Oh, I'm so glad," Aaron said, pressing his forehead into Zack's chest.

Zack rubbed his back. "Me too."

Aaron looked up at him. "I meant to ask," he said, "before I got distracted by the weather scare. All that stuff about the seals… Is that okay? I didn't scare you off, did I?"

"Freak me out, yes. Scare me off, no." Zack hugged him tighter, though he was aware of Aaron's parents surely watching them.

"Oh. Okay. Well, good." Aaron seemed to ponder something for a moment. "Another question for you."

"Yeah?"

"Want to come to Nationals? To watch?"

"Oh!" Zack was surprised, but pleasantly so.

He hadn't imagined being included that way when everything between them was still so tenuous and under-discussed. It was a given that Aaron's season came first, but to be a part of it felt huge.

He didn't even know where Nationals were. Hopefully he wouldn't have to get on another plane. Yet there was only one answer he could give.

"Yes," he said. "Definitely."

29

U.S. National Figure Skating Championships

Boston, MA

Walking into the draw was always a little bit like walking into a high school cafeteria – at least as far as Aaron could tell. His schooling hadn't exactly been typical. But it seemed like the sort of tension and drama high school cafeterias had on TV. Who sat where and what that meant was a big deal.

"Hey Sheftall, welcome to the big kids table!" Cayden shouted.

At least Aaron's read on the situation wasn't wrong. He narrowed his eyes at him. "This is my sixth senior nationals."

"But you're having a year!"

"I am, aren't I?" he said with a smile he didn't feel. He was either going to have to sit with Cayden and his hangers-on or he was going to have to pointedly reject his not remotely sincere friendliness, which would create a whole new drama.

He scanned the seats looking for a better, more plausible option, but Katie and Brendan didn't have any other U.S. senior men and were currently with their pairs skaters who had practice ice.

To his relief, Rasmus Tamm caught his eye and waved at him. "Aaron!" he said warmly, patting the empty chair next to him. "I haven't seen you all season. How are you?"

The rescue was obvious. And immensely welcome. That it probably annoyed Cayden on both those counts was only a bonus.

Aaron stepped across the aisle and into the seat Rasmus had indicated. He'd competed for Estonia years ago before moving to the States, and now was one of the oldest skaters in the U.S. field. Everyone called him 'Uncle Ras' – fondly and not to his face. If someone needed a ride at a competition, or a rescue from unwanted advances or social awkwardness... Uncle Ras was there.

What the fuck Rasmus was doing with his life, Aaron did not understand. He'd never won nationals – in the U.S. or Estonia – had almost no international competition experience, and had certainly never been to an Olympics. At thirty-two that wasn't going to change. And yet he kept showing up. Aaron didn't know how he had it in him. Surely it was a sign he was a better person than all of them. Because Rasmus just loved to skate, results more or less be damned.

He twisted his hands together in his lap as Rasmus asked him how his family was doing. He replied on autopilot, probably inanely, and was grateful again when Rasmus didn't take offense at his distraction.

This was the U.S. National Figure Skating Championships. How he placed here would determine whether he secured a spot on the Olympic team. Jack and Cayden were here and their careers were on the line, too. This was it. If he didn't perform at his absolute peak, if he didn't make the cut, in seventy-two hours the season and Aaron's Olympic dreams would be over.

An official stepped out, holding the bag of numbers for the draw. Aaron took an involuntary breath.

Rasmus reached over and patted his knee. "You'll be all right."

Aaron wasn't so sure he would.

✦

Despite the fact that he'd invited Zack to Nationals, they didn't see much of each other. Separate hotel rooms and no plans for socializing until after the competition were essential; he needed to keep his head in the game. So while Zack occupied himself, Aaron went to his practice sessions and kept his focus where it needed to be: skating.

By the morning of the men's short program, Aaron could feel the uncertainty trying to push its way through the well-managed nerves he'd been able to keep in check for the rest of the season. Competitions were always nerve wracking, but this was different. There was so much on the line, and in a season filled with surprising success, there were now expectations on him. Aaron was unfamiliar with the sensation, which was the emotional equivalent of not being able to settle over his blade on the ice. He wanted to find somewhere safe and dark and hide.

I've trained for this, he reminded himself as he laced up his skates for the warmup. *I trust my training. I trust my coaches. I trust myself.*

Aaron hated skating early in the draw. The crowd was never filled in yet, there wasn't much energy in the arena, and judges, he believed, needed to warm up as well. Not to mention, with so many people coming after him it was easy to get forgotten in the commentary of the day.

But no matter when he skated, he still had to turn in the performance of his career.

At the end of his short program, he wasn't sure he had. He'd skated cleanly, that was for sure, but there had been no magic, no energy, pulling the crowd along with him.

Still. Clean was nothing to be ashamed of. The judges agreed. It was still too early in the day for it to really mean anything, but when his scores were announced, he was in first.

Which should have been a relief, but as Aaron left the kiss and cry with Katie's arm around his shoulders all he could think was that there were three more groups of skaters to go and every chance his name would fall too far down in the standings. And with his own skating done for now, there was nothing to do but watch everyone else skate.

Katie and Brendan always did their best to keep their people from calculating their own ranking or keeping track of other people's scores, but Aaron was the restaurant's bookkeeper. He was good at mental math and had an excellent working memory. It was far easier for him to do the math than it was to stop himself from doing the math.

Finally, in one of the rooms backstage, with the final group about to go on, Katie looked up from where she was sitting cross-legged on the floor with her laptop.

"Aaron," she said.

"Yes?"

"Stop pacing," she ordered. "Go get a snack. Watch cat videos on your phone. *Something*. You can't change anything now."

"I know, but –" Aaron protested

"Go," she said. There was understanding in her face. "Twenty minutes. You can do it."

Aaron reluctantly nodded. He reached into his bag for his phone. Zack was watching from the stands, maybe they could meet up somewhere afterward.

Once outside the room he took a moment to first swipe away various congratulatory texts from family and friends.

He could deal with those later, when he actually knew how he felt about his scores.

But as he did, he realized that it wasn't just texts he was dealing with. There were notifications from every social media platform he used – and from some he had signed up for only at Brendan's insistence.

Odd.

They all seemed to include links or talk about an article… Aaron clicked one of the links at random. It led him to *Athletics Monthly*, and the article Zack had written.

This was obviously not the time to look at that, but here it was. His own name leapt up at him from the page, and he settled himself down on a bench in the hallway to read.

Curiosity turned to dismay, then to horror as he got further into the piece. The writing was incredible, no doubt about that – but it was about him. Aaron. And only Aaron. No mention of Cayden or even of Jack, other than that they existed and were also vying for a U.S. Olympic spot. Aaron knew Cayden was being difficult, but he hadn't realized that this would be the result. Especially after he'd put himself out on a limb way back at camp to try to help Zack.

And then, towards the end, was a paragraph, not about skating at all. But about the island. The most private part of his life, that he had trusted Zack enough to see. And there was a picture – Aaron recognized it. Zack had taken it their first day there, when they'd taken a walk along the shore. *How dare he.*

Somehow he got to the doorway of the room Katie was in. He grabbed the frame and said her name as softly as possible; he didn't want to draw attention to himself, and he didn't want her to yell, but mostly, he didn't want to let go of the door frame in case he fell down.

Katie looked up from her laptop, and Aaron watched as the thing where they were alike kicked in. He didn't have to say anything, but her forehead creased in concern.

"What's wrong?" she asked, just as quietly

With one hand still on the doorframe, he texted her the link to the article, and nodded at her phone when it dinged.

Aaron watched her face carefully while she scrolled through the piece. She was too studied in the need for neutrality, though, to betray any reaction.

"I see," she finally said when she finished.

Aaron, finally reasonably sure his knees would hold him, let go of the doorframe, crossed the room, and dropped down on the floor next to her.

"I forgot that was coming out," he admitted.

"I hadn't. It's good timing," Katie said, her face and voice still neutral. Aaron felt his anger extend to her, too.

"What do you mean it's good timing?" he protested. "I'm in the middle of Nationals! And he doesn't talk about anyone else in the field!"

"That's wildly to your advantage."

"He wrote about the island!!" The sense of betrayal nearly choked him.

"He's allowed," Katie said. Her tone was quiet, but the words were relentless. "You invited him there."

"Not for that." Aaron stared at her. "I can't believe you're taking his side"

"I'm not taking anybody's side," Katie said firmly, even sternly. "He came here to do a job. He did it. I asked you to make sure it got done a certain way, and it did. And yes there were bonus complications, but you've seemed to mostly enjoy those. He's a good enough guy. Everyone's done quite well, as far as I'm concerned."

Aaron couldn't be that dispassionate. "He broke up with me because he was worried about journalistic ethics!" he exclaimed. "Doesn't that make this sketchy?" He waved his phone around. "I'm not just having emotions because I'm me and I'm cagey about the shit I'm cagey about!"

"I get that, Aaron. I do. But this article only does you well. And your personal feelings about it can wait until you're on the side of a cereal box. Okay?"

"Everyone's going to be talking about it!" Aaron protested

"That's the goal." Katie wrapped an arm around his shoulders and gave him a sideways hug. He slumped his head down on her shoulder. "Also, Cayden just finished."

Aaron sat bolt upright again. Cayden had drawn the last slot for the day. "How'd he do?"

"You're in third."

Aaron took a deep breath. That meant Cayden was ahead of him for now. Which wasn't great, but also wasn't fatal. "Okay. I can work with that. After I yell at Zack, of course. And go to the press conference, I guess."

He was trying to be funny and trying to remind himself that he was within striking distance of what he wanted. But he was too angry. He felt exposed, in the worst sort of way. He'd trusted Zack, and Zack had laid out all his deepest secrets for everyone to see. He was also in the middle of Nationals and had exactly no time to deal with this.

Right now he had to get through the press conference. Aaron had never loved these things and now he was furious and trapped, a selkie without its skin and under someone else's control. But he knew how to do these things, and was safe from questions about Zack's article. No journalist was going to ask about someone else's journalism.

As the day went on he was sure he could track the spread of the article, as people's eyes and not-so-subtle whispers followed him. He tried to keep to himself as best he could, but that wasn't much. After the press conference and the testing, he had a team meeting with Brendan and Katie and the rest of the TCI crew, after which they all went out to dinner. At least these were the people who knew him and could insulate him from the whispers and stares of others. In other circumstances, Aaron would have had Zack come along. But he was sure he couldn't see Zack without screaming right now, and that didn't need to happen in front of everyone else.

At least at dinner the other skaters were more focused on some drama that had happened that afternoon in the free dance than anything involving himself. He wasn't interested in it, but he was grateful for it.

After that, he had every intention of crashing early. Instead he lay in bed and stared at the ceiling for hours, trapped in the narrative of his life – from everything the article shouldn't have covered but did to everything no one could understand but he desperately wished they would.

✦

The next morning at breakfast, while Aaron picked at scrambled eggs from the hotel buffet, Katie and Brendan finally came to intervene. They slid into seats at the table where he was sitting by himself, each carrying their own breakfast.

"How are you doing?" Katie asked, while Brendan gave Aaron his best concerned-coach look.

"Trying to be chill. But really, really pissed. And I didn't sleep well," he admitted.

Aaron didn't miss the look of concern that Katie and Brendan gave each other. Knowing his coaches were worried about him didn't exactly help his equanimity. He was on-edge enough as it was.

"This is a thing you need to deal with," Katie said simply.

Aaron wanted to snap at her that he *knew* that, but before he could, she kept talking.

"And it's a thing you *will* deal with, with Zack, after this competition is over," she said. "You two will sort it out, one way or another, but for now, you need to put all your feelings about him and that article in a box. There will be time when this is over. There isn't time now. Okay?"

"I've been trying," Aaron said, petulant.

"Try harder," Katie said, the same way she would tell him to fix his footwork or a jump he should have been able to execute but couldn't. Her words were crisp, but her face was sympathetic. "Because right now, you don't have another choice."

✦

Several hours later Aaron was jogging up and down a hallway deep in the maze that was the venue's backstage, keeping his muscles warm. He wasn't sure he was allowed to be back here. He'd certainly seen no one else. But the solitude had been necessary.

He was surprised, therefore, to see Brendan coming down the hall toward him. He wondered how he'd found him. He slowed his pace as Brendan approached, then stopped when they met.

"I thought I had Katie today?" he said, which wasn't very kind, but it was usually Katie with him backstage during competitions whenever possible. Also, Brendan was better at ice dancer drama; it just made Katie yell.

"And you will, we're just trading off for a minute." Brendan seemed unperturbed by Aaron's rudeness.

"What's up?" Aaron asked warily.

Brendan looked him square in the eye. "I want to tell you that I know you can do this, and more importantly you know you can do this and who you are is worth showing the world." Brendan's voice was low, his words intent. He meant them.

Aaron stammered, suddenly overwhelmed.

"Sometimes it helps to hear it from the people you don't have as natural a connection with," Brendan added.

"Maybe?" Aaron said, his voice strangled. He knew why Brendan's observation was important, but he wasn't sure he wanted to deal with it.

Brendan shook his head. "Look. I know how it is to be a man in this sport and navigate what other people think and what judges want and what people think judges want. It's weird. Maybe not as awful as the women get, but odd. You're a fantastic skater. You're also a very specific skater... and a very specific person. Be that person today. Put the rest of it down. Fuck what anyone else thinks. Get it done. Even if you'll probably find a way to give me a heart attack. Again. Okay?"

Aaron nodded automatically. It wasn't the pep talk he'd expected – and certainly not from Brendan, whose fierceness and troubles didn't usually show through as strongly as Katie's did.

"Yeah," he said, still nodding, while Brendan's eyes peered keenly at him. "Yeah, I can do that."

Brendan clapped him on the back, then pulled him into a hug. "Kill it out there."

Aaron closed his eyes and exhaled into Brendan's shoulder. "Yeah."

✦

Brendan led Aaron back to the main backstage area, bustling with competitors and coaches and federation staff, and left him with Katie with a last parting hug.

"Are you ready?" she asked.

Aaron wasn't sure. "Yes," he said, because he had to be.

He paced the hallways while the first groups skated, trying not to pay attention to how anyone else did. *Keep your eyes on your own paper.* But the buzz of the competition followed him while he paced, coming from TV screens and people's personal devices. He wished he'd stayed in his hidden hallway.

Because Aaron had finished third in the short program, he was in the final group for the free skate. Which meant he and the other five in that group had to wait the longest to skate – and had to spend the most time trying to block out how everyone else was doing. By the time the ice had been resurfaced, and the final group – Aaron, along with Cayden, Jack, Rasmus, Eric, and Misha – were lined up for the six-minute warmup, Aaron knew there was room. Not to win – Jack would do that – but to come in ahead of Cayden. That was all he needed.

You finished third at the Grand Prix Final, he reminded himself, rolling his shoulders to loosen them. *You can do this.*

At his side, Katie folded her arms. "No jumps," she warned him. "Not for the warmup. You're too wound."

"I'm fine."

Katie looked unconvinced. "Show me your footwork," she instructed. "And don't forget your edges."

Stepping on to the rink was a relief. With the rush of the ice under his blades, everything else in the world fell away, if only for a moment. This was where he belonged. This was what he was meant to do.

Aaron was finishing his step sequence, aware of Katie's gaze following him coolly around the ice from her spot at the boards, when someone nearly collided with him.

"Sorry, Seal Boy!" Cayden called, sounding not sorry at all.

He'd spoken loudly enough to be heard by the nearest audience members, and there was some rustling in the stands. Aaron wondered if they were upset about Cayden's near-collision with him, or talking about him. And the island. And his seals he'd never meant for anyone else to know about.

The calm he had felt for a few brief moments was shattered. He was shaking as he stepped off the ice at the end of the warmup.

"I hate everyone," he told Katie.

"Believe me," Katie said, handing him his skate guards and then his water bottle. "I know the feeling."

She had her face schooled into a mask of neutrality, but her fury flickered through. Aaron could see it in her eyes.

"As soon as this is over, by the way, we'll be filing an official complaint against him for that," she said.

Aaron didn't have the energy to protest. And he wasn't sure he wanted to. Thankfully Misha Khovanski was being announced, and Aaron could turn his attention to watching him skate. This was Misha's first year in seniors, and he'd had a strong showing all season. Aaron knew he hoped to finish well. Which it looked like he would… until he fell on a triple axel that had never given him trouble before, then fell again on a quad lutz that should have been part of a combo.

Nerves, maybe. Nationals was, after all, A Big Deal, even if you weren't counting on it to make or break your Olympic dreams.

But the ice had moods. And if the ice was having a bad day so would everyone who skated on it. That wasn't one of Aaron's personal superstitions; skaters talked about the moods of the ice the way people who played outdoor sports would talk about the weather. And there were competitions that were notorious because everyone had performed below expectations due to strange slips and excessive falls. U.S. Nationals a few years ago was still referred to as 'Failtionals.'

Aaron very much needed the ice not to be in a bad mood right now.

Jack fell on his first jump and never fully recovered. That was two skaters in a row. Aaron tried not to panic, willing him through every takeoff. But none of it really worked. Jack would get great program component marks, he always did, and manage to walk away with gold, but yikes.

Aaron forced himself to breathe, to do what Brendan had said and let everything else go, as he warmed up and Jack waited in the kiss and cry for his scores.

Be good for me, he pleaded with the surface under his blades as he stroked around the perimeter. He had to get through the next four minutes. Even if passing out on the ice right here felt like a more comfortable option right now.

What is everything thinking about the seal boy now? Was his last thought as he took his starting position in the center of the ice.

It didn't help.

Aaron got through his program without any falls, but that was the best he could say about it. He popped his triple axel, the one he'd frightened the judges with at camp that seemed so very long ago, and he two-footed the landing on his quad sal. His energy was wrong, his timing was off, and altogether it was a chaotic mess.

Aaron pried himself back to his feet for his bows. The audience was cheering, but the energy felt... flat. Polite, but uncapitulated. Frantically, his mind tried to reassure him that everyone was a mess today, and he'd be fine and pull it out. But as he skated to the door of the ice, where Katie waited for him so they could sit together in the kiss and cry, he couldn't shake the feeling that his career might have somehow peaked on that strange night in Saint Petersburg and that Ari, when she saw the article, would blame him for giving their secrets away.

Aaron twisted his fingers in his lap while they waited for his scores. When they appeared, he let his head fall into his hands, tense with nerves. He was currently in second, behind Jack. Good. For now. With Eric and Cayden still to skate, anything else would have put a medal completely beyond him. Either of them could beat Aaron on his best day, and Aaron had definitely not just had his best day.

Please let me finish ahead of Cayden.

At least it was Uncle Ras skating at the very end. Aaron was very fond of him – and deeply grateful – but he had barely squeaked into this last group; the long program wasn't going to be easier for him. There was no medal risk there.

Backstage, Katie gave up on trying to get him to pay attention to anything other than the other skaters for the remainder of the event. They sat together in the seats set aside for competitors and staff, and soon were joined by Brendan and the rest of the skaters from TCI.

Aaron didn't like to root for other skaters to fail. That kind of mentality went against everything he strived to do and be in this sport. For him, figure skating may have been a solo event, but all the skaters were on this strange journey together.

So he felt torn when Eric struggled with the ice the same way the rest of them had. Still, even with more than one fall, he might have been able to hold it together… until he fell out of his final spin.

"Oh no," Aaron muttered.

Katie hissed in sympathy. "Injury? He went down *hard* on that one fall."

Injury or not, it didn't make a difference to the scores. Eric was in sixth, and Aaron was still in second, when Cayden took the ice.

…And fell on his first jump. Aaron clenched his hands into fists and huffed out a breath. Okay, maybe he did want Cayden to fail. Just a little.

But he didn't. His performance wasn't any cleaner than Aaron's, but the base value of his program was higher, and this was a sport where fractions of a point could matter. And when the scores came, Cayden had squeaked ahead of Aaron by only two points.

Third. I can live with third. The Olympics can still happen with third. My international record is better than his. They can still choose me. Aaron told himself this over and over. He knew it wasn't guaranteed, but he'd had a strong season. Stronger than Cayden's, and maybe that nightmare article

Zack had written – and that Aaron still needed to address with him – really would work in his favor.

Nothing he could do about it now though, that much was sure.

Rasmus took the ice.

Aaron turned to Katie. "I hope he does well. If anyone doesn't deserve a bad run, it's him." He said it with an intensity that surprised himself; in all this whirlwind of a season, Rasmus had been the one skater outside of TCI who had been reliably kind and welcoming to him. Aaron had no outlet for his gratitude in this moment than that fervent wish.

Aaron hadn't been following Rasmus's programs much this season and regretted that as the music started. This was a good choice, well suited to his energy and the presence he had on the ice. It would have been fun to watch it develop.

In fact, Aaron was so captivated by the performance that it was almost a minute into it before he noticed that Rasmus hadn't fallen. Hadn't struggled. Wasn't bobbling anything. And did, in fact, have the rapt attention of the entire arena.

He squeezed Katie's hand tighter, his own concerns momentarily forgotten, while he got swept up in Rasmus's skating along with everyone else. Figure skating had these moments, sometimes, where someone would break out of the pack and blow everyone's expectations away. They were magic to watch.

When he finished Aaron was on his feet with the rest of the audience. He cheered wildly while Rasmus took his bows, tears streaming down his cheeks and his grin stretching from ear to ear.

Rasmus staggered off the ice and into the waiting arms of his coach. He said something that Aaron couldn't make out from this distance but that made everyone around him laugh. Aaron was sure that, whatever it was, by tomorrow it would be a meme on figure skating social media.

The reality of the situation only crashed into him when the scores were announced.

He, Aaron, was in fourth. Rasmus had beat him out to come in third.

Aaron felt like the walls of the venue were closing around him, the cavernous space shrinking and the excited noise of the crowd fading into the distance. He shrank down into his seat, unaware of Brendan's worried face or Katie's calculatedly calm one.

He'd come in fourth. The federation wasn't going to send the fourth-place finisher at Nationals to the Olympics. Jack and Cayden would go. Aaron would get named an alternate and left at home. He felt like the ground was sliding out from under him, and he did not want to do this in public.

Unfortunately, there was a lot of public left to get through. Katie managed to urge him to his feet and shepherd him through the backstage hallways. At least fourth place didn't have to go to the press conference, which was the very smallest of silver linings.

He did, however, have to talk to journalists in the mixed zone and pretend he wasn't crushed and that his dreams hadn't just been shattered. He would also have to put on a smile and congratulate Cayden because that was what good sportsmanship demanded.

At least there was Rasmus. The man was tucked into a quiet corner, looking overwhelmed but ecstatic; the tracks of happy tears marked his face.

"Aaron!" Rasmus's face lit up even brighter when he saw him, and he pulled him into a hug. "You did well."

"You did better," Aaron said, without any bitterness, hugging him back. "You just made history. That skate was *incredible*. I'm so glad I got to see it." He meant that, too; as upset as he was, he couldn't be anything but happy about

Rasmus's placement and that he'd gotten to see such an iconic performance live. That was a thing to cherish.

But it was perhaps the only thing today he could say that about. Soon Katie was herding him through the crowd again, and Aaron realized with relief that they were heading for the doors.

Brendan joined them outside and together they made it all the way out of the arena, down half a block to the hotel and into the lobby.

When suddenly, Aaron pulled up short.

Katie bumped into him from behind. "What is it?" she asked. Then, "Oh," as she saw why Aaron had stopped.

Zack was striding toward them across the lobby, concern etched into his face.

"Aaron!" he called, his hands already spread, as if ready to pull Aaron into a hug.

And Aaron wanted to be hugged, wanted to collapse against Zack's warm, muscled chest and let himself be comforted. But that was a fantasy that belonged to a world where Zack *hadn't written about the island.*

So he glared at Zack, and felt a small flare of satisfaction when Zack stopped in his tracks.

"What's wrong?" he asked.

"Do you want me to punch him for you?" Brendan muttered, quietly enough for just Aaron and Katie to hear – Aaron hoped.

"You'd miss," Katie said flatly.

Aaron looked at Zack and realized the other man had almost no idea what was going on. He surely knew the article had come out yesterday, but he didn't know Aaron had read it. He'd seen Aaron underperform today, but then, everyone in that final group had underperformed. He didn't know how Aaron had struggled to pull off the sub-par performance he had. If he was worried about Aaron's placement regarding the Olympic team decision, he likely didn't understand quite how dire a situation it was. And certainly, he had no idea how to comfort an athlete whose one dream was about to slip away.

Aaron was furious with him for all of it, but most of all the part where he'd have to explain it, in very small words, when he was dizzy with grief and somehow even more terrified than he'd been by the Neva in Saint Petersburg.

"I am so angry at you." It was easier than explaining why.

"Okay," Zack said, his tone neutral, his eyes darting between Aaron, Katie, and Brendan. "If there's something we need to talk about, we could –"

"We already talked! You and me! Lots and lots of times!" It was so much simpler to yell, to be upset at Zack about this. If he was angry at Zack, he didn't have to think about his inadequate skate and the fact that he wasn't going to the Olympics and that everything, this whole year, had been for nothing.

"Okay," Zack said again, still that studied neutral, which only served to infuriate Aaron more. Why couldn't he react?

"Your article came out! The one you wrote about me!"

"All right," Katie said, cutting in verbally and partially stepping in front of Aaron. He was mad at her too, now. He wanted a fight. His season was over, but she wasn't letting him have it. "We're not doing this here."

"I'm still not one hundred percent sure what we're doing," Zack said, slowly putting his hands up in front of his chest.

Aaron ducked around Katie. He kept his voice low; after all, they were in a public space. But if it was possible to whisper shout, whisper shouting was what he was doing.

"I didn't invite you because of your job! You said you were done. But then you added things about the island to the article! You said the article was about the race for the other slot, which means me and Cayden. But somehow, that's not what happened! Cayden wasn't even in the article!"

"He wouldn't take my calls," Zack said. "You knew that. You talked to the guy!"

"I didn't know you'd given up on him and changed the focus to me! Did you see Cayden almost crash into me in warmup?"

Zack looked eager to grasp at the subject change. "Yeah, that was fucked up right?"

"It sure was!" Aaron exclaimed. *Fuck whispering.* "He called me 'seal boy,' and that's all your fault."

"Boys!" Katie said sharply. "Elevator."

Aaron let her shepherd them, but that didn't mean he was going to let up. His true disappointment, the text with the names of who would be going to the Olympics, hadn't come yet. He wasn't going to be on that list now, but when it came – and it would at any moment – he'd probably cry. So if he was going to yell, he needed to get his yelling done now.

He tried to lay into Zack again in the elevator, but Brendan just made a soft noise and pointed to the obvious security camera and the large mirrored walls. No one cared about figure skaters, until they did.

Aaron keyed into his room and everyone else followed. Housekeeping had made the bed, but his short program costume was draped over the vent to air out, his laptop and chargers were in a tangle on the nightstand, and his snack stash was an unorganized pile on the desk. His other clothes were scattered messily around the room. If he'd known his coaches were going to be in here, he might have tried to tidy up, but then, maybe not. Which was probably one of those figure-skaters-have-weird-boundaries things that had perturbed Zack at first, but Aaron didn't care right now.

"Do we all need to be here for this?" Aaron asked at full volume once the door was shut behind them.

"You're yelling at me," Zack pointed out. "So I probably need to be here for it, yes."

"We're here until the team announcement," Katie said quietly, sitting down on the edge of the bed.

Aaron stared at her in disbelief. "I'm not going to be on the team! We're not going to have to go back there to deal with it. You two can go break up whatever fight the ice dancers are having or whatever it is you do when you're not watching your athletes fail." He started pacing up and down the room, mostly so he didn't have to look anyone in the eye as his started to fill with tears.

"You didn't –" Brendan started.

"I did!" Aaron was shouting now. "And it's a hundred times more embarrassing be because *someone* –" he pointed at Zack – "completely misrepresented everything about the article he was writing, the article that *you* –" he whirled to face Katie "Insisted I find a way to make myself the star of."

"Insist is a strong word," Katie said. Her calm was infuriating. But before he could lash out again, at her or anyone, Zack touched Aaron's wrist gently.

"Hey. Aaron. Hey," Zack said quietly.

If he'd tried to grab his arm Aaron would have pulled away and might have tried to hit him, which Zack probably knew. Aaron gulped a breath and stopped pacing.

"Aaron, I'm sorry. I didn't mean for this to happen."

"That doesn't change anything, now does it?" Aaron snapped. But his anger was burning itself out, although maybe that was the effect of Zack's fingers, now intertwined with his.

Zack pulled him closer. "I know it doesn't. But it's still true."

Aaron closed his eyes and let his head fall into Zack's shoulder. Zack's arms went around him. And it was so, so tempting; he could just stay here and cry and let Zack make him feel better.

Aaron's phone barked in his jacket pocket. He jumped, jolting the top of his head into Zack's chin.

"Ow," they said at the same time, though Aaron had barely felt the pain. His body was suddenly awash with adrenaline.

"I know what it says, but I don't want to look."

Katie and Brendan's phones also chimed, but they made no move to look at them. Everyone was frozen in place. Zack had dropped his arms from around Aaron, but they stood so close Aaron could feel the rise and fall of his chest.

Zack finally broke the silence. "Someone should look."

"I can't," Aaron whispered.

Katie, still perched on the edge of the bed, moved slowly for her pocket, and just as slowly drew out her phone and unlocked it. As if her movement had unfrozen his, Brendan did the same.

Katie's eyes darted across the screen. "Aaron," she said, her voice somewhat strangled.

"What?" he demanded. Everything else in the room was silent except for the pounding of blood in his ears.

"You should look at the text," Katie said.

"Am... am I on the team?" Aaron couldn't hope. He *couldn't*. But he had to ask.

"There will be no U.S. Olympic Team announcement at this time," Brendan read out. "The U.S. will be represented at Four Continents by..." He hesitated, glancing up at Aaron. "Cayden Sauer and Aaron Sheftall."

"Four Continents?" Aaron squeaked. In a normal year it was the biggest competition before Worlds, but this was an Olympic year. Nobody cared about Worlds or anything after the Grand Prix and Nationals. He hadn't given Four Continents a thought.

"Jack Palumbo isn't going to Four Continents," Katie said.

"And he doesn't need to," Brendan put in. "He's a given for the Olympics."

Realization hit Aaron like the ice rushing up to meet him in a fall. His heart drummed wildly. "They're letting Cayden and me battle it out. For the last team slot."

Katie nodded. "Looks like."

"That's – Aaron, that's fantastic!" Zack exclaimed. He reached for Aaron, as if to take his hands again, but stopped himself. "You still have a shot!"

And maybe it was, or should have been, but all Aaron felt was panic and dismay. His mind was a whirl, adrenaline was coursing through him, and his heart was a wreck of so many emotions – fear, excitement, elation, dread – that he couldn't begin to sort them out. He felt, suddenly, so very, very tired.

"It's not fantastic," he snapped, stepping back from Zack. "It's horrible! It means I have to do all this *again* with your article floating around and all that rest of it. If today had to go badly, at least it was going to be the end. And now it's not!"

"Okay, but –"

"*Auuuughhhhhhhhh!!!*" Aaron yelled in frustration. He was intensely satisfied when Zack jumped back.

"Does anyone need me for anything?" Aaron asked, looking from Katie to Brendan.

"Not 'til the gala," Brendan said.

"Good. I'm going for a walk. You all can do... whatever."

And with that Aaron stormed out of his own room to wander around this city with his only true wish being not to run into any goddamn seals.

30

One Week after Nationals

Minneapolis and Saint Paul, MN

A week after the disaster – on so many levels – of Nationals, Aaron was in Salt Lake City for Four Continents and Zack was in the middle of the kitchen in his new apartment in Saint Paul. The cardboard boxes and bubble wrap surrounding him reminded him of the day he'd been beginning to pack up in Miami when Sammy had called with a job offer that had shifted the course of his life. He'd been at the end of a relationship then, and he wasn't sure if he was at the end of another relationship now.

You probably are, the reasonable part of his mind told him. *Scratch that. You almost certainly are.*

Aaron was still angry – justifiably, as it turned out. At least that was the firm opinion of Katie, Sammy, and Matt, which sure seemed like enough to make it true. Zack hadn't communicated clearly about the shifts the initial article was taking when Cayden had proved to be so resistant to participating. And cutting the guy entirely so Zack could shove in the stuff about the island at the last minute had been straight up duplicitous and a not-insignificant breach of trust. The photo had been a reasonable choice, but he should have told Aaron first. And he'd mentioned the seals. In passing, as an inland colony of freshwater seals. No myth, no whisper of magic.

You were threading a needle, Katie had told him, after Aaron had stormed out of his own hotel room in Boston. *And you did it well. But he's not in a place to deal with that right now.*

It was, his triumvirate of personal counselors assured him, the sort of thing that could be apologized and made up for, but not while Aaron was trying to go to the Olympics. Still.

So Zack was letting it lie. And spending a lot of time thinking about his need to process his life through words and the way that had an impact on the other people in his life. While he still had hockey and his work on his memoir to keep him busy both those things felt complicated now. *Maybe Sammy will find some other sports emergency I can write about this year*, he thought.

As he pondered that possibility – surely something at the Olympics would want covering? – his phone, buried somewhere on the counter under various packing material, rang. Zack fished it out, expecting it to be Matt; they'd talked about grabbing food later.

Instead, *Katie Nowacki* flashed up at him from the screen. Odd. And concerning. Katie was in Salt Lake too, with Aaron. Why was she calling him?

When he picked up, there was a rush of static and background noise – a crowd, of some sort. A pocket dial, in all likelihood; he moved to hit *end call* but before his thumb could find the button Katie's voice crackled out at him.

"Zack?"

"Yeah?"

"It's me. Katie."

"Yeah, I know. What's going on? Is he okay?"

"We're at Four Continents and I need you to get out here." Katie's voice, raised over the sound of the bustle around her, was a command.

One Zack did not comprehend, because it made no sense. "What? Get out where?"

"Salt Lake City."

Did she think he'd travelled there on his own to watch the competition? Because he definitely hadn't. "I'm in Saint Paul."

"I'm aware of that! Hence the verb *get*."

"Is it Aaron? What's going on?" he demanded. He couldn't help thinking of how he'd come to be in the Twin Cities and of Luke Koval's accident that had sent them all on this journey. *Is he hurt? How badly?*

"The short program just ended. Aaron finished behind Cayden. He can still pull ahead, there's room, but his head is a fucking mess and I need you to get out here and fix it." Katie's voice was terse, businesslike, but there was an edge of panic under it. One that Zack recognized all too well.

As much as he sympathized, however.... "I can't do that," Zack protested.

"Yes, you can," Katie said firmly.

"You were in the room when he yelled at me a lot – fairly – for a bunch of different things."

"Yes. And?"

"I helped cause the mess he's in, in the first place. Because of how he is wired and attached to that island I cannot actually fix anything for him. And even if I could, he still needs to ask for it or at least consent to having you ask me for it. This is his life, not a fucking rom-com."

Katie laughed darkly. "Believe me, I am well aware."

"Katie," Zack said. She couldn't seriously expect him to do this, could she?

"Zack," she replied. "I know my athlete. Who is also a gossip. I know more details of the mess you two are in with each other than any of us want. So. To be very clear. The men's long program starts in thirty hours, and I don't care how you get your ass here, just do it."

With that, she hung up.

Zack pulled his phone away from his ear and stared at it. That was all sorts of data points. About Aaron. About Katie. About, by extension, Brendan. He half-sighed and half-laughed. What a damn mess.

"Respect to you, Katie," he muttered at his phone.

Then he called Matt. It was after six, his shift was over by now, and Zack desperately needed advice.

Matt answered, sounding as cheery as ever. "Hey, what's up?"

"I have a problem," Zack said. He wandered out of his new kitchen into his new living room, which was empty except for a futon and a folding lawn chair. He dropped down onto the futon.

Matt's tone shifted instantly to one of concern. "What's going on?"

Zack did his best to explain. The things that had led up to this moment, at least, Matt already knew. "Katie wants me to go to Salt Lake to help get Aaron's head screwed on straight but I am the one who unscrewed it in the first place, and I am sure he has no idea Katie called me."

"Okay," Matt said slowly. "What are you going to do?"

"I don't know!"

"What do you want to do?"

Rewind time and not put in that damn paragraph about the island. Or the picture. But that wasn't an option. "What I want doesn't matter. What matters here is what Aaron wants, and making sure I don't intrude where he doesn't want me." Saying that out loud helped. How on earth could he be considering taking such a step? And yet, he was.

"You think he doesn't want you there?"

"Given that the last time we spoke he was shouting at me, I do think that, yes. If there's time or space to start making what I did right, it is not during the latest most important competition of his career."

"Then don't go," Matt said simply.

Zack felt his heart lurch in disappointment. He knew Matt was right, but that hadn't been what he wanted his friend to say.

"So you do want to go," Matt said, too knowingly, when Zack didn't say anything.

"What I want doesn't matter," Zack said firmly.

"Okay. Yes. In this instance, you're right," Matt said. "He's a big boy who gets to make his own decisions. And based on what I know of her, I am also sure Katie didn't tell Aaron she was calling you."

Zack dropped his forehead into his free hand. "If I show up there without warning he's going to murder me. Why couldn't Katie just tell me to call him?"

"Because she's his coach, and that's not what she thinks he needs. Okay. Zack. I need you to listen to me."

"Okay?" Zack asked warily. His head and his heart were a mess. He honestly didn't know what to do. But he could listen to his friend.

"The stakes for Aaron here are like, massive, right?"

Zack nodded, even though Matt couldn't see him. "The most massive," he said.

"Do you trust Katie to have his best interests at heart?"

"Absolutely." There was no question of that.

"Do you trust Katie to have the knowledge to accurately assess what Aaron's best interests are?"

"Unfortunately, yes." *I know more details of the mess you two are in with each other than any of us want.* But just because Aaron liked being tied up didn't mean he had a subby bone in his body. Zack was entirely sure he didn't. And even if he did, Zack still didn't have the right to make decisions for him.

Matt continued. "If you go, will you make things worse?"

Zack thought about that one. "Probably not. Aaron might hate me forever but that's kind of already what we're dealing with."

"If you go, will it help?"

"Katie thinks so."

"Then trust Katie. Because yeah this is fucked up, but so's figure skating. If he didn't need you there, she wouldn't have asked."

It was a gamble. A wild, long-shot gamble both for Aaron's Olympic dreams and their relationship. Which probably wasn't going to come through this intact. But if Zack could save his dream, he had to at least try.

"How far is it from here to Salt Lake City?" he asked, not expecting Matt to have an answer. But he did.

"Nineteen hours by car. I just googled."

"How long by plane?" Zack asked.

"You hate flying."

"I can't drive nineteen hours alone and get there alive!"

"Which is why I," Matt said grandly. "Am coming with you."

✦

"This," Matt said as they pulled out from a gas station where they'd stocked up on extremely unhealthy snacks that would probably appall real athletes, or at least their nutritionists. "Is a nearly heterosexual level of disaster you are engaged in."

"Uhhhh, thanks?" Zack said, having no real idea how to interpret that. It was his turn to drive, and his focus was marginally occupied by figuring out how to turn on the windshield wipers in Matt's truck. Their stuff, including Zack's camera bag, were stashed behind their seats.

"It's like a romantic comedy," Matt said. "Filled with things you shouldn't do in real life but work in the movies.

Because I used to try to do things like the dudes in romcoms, and girls super told me to stop doing that."

"You know the gays have romantic comedies too, right?" Zack asked.

"Yes. But are they this ridiculous? Really?"

It was, Zack thought, a nearly fair philosophical question. And to the extent it wasn't, it was perfect for a useless road trip debate.

✦

"Okay," Matt said as they approached the Wyoming state line and the clock approached midnight. "We're going to stop for the night, right? Because I am all for true love and shit but not for one of us falling asleep at the wheel."

Zack decided not to argue. Death was, after all, bad.

"Will we still be able to get there in time?" he asked.

"When's his thing?"

"Five-thirty p.m. tomorrow," Zack said.

"Which time zone?" Matt asked.

"Which – fuck!" Zack fumbled for his phone. "Uh. Mountain Time. Which apparently we crossed into like an hour ago."

"Okay. So it's midnight now, we have...." Matt tapped his fingers on the steering wheel, his mouth moving as he counted. "Seventeen and a half hours. We'be fine."

"Fine like, we'll have a couple of hours so I can do whatever Katie thinks I can do or fine like we'll roll in just as his skate starts?"

"The first one. What are you going to do when you get there?"

"Call Katie. Beyond that. I have no damn idea. She says she has a plan; I'm letting her have a plan."

"Do you think she knows how much boys like doing what she says?" Matt mused.

"I'm going with yes."

✦

Zack assumed that they would not have any problem finding a hotel room somewhere along I-80 in the middle of the night on a random weekend in January. He had, however, not counted on a business tech convention taking place in Cheyenne.

"I've just got the one room," the clerk told them at the first hotel they pulled into.

"That's fine," Zack said. Anywhere with a mattress and a pillow – and a shower – sounded great at this point.

"It's, uh, the honeymoon suite," the clerk said.

"Oh for fuck's sake." Zack strongly considered putting his head down on the check-in counter.

"That's fine," Matt said, stepping up.

✦

"Should I carry you over the threshold?" Matt asked as they reached the door.

"I think that's for when you get to your own house? Also no. No marriedness."

Matt cackled and keyed them into the room. "Aww!" he exclaimed, dropping his suitcase in the middle of the floor. "The towels are all folded up like swans! And hearts!"

"How is this happening?" Zack muttered, mostly to himself. This trip was becoming too absurd.

"Because we are two very lucky men in pursuit of true love, in your case, and a deeply excellent story I can tell forever, in mine."

"I suppose I should thank you for being cool about this," Zack said, eyeing the one bed. Which at least was a king. Hopefully Matt didn't hog blankets.

"Fuck cool, this is hilarious! Now help me take pictures." Matt dug out his phone. "I wanna make people on social media scared I got married!"

Zack shook his head and laughed. Matt was ridiculous and also a good, kind, and fair friend.

✦

They were on the road by seven the next morning, multiple cups of hotel breakfast coffee in the cupholder between them.

"You know," Zack said as he got up to speed on the highway. "This is everything I used to love about war reporting, without the getting shot at." There was a thrill in this, on the road before dawn, a deadline to beat and the rush of adrenaline and uncertainty.

Matt looked over at him from the passenger seat. "You've got a therapist, right?"

"Oh yeah."

"Good, good. 'Cause you're a fucking mess. Got any more of a plan than yesterday?"

"Nope. Not a clue."

✦

They rolled into Salt Lake at three in the afternoon. For all the travel he'd done, both internationally and domestically, Zack had never been there before. It was beautiful. The sky was a dazzlingly blue dome above them, curving down to touch the mountains that ringed the city. He wondered if he'd have a chance to get out and take any photos. *Probably not.*

As soon as they found a parking spot, Zack pulled out his phone and called Katie. Next to him, Matt drummed his fingers on the steering wheel. He was enjoying this entirely far too much.

The call connected, and she answered immediately.

"I swear to God, if you are still in Saint Paul...." Katie began.

"I'm in a parking garage two miles away from the venue because this is the closest we could get," Zack said.

"We?"

"You wanted me to get to Utah in thirty hours," Zack said. "That was not a one-person drive. One of the guys from hockey volunteered."

"Sure, but planes are a thing?" Katie sounded baffled.

"Yeah, I hate planes," Zack said. He paused. "Aaron's mentioned that, hasn't he?"

"Maybe," Katie said. "*At any rate*, so glad you're here. I got you tickets, and I guess we can get your friend tickets. Anyway. Whatever. Just get to the venue. Brendan will meet you with credentials and we'll sneak you back before the comp starts."

"Does Aaron have any idea this is happening?" Zack asked, though he already knew the answer.

"No. But he's a jittery, unfocused mess," Katie said. "And his sister keeps texting him. Even if he wants to murder me for this and hates you, it'll at least give him some focus."

"Uh. Great. At least you're clear about how this is probably going to go."

"I am a mean, anxious, unpleasant person, Zack Kelly. But my instincts are fantastic. Get out of your damn car and start walking."

Zack hung up the call and looked at Matt. "You wanna go watch some figure skating?"

"Does that come with you getting your ass handed to you?"

"I think so."

Matt was definitely enjoying this way too much. Zack tried to focus on being annoyed at him for that, instead of wildly apprehensive about what he was about to do.

"Cool. Sounds great," Matt said and held up his phone to snap a picture of Zack for his latest social media update.

✦

"Here we go," Matt said, as they stood on the sidewalk looking up at the concrete and glass structure that was the Salt Lake City Ice Center. It was growing dark outside, and bright lights gleamed from inside the building, illuminating the staircases that zig-zagged between floors.

"Yeah." Zack took a deep breath. *Here we go.* "You ready?"

"More than you."

The venue was packed. Zack thought he had seen the peak of competitive figure skating crowds – outside the Olympics, at least – at Nationals, but that paled in comparison to this. There were throngs of people, speaking multiple languages, all jostled together and buzzing with excitement. A lot of them were holding stuffed animals, flowers, or both. Zack narrowed his eyes at a girl standing by a giant cardboard cutout of a skater he didn't recognize. Was that a *seal* plushie under their arm?

He was wondering how Katie thought he'd be able to meet up with her when there was a sharp whistle from above; looking up, he saw Brendan on the steps leading to an upper level, waving at him.

Zack weaved his way through the crowd toward him, Matt following behind. When they reached Brendan's step, he pulled Zack into a hug. "Glad you made it."

"Uh. Yeah." Zack hugged him back.

"Come on, he's this way."

Brendan led them through a dizzying route of hallways, up and down flights of stairs and through hallways that didn't get less crowded, but were definitely filled with skaters and team staff instead of spectators. The further they went, the more worried Zack got.

This is a terrible idea. He's going to hate me forever. And I'm going to ruin his career —

"Holy shit," Matt breathed, interrupting the churn of Zack's brain. "Is that – Isao Chiba?"

"Yeah," Brendan said looking at the man walking down the hall in sequined trousers, a Team Japan jacket zipped up over his shirt.

"He's set so many world records. He got gold at the last Olympics, in Harbin," Matt breathed. His eyes were actually starry. "His free skate to Carmen is *legendary.*"

"Yeah," Brendan said. "He's a nice kid too. He tries to bake for everybody."

"How do you know that?" Zack demanded of Matt.

"I follow him on Instagram. How do you not know that? You're the one who wrote an article on figure skating for the country's biggest sports publication!"

Zack, however, had stopped listening. They'd reached a room at the end of a hallway and in the doorway stood Aaron. His hand was on the doorframe, and Zack didn't think he was imagining how white his knuckles were from gripping it too hard. He was dressed in his free skate costume, and staring at Zack like he'd seen a ghost.

"Uh, hi," Zack stammered.

"Here for the final chapter?" Aaron asked, sharp and sullen. But it was all defensive bluster, Zack could tell. His heart wasn't in it.

"Here because Katie ordered me to be here," he said. "And while I could say no to her, I wanted to give you the chance to say no to me yourself." Zack was distantly aware of Brendan and Matt in the hallway behind him, along with the other staff and skaters moving past. "Can I come in? We probably shouldn't be doing this out in front of people."

Aaron looked about to make a cutting remark, but then he stepped back to let Zack in.

The room was small, cinder block walls painted white and blue under a glaring fluorescent light. There was a folding table and a few chairs, all looking somewhat the worse for wear. Aaron's skate bag was in one corner, the contents spread out on the floor. What must have been Katie and Brendan's things were piled together against another wall. A garment bag hung from a hook, and Aaron's street clothes were draped over the back of a chair.

Behind them, Brendan cleared his throat. "I'm gonna go," he said awkwardly. "But there's about fifteen minutes before we have to get on to actually doing this thing. So if you're going to sort yourselves out, I'd do it quickly."

Zack almost laughed as he and Aaron nodded in unison.

"Katie's got your tickets, let's get you settled," Brendan said to Matt, leading him off in the direction of, Zack could only assume, the arena itself.

Aaron pushed the door shut, the sounds of the hallway outside instantly falling away.

"I didn't ask for this," he said, his shoulders slumping. More than angry, he looked exhausted.

"Yeah, well, neither did I," Zack said. "But here I am."

"I'm still mad at you."

"If yelling at me is what helps right now, I'm fine with that. I know this is a lot."

"You're damn right it's a lot!" Aaron snapped, jerking his head up to glare at Zack, and there, *there* was the fire Zack had seen so often on the ice.

That was one way to help, Zack supposed.

"I said yes to Katie because she asked me to come and because I trust her. I know this is way beyond weird skater boundaries and into plain old bad boundaries, but if there was even a chance I could help, I wanted to offer it."

Zack hesitated, waiting for Aaron to say something, but Aaron just stood there glowering at him. But maybe – just maybe – that fire was starting to melt something in his gaze.

Zack decided to keep talking. "When this is over I am going to apologize again for everything. Then we can do the work or not do the work or whatever you want. If you want I will walk right out of this room and you'll never have to see me again. But all I am here for, right now, is to do whatever I can so you can go have the skate of your life," Zack said.

"What if I don't want that to be the only reason you're here?" Aaron's words were hesitant, more than they ever had been with Zack before. But his eyes caught Zack's and held them.

Zack decided that was enough of a cue that it was worth reaching out to touch Aaron's hand. Touch was, he was fairly sure, the only thing that was going to settle him anyway.

Sure enough, Aaron didn't pull away. As their hands slid together, Zack expected that they would simply interweave their fingers – a bit of quiet, of reassurance, maybe even a promise for a future with or without the Olympics. But Aaron was always full of surprises and didn't stop moving until his wrist rested in Zack's palm.

Slowly, carefully, Zack closed his fingers around the delicate bones.

"Give me the other one," he said softly. It wasn't any sort of question, and Aaron did as he was told, with an exhale that sounded to Zack like gratitude.

"Better?" he asked, when Aaron had closed his eyes.

Aaron nodded, but said nothing. Under any other circumstances, Zack would have prodded for more. But this was not that.

"Okay. Then I need you to listen to me. Can you do that?" he asked.

Aaron, eyes still closed nodded. Then, as an afterthought, answered him with words. "Yeah. I can."

"Good. So the other thing I need you to do is stop skating like you're scared. I know you are, and I know there's nothing you can do about it. But I need you to go out there and frighten the judges and your coaches and me, whether that's because your jumps are better with your eyes closed or because you're not even human – I don't know, and I don't care. But I need you to be who you truly are out there. Everyone else be damned. Very much including me. Okay?"

Aaron bit his lip and nodded fiercely. "Okay," he said.

"Good. Now is there anything else I can do?"

Aaron opened his eyes. "You can kiss me."

"Right now?" Zack asked. He adored Aaron, but the boundaries of this situation were already so bizarre. He simply had to double check.

"I don't mean on the ice," Aaron said.

Zack knew he meant the arena, but he couldn't help but think of the island.

He took Aaron's face in his hands. "Can I kiss you, like I did at your home, next to the cold of your lake?" he asked.

Wide-eyed, Aaron nodded.

So Zack did.

31

Four Continents Men's Free Skate

Salt Lake City, UT

Aaron moved through the crowded backstage area toward the ice. His motions were slow but his limbs felt weightless, and all sounds seemed very far away. Even his emotions felt distant, like he was looking at them through deep water.

Zack was here. Zack had come to – to what, Aaron still wasn't sure. He also didn't care. Zack had driven nineteen hours to give him one directive. And maybe that was messed up, but maybe it was also what they both needed. Even if Aaron was still angry at him and still wanted to yell.

There were all sorts of conversations they needed to have. But that wasn't going to happen right now. Because right now, Aaron had to skate. And to do that, he needed to be exactly who he was.

Other skaters in his group took the ice; he ignored them. Cayden skated, and Aaron had no idea how he'd done. It didn't matter anymore. As he waited for his turn, he closed his eyes. The distant hum of the music and roar of the crowd was like waves on the island, pounding and retreating, leaving the shore rocky and water-swept after a storm.

Eventually, Katie patted his shoulder. "It's time," she said.

He opened his eyes.

The sound of the world and the awareness of his own stomach-clenching limb-freezing nerves came slamming back. Aaron breathed through the sensory onslaught, both internal and external. He would let the fear go when it was time. And if he couldn't, he would work through it. Either would be fine. After all, this was what he had trained for.

Aaron skated laps while the skater before him, Aizat Beysenov, waited for his scores in the kiss and cry. There would be no beating him this time. Aizat had turned in a flawless performance. Aaron didn't mind. Aizat was a good guy and an incredible skater.

He couldn't help smiling at the feel of the ice under his blades, of the wind of his own speed in his face. This was who he was: A boy with skates on his feet and the water in his heart.

Aizat's score was announced, Aaron's name was called, and he raised his hands to acknowledge the cheers in the crowd. He found center ice, took his starting position, and closed his eyes.

He could feel the tension of the audience when he started skating, his eyes still closed. That was what he needed, to carry them along with him while he told the story of what he had once been and would be again.

Eyes still closed, he set up his axel, the sound of his blades echoing through the arena as they cut through the ice, building up speed. *Right back outside. Left forward outside.*

Jump.

Aaron snapped his eyes open on the landing – and there was Zack. He was in one of the seats behind the judging panel, his elbows on his knees, his hands pressed to his mouth. Rapt.

Aaron smiled, a feral come-hither, for Zack and the judges, for the audience, and for the journey he was going to take them on.

✦

Five minutes later Aaron was sitting in the kiss and cry between Brendan and Katie, clutching a seal plushie on his knees. Ari would probably be furious. Ten minutes ago, he'd have been furious too. But right now, he could only laugh at it and the scatter of other seal stuffed animals the sweepers had picked up off the ice. Zack had told the world about his seals, and people had, apparently, taken them, and him – the seal boy – to heart.

Also he'd skated brilliantly, and he knew it. But waiting for his scores was always the worst.

Plus, he *really* wanted to see Zack.

"And the scores for Aaron Sheftall…." Aaron startled at the announcement; he could feel Katie and Brendan tense beside him too. When the numbers were read out, Aaron shrieked, covering his face with the plush seal while Katie and Brendan shouted joyfully and hugged him between them.

A season's best, a personal best, *and*, absolutely crucially, ahead of Cayden. By several places. It wouldn't get him on the podium, but the podium here had never been the goal.

"You did it!" Katie was chanting in his ear as she rocked him back and forth on the bench. "You did it, you did it you did it!"

"It's not over yet!" Elated as he was – and hopeful as he was – the Olympic decision hadn't been made yet. He wiped his tear-streaked cheeks on Katie's shoulder and grinned when she glared at him.

"You're gross," Katie complained.

"You're going to jinx me!" Aaron protested.

"Let's go watch the rest of this thing, okay?" Brendan said, urging them up and out of the kiss and cry as the next skater's program began. They passed Cayden and his coach; Aaron could feel the strength of his glare boring into him. Evidently, he was as pissed at Aaron's final standing as Aaron was elated. But for once he said nothing.

Brendan led the way further backstage and down a small hallway that was mercifully quiet and somehow empty of other people.

"I have to go find Zack," Aaron said. He liked to think of himself as a good competitor and knew he should go back and watch the rest of the skaters coming after him, but Zack had driven all this way for him under the most uncertain of circumstances.

"Not if he finds you first." Katie said smugly, looking somewhere over Aaron's shoulder. Aaron turned to follow her gaze and there, once more, coming around a corner into the little hallway, was Zack.

Aaron was already trembling with spent nerves and adrenaline. His knees went even weaker at the sight of him.

Zack stopped in front of him. "Hi."

Aaron smiled up at him. "You didn't catch frostbite out there. Impressive."

Zack grinned back. "I brought layers."

It was then Aaron noticed the guy standing next to Zack, who looked vaguely familiar.

Aaron squinted. "Who are you?"

"Oh, yeah. This is my buddy Matt, from hockey."

"I thought I recognized you. Why are you here?" Aaron was genuinely curious. And far too wound up to be more polite.

"He needed a co-pilot." Matt jerked a thumb at Zack.

"You drove out here with him?"

"Well, yeah. What are friends for?"

Before Aaron could reply, his phone, tucked in the pocket of his jacket, barked. He stilled. He'd muted every single contact he had, except one.

Katie's phone chirped too. So did Brendan's.

"I still hate this part," Aaron said.

"Don't strangle the seal," Zack warned. Aaron looked down at the poor plushie he'd been unconsciously twisting in his hands.

"We looked last time," Katie said. "Your turn now."

"I hate you, too."

"You'll thank me someday."

"Ugh!" Aaron shoved the seal at Zack and dug the phone out of his pocket. His hands were too sweaty for the fingerprint sensor to work and shaking so badly it took three tries to get his unlock code right.

Once he did, he stared at the text.

"Okay technically," he said, looking up at Zack, his voice somehow steady. "I'm not supposed to tell anyone about this." He was glad there was no one around but his coaches, Zack, and Zack's random friend.

"I'll get out of your hair," Matt said, stepping back a few paces.

Katie gave a muffled shout, her hands clapped over her mouth. "Oh my God!"

"Yeah." Aaron's face hurt. Possibly from smiling so broadly.

"Okay, all of you" Brendan wrapped one arm around Katie's shoulders and one around Aaron's. "If you're not going to have poker faces, let's get you somewhere people aren't going to stumble in on you."

"My hotel is walking distance from here," Aaron told Zack.

"You'll want to get your skates off first." Zack smiled.

32

Eleven Days Before the Olympics
Almaty, Kazakhstan

There were eleven days in between the one where Aaron was named to the U.S. Figure Skating Team for the Olympics and the opening ceremonies in Almaty. Which to most people probably was a laughably short space of time to prepare for intercontinental travel and also being in the Olympics, but Aaron had his coaches and federation to help him, and Zack had been sent off on assignments into combat zones on shorter notice than that.

Olympic prep was much more fun.

Zack could even be useful. While Brendan dealt with the federation and Katie dealt with Aaron's skating, Zack packed for Aaron and worked with his family to make sure they all got to Kazakhstan. And when the major news networks started calling wanting to do human interest pieces about Aaron and his family and his island... well, Zack knew how to manage that, too. Often by talking to Aaron and agreeing that the lesser of two evils was human interest pieces about their relationship and not a camera crew descending on the smallest inhabited chunk of rocks in the middle of Lake Erie.

Zack suspected Aaron would have spent more time yelling about that if he hadn't been training every waking hour.

◆

Zack travelled with Aaron's family and they all stayed in a rented apartment in Almaty. It should have been awkward, and on some level, probably was. But he was a welcome distraction as they fretted about Aaron and navigated the chaos of an Olympic city. They didn't question his fear of flying, and he didn't question Ari's scowls in the face of so much land and so little water.

He didn't see much of Aaron in the days leading up to his skates – after all, Aaron had an entire Olympic Village to explore, friends to make, and experiences to soak in – but whenever he did, Aaron radiated with happiness and bubbled over with stories about the adventures he was having with Huy and the other skaters who were there. The media – both U.S. and international outlets alike – adored him, and the audience was rapt at his performances. They kept throwing the seal plushies onto the ice, too.

In the end Aaron didn't win or medal, but they all knew that going in. That wasn't the point. The point was being an Olympian and getting to be in the one place in the world other than his island where people were at least a little bit like him. Besides, coming in seventh was a hell of an achievement for someone who hadn't even been an also-ran a year ago.

Aaron might not have gotten a medal, but when he got back to Saint Paul he did get his rings. Zack went with him when he went to get them tattooed below his ribcage, where they'd never be seen in any competition-legal costume.

"I want to go back," Aaron said, gripping Zack's hand tight as the tattoo artist worked her magic. "Another four years. I want to do that again."

"Whatever you want," Zack said, gripping back.

✦

But of course the island and the lake and the seals called, and Aaron had no idea what to do but fret about the cost of four more years of hard work away from home, and Zack had no idea what to do other than say he'd be there for whatever Aaron's choices turned out to be. It was nice to follow something other than destruction for a change.

In the short term, for Aaron, there were ice shows and tours across the country and around the world. Which was evidently a first for him; as he told Zack, he'd never before felt like he could leave the island in the summer when his family needed him most.

But he spent most of the previous summer away to no dire consequences, so there was no reason not to do it again. It turned out there was quite a bit of demand among figure skating fans for that year's surprise star.

So they spent a lot of that summer apart, but that also worked for them. With distance, they could slow things down and not rush completely headlong into a relationship that still needed time and work to heal and deepen and grow. Zack could sit in Saint Paul and write while Aaron travelled, and the adult hockey league didn't stop playing just because the pros took the summer off or someone's boyfriend had gone to the Olympics.

Katie and Brendan started inviting Zack to the farm for dinner on the weekends – at least the weekends when they weren't off travelling for their own ongoing skating careers. Zack was pretty clear they hadn't hated him in a while, if ever, but he was never quite sure when the turning point had been. Now he worried they liked him enough to ask him to babysit the cows while they were on the road. The cows still freaked him out.

Zack went to the last show of Aaron's tour, one Aaron, Katie, and Brendan were all skating in together. Since it was in Saint Paul Matt went too and somehow smuggled in both another seal plushie for Aaron and flowers for some skater he'd been talking to since the whole ridiculous Four Continents road trip situation. They sat in the front row, in the seats basically on the ice. Zack spent the whole time in awe of the art Aaron and his fellow skaters could create and anticipating the moment when he could, finally, have Aaron back in his arms. They'd been apart for weeks.

Also, wow did Katie and Brendan skate like they were about to fight or fuck. He had suspected that from the beginning, but now he knew that was just how – and why – they worked.

Zack got himself backstage at the end of the show, and threaded his way through bustling crew and chattering performers to find Aaron outside the dressing rooms talking with one of the other skaters. Zack knew Aaron had had his eyes on him the whole night, but Aaron still gave a happy shout when he saw him.

Time seemed to slow down as Aaron ran toward him and threw himself into Zack's arms. He was so warm, so real, and Zack drank in the feel of him.

"You did amazing," Zack told him, kissing the top of his head. His curls were sweaty and sticky with gel.

"I know." Aaron tipped his head back to beam up at him. That smile still made Zack go weak at the knees. "Let's go home."

Home. Zack loved the sound of the word. "Yours or mine?"

"Oh for tonight? Whichever. I think you're closer. But I meant the island."

"I thought you were off the hook for the summer," Zack said, hesitating. He very much wanted to be on the island again, sharing that space with Aaron. But the thought of doing that flight again was almost too much.

"I am. Technically. But there's only a few weeks left before pre-season starts, and I want to spend them there. Maybe take an actual break for once. I know I should have talked to you about it before, but I didn't want to do it from the road, and…"

"Shhhhhh, that's not what I meant," Zack said, rubbing his thumb through the short hair at the nape of Aaron's neck. "Just… seriously. That flight."

Aaron stared at him with that look that said once more, Zack was ignorant of a basic fact of his world. "Ice melts in the summer. The large island is a resort, remember?"

"Are you telling me we can have a lovely summer vacation?" Except for the flight, the idea was more appealing than Zack could say.

"No," Aaron said laughing. "I mean yes, we can, even though we'll probably end up doing work at the restaurant anyway. But no, I'm telling you we can take a boat."

32

The Next Summer

Whisker Island

Aaron sat at the end of the dock, his feet dangling in the water. The glaring rays of the setting sun had faded into rosy pinks and oranges at the horizon. Behind him, to the east, the sky was already dusky blue with the coming night. In a few days, he and Zack would head back to Saint Paul so Aaron could start training for the coming season. For now, the air was muggy, but rapidly growing cool as the light faded. The gentle lap of the waves on the shore made him smile with the memory of a thousand childhood evenings spent just like this.

Footsteps behind him made the dock creak and sway. There was a warm hand on his shoulder and then Zack was sitting down next to him.

"You finish your chapter?" While Aaron had been spending much of his time pitching in with the restaurant, Zack had been pounding away at his book.

"Close enough for now. I thought I'd come out and say hi."

"You missed the sunset."

"There'll be more."

Zack put his hand on Aaron's knee, and Aaron twined their fingers together. With the ups and downs of the last season, he'd had plenty of occasions to appreciate how capable Zack was in a crisis, even in crises of his own making. But the last several weeks here on the island had been good, too. They could just exist like this, quiet and together, through the ordinary as well as the dramatic.

"I can't believe we have to leave so soon," Aaron said.

"I thought you were excited to get back."

"I am." He'd been texting back and forth with Katie and Brendan the entire time he'd been away discussing new program ideas. He had momentum now, and couldn't wait to see what the new season would bring. But....

"Leaving always feels so hard. Though I guess…" he gave Zack a sly look from under his lashes. "It feels less hard this year."

"Because you've shown the world what the skating seal boy can do?" Zack said, his voice teasing and apparently not taking the bait.

Aaron laughed; what had started as an insult from Cayden had now become, somehow, the audience's fondest nickname for him. Aaron didn't hate it anymore. How could he, when he'd finally found the way to be who he always was?

"Yeah, I guess so," he said, leaning over to kiss the edge of Zack's jaw.

"Question for you," Zack said, when Aaron pulled back.

"Yeah?"

Zack looked apprehensive. "We still take the ferry when we go, right?"

Aaron squeezed their twined fingers together. "Yes, of course. It runs until after Halloween." He sighed, letting himself indulge in wistfulness for the moment. Unlike summer evenings, he had a lot fewer memories of autumn here. "Do you know how long it's been since I've been here in the fall?"

Zack shook his head. "I know better than to hazard a guess."

"Not since I was seventeen, and even then I was flying out all the time for skating things."

"Do you want to come back, when you're done?"

Aaron shrugged. "What does even mean? I can't skate or tour or coach from here. That's why I had to leave in the first place. I don't know what my career looks like after skating. Or if there ever will be an after. Maybe I'll be like Uncle Ras. Or maybe I'll coach. Who knows."

"Does it still bother Ari?"

"No." He and Ari had had a long conversation after Almaty. As displeased as she'd been about Zack's article – and the attention it had drawn to their island and the seals – as time had gone by she had come to tolerate, if not embrace it. Aaron suspected that both bringing Zack to the island and travelling to Kazakhstan herself had helped. She was still connected to the island in a way even more profound than Aaron was, but they understood each other better now.

"I think it helps that – well. It's not like things could get weirder than they were this season. If we – she and I and the island – survived that, we can survive anything."

"I'm glad."

"Me too," Aaron said sincerely. "She still hates my ringtone, though."

Zack laughed, his face creasing in a broad smile.

Aaron gazed at him, his strong jawline and the lines of his shoulders under his t-shirt. He traced a fingertip down Zack's arm, tracing the swirling pattern of ink.

"I'm lucky you're crazy about me," he said. "I know this isn't the sort of place where I can ask people to follow. And, to be clear, I'm not doing that. I'm just happy to have you with me as long as you want to be."

All of which was true. Aaron knew Zack loved him, his family, and his island, as much as anyone not from it could. But Aaron didn't know how to look too far into the future, because he didn't know how to have both Zack and this place forever.

"Isn't it?" Zack said. He sounded surprised. "Your island. Who wouldn't want to follow you here?"

"People less enamored of hard work, dangerously isolated winters, and fish?"

Zack fixed Aaron with an intent gaze. "Hey. I am in this adventure with you. If I'm not scared off by skating, your meal plan, an entire Olympic cycle, or my general incompetence at relationships, I'm not scared off by this place or your stories about it."

"Or gutting fish in the family restaurant?" Aaron asked.

"Or that," Zack said gamely. "And I get that we're taking things slow and being reasonable people with separate places, and if that's what you need for the next four years, I'm on board. But I'll be wherever you are, waiting when you're done. And if you need something else, I'm here right now too."

Aaron opened his mouth to say something in response to that – or at least kiss Zack like he deserved – but in the distance, something on the water caught the corner of his eye. He turned his head sharply to try to get a better look at it.

"Are you fucking kidding me?" he whispered under his breath.

He stood up and held his arm out behind him.

Zack took his hand, but didn't get up. "What is it?"

With his other hand Aaron pointed deep into the lake, towards the horizon "What am I looking at? Out there?"

Zack squinted. "I know what you're asking, but I'm not sure. I wouldn't even know what they look like."

It was then that the barking started.

Aaron turned to him very slowly. "Oh my God," he said. What had been terror in Saint Petersburg was simply wonder here.

"Do you want to go and see?" Zack didn't sound concerned, only eager, as ever, to follow Aaron into anything as if it were nothing more unusual than a walk in the park.

"I'd have to swim," Aaron said. "If they're real, the boat has always scared them."

"I can swim, too, you know," Zack said.

"I know," he told Zack. "But this isn't your problem." Truth be told, he didn't know what the seals, if were even real, would do if confronted by an outsider. But then, if they were showing themselves now to the two of them, perhaps that meant they approved of Zack.

"Considering how much I want to keep you with me, and know I can only do that by going where you go, I'd say it's absolutely my problem."

Aaron stared at him, his heart fluttering at the warmth in Zack's eyes. In the distance, the barking started again.

"Before we go," Zack said. His fingers tightened on Aaron's. "There's something I want to ask you."

"Go on then. Before they leave."

"Aaron Sheftall." Zack reached for Aaron's other hand, pressing both of them together so they were clasped between his own. "Can I marry you?"

Aaron could feel the smile broadening across his face, his skin heating with a flush of joy. He hadn't known there would be a way to make this evening more perfect, and yet, here it was.

But still. *Priorities*. Zack, he was sure, would wait a moment. The seals might not.

Still smiling so widely his face hurt, he gently withdrew his hands from Zack's and pulled his t-shirt over his head. He kicked off his sandals, delighting in the moment of pure confusion on Zack's face as he dove in the water.

When Aaron resurfaced a moment later pushing his wet hair back out of his face, the bobbing shapes in the water were closer. *Yes.*

Zack, still on the dock, was now also shirtless and poised to jump. But his eyes were fixed on Aaron's face, and Aaron knew Zack wouldn't move until he had his answer.

"Yes, of course!" he called, slapping the water to send a splash up at Zack. "Now come on," he hollered as he turned and kicked off towards the open lake.

For a split second, he was terrified that Zack wouldn't follow, but then he heard a splash, far clumsier than his own.

Aaron laughed as he pulled himself through the water, the gentle waves cool and flowing over his skin. He didn't know what the future held – not in the next four minutes or in the next four years, but for the first time in his life he knew he was real and loved and tethered, truly and joyfully, to a world so much bigger than himself.

Whatever happened next was going to be amazing.

Also by Erin McRae and Racheline Maltese

The Twin Cities Ice Series
After the Gold
Ink and Ice

The Royal Roses Series
A Queen from the North

The Love in Los Angeles Series
Starling
Evergreen
Doves
Phoenix
Cardinal

The Love's Labours Series
Midsummer
Twelfth Night
Tempest

Standalone Novels
The Art of Three
The Opposite of Drowning

Non-Fiction
Self-Publishing for Perfectionists
You've F*cking Got This!: Daily Motivation for People Who Hate That Crap

Novellas and Short Stories
Alpha Bodyguard: A Forbidden Omega Story
The Anniversary Gift
Backstage Beginnings
The Hart and the Hound
Off-Kilter
The Omega's Reluctant Alpha
Room 1024
Sample and Hold
Second Chances
Snare

9 781946 192165